TRUCKTRESS

Book Two

Mother Trucker Book Series

Library of Congress Cataloging-in –Publication Data

p.   cm

ISBN: 978-0-9972129-1-4   PCN: 2016939837

I. Truckers—Fiction II. Trucking Industry—Fiction III. Adventure Fiction
Fic Mit   PS 3606.A775M46

Editor-in-Chief: Mindy Reed, The Authors' Assistant
Interior Designed by Danielle H. Acee, The Authors' Assistant
Cover Design by Douglas Brown, Album Artist

Printed in the United States

TRUCKTRESS

a novel by

ROBYN MITCHELL

PUBLISHING
Odessa, TX

Chapter One

Assistant District Attorney Mary Polk was briefing Sergeant Arnold Petersen of the Utah State Police when there was a knock on her door. "Come in," she said. Her secretary entered and handed her a report across her desk. She nodded her thanks and the secretary left. Mary lifted the front cover and read the summary. "Betty Burton's psych report," she told the officer. "She's definitely a psychopath. We should be able to put her away, just on this information alone."

"I thought you couldn't try a case based on a physiological profile," Petersen said.

"We can't, which is why your testimony is so critical."

Petersen had been assigned to clean up the mess and head up the investigation after the husband, fellow truckers, and biker group went rogue in their successful attempt to save Shelby Mathews. His superiors, who considered the rescue vigilantism, wanted the men charged with obstruction and endangerment of the public, but Petersen had convinced them the public would not take kindly to arresting true American heroes, especially in an election year.

"Are you sure we can't tie this Burton woman to Ted Simon's death? I'd much rather get her convicted for first degree murder than attempted murder."

"I appreciate your suspicions. Betty and Ted were involved. There was nothing left of his truck but some charred embers. All we found of him was enough to match his dental records. From the truckers' statements, Betty was riding everyone hard. Still, claiming his going over the side of the mountain was anything other than an accident is nearly impossible to prove."

"Didn't his wife discover the emails Betty wrote?"

"Yeah, but they only talk about wanting to get Shelby."

"Well, let's get through this trial. Hopefully there are other charges we can add later."

◊◊◊

Betty lay on the cold steel bunk and stared up at the ceiling.

"Ain't you going to court today, Balls?" Darlene called from a neighboring cell.

Balls was the name Betty Burton had earned after numerous confrontations with fellow inmates. She liked it because not only did she think of herself as having a pair, she would bust the ones on any man who crossed her.

"Yeah. Once my lawyer springs me, I'm going to make that bitch pay for putting me in here," Balls responded.

"You really think he's gonna get you out of here?"

"He better. I have a score to settle and I can't do it in here."

"Hope you're right. Doesn't seem right what they done to you."

Balls took a deep breath of the musty air and turned over. She slowly moved her fingers over the cinder block wall…over the numerous hash marks she'd made from her own blood, drawn from sinking her teeth deep into her wrists. "He'd better come through," she whispered to herself, "Or, like Barbie, he'll find himself in the morgue."

◊◊◊

Noisy chatter permeated the crowded courtroom. Shelby sat stiffly in a chair flanked by Eddy and Sandy on each side of her. *I never thought I'd be back in this town,* she thought from her seat directly behind the prosecutors' table.

Sandy leaned over and whispered, "This is some big shindig."

"I never expected this many people to show. Did you?" Shelby glanced around and recognized several people.

Sandy shrugged. "It's a little town. This is probably the biggest event of the year for them. Where's Jack, anyway?"

"Working." Before Sandy could question her clipped response, Shelby waved at two friends a few seats away. "Hey, look! There's Snowmobile Flyer and Richie Rich."

Sandy was not deterred. "Work? Must have been really important for him to let you come all this way by yourself. He's been so protective of you over the last few months I figured you would be surrounded by body guards."

Shelby just shrugged and looked down at her lap.

"I know you too well, Shelby. Something's up. You don't have to tell me right now, but we will talk later."

Shelby crossed her legs and arms. "Work, Sandy. It was just work."

"We'll talk later."

A hush came over the courtroom. The bailiff opened a side door and held it while Betty and a female jailer walked through. "Wow. She looks horrible," Shelby whispered.

The anklet chains shuffled across the floor as the gaunt Betty was escorted to the defense table. Shelby felt of pang of sympathy for the haggard woman. But the minute Betty mouthed the words, "You're mine, bitch," the disdain Shelby felt for her nemesis returned.

The spectators murmured amongst themselves as the jailer forcibly pushed Betty down into her chair.

Shelby leaned back in her chair in an attempt to avoid any further eye contact with Betty. Sandy patted Shelby's leg. "Don't worry about her, Shelby. That vicious attitude will be slapped out of her by the time this trial is over."

"I know. She's handcuffed and surrounded by cops, but she still intimidates me."

"Maybe it's the way she looks. Hell, that bony witch scares me."

Shelby laughed with Sandy, but as she turned back to look toward the front of the room, she saw Betty staring at her, her eyebrows furrowed. As their eyes met, Betty mouthed, "Laugh now. You'll be crying soon."

◊◊◊

On the fourth day of the trial, Shelby learned she would be testifying. As a result, she was not allowed into the courtroom until the prosecution called her. She paced the hallway, chewed her manicured nails, and fiddled with her bleach blonde hair.

"Shelby, sit down. Everything is going to be fine," said Sandy, patting a space on the bench beside her. "That state trooper Petersen is almost finished testifying. Then all you have to do is tell the truth about what she did to you."

"I know, but I'm so nervous."

The courtroom doors opened, releasing a sea of angry voices. Shelby stood up but a guard approached her. "Best if you ladies stay seated over there until this mob clears out." The mob of spectators poured into the hallway.

"What's going on?" Sandy demanded.

The guard shrugged and stepped toward the mayhem. "Don't know." He announced to the crowd, "Okay, folks. Move it along, this way."

Before long, Eddy emerged and made his way to the two women on the bench.

"What the hell is going on, Eddy?" Sandy asked.

Eddy sighed. "Apparently, the trooper did not mirandize Betty properly. She was still under sedation in the hospital when they came to make the arrest, so she was unable to concur that she understood her rights. She also claims they sedated her without her consent."

Sandy muttered a series of obscenities. Shelby was stunned. "Seriously, how does this happen?" she asked. "How do you get consent from a crazy person?"

"She's claiming they took advantage of her emotional state after Ted took his dive over the mountain. Temporary insanity due to emotional trauma."

"What does that mean for us?"

"I'm not sure. We have to wait and see what the judge decides. The attorneys are in his chambers right now."

Sandy stood and crossed her arms in front of her chest. "This is crap. That psycho can do whatever she wants to do, to whomever she wants, and gets away with it because of a technicality? She gets to go free because she received medical attention rather than being left beside the road?"

Eddy reached for Shelby's hand. "Let's go inside the courtroom and see what the judge does before we jump to any conclusions. It's going to be okay, even if she does get off here in Utah. There are still charges pending in Texas. She'll definitely pay for her crimes there."

Shelby didn't say a word as she rose in a daze and walked back into the courtroom. The courtroom was chaotic as she and Sandy found their seats and sat in silence next to Eddy. Betty was sitting next to her attorney with a devious smirk on her face. *How can this be happening?* Shelby thought, as the judge returned to bench. Everyone left in the room stood up.

The judge used his gavel to quiet the courtroom. Shelby's heart was beating so fast. *Is this ever going to end?*

"Ladies and gentleman, I find that it is my duty, no matter what my personal feelings might be, to always uphold the law in every case. I, therefore, have to rule in favor of the defendant and grant a mistrial. I suggest that the prosecution bring me new evidence against this defendant before presenting a new case. Make sure this time that her rights are not violated."

There was a series of boos in the room as the prosecuting attorney stood. "Your Honor, I would like to request that Miss Burton remain in the custody of the State of Utah as we are currently waiting on extradition papers from the State of Texas for her charges there," Polk said.

The defense attorney rose. "I object, Your Honor. The prosecution should have taken care of that before this trial."

"Calm down, Mr. Fox. He's correct, Mrs. Polk. It is not this court's practice to hold defendants on so-called 'paperwork.' If you want Miss Burton to remain in the State's custody, I suggest you come up with something better than that."

"Your Honor, we are just waiting on the paperwork."

"Not good enough. Miss Burton, you are hereby released from the custody of this district, but it is the court's request that you remain here until your paperwork from Texas is completed."

Betty conferred with her attorney and, with a smile of revenge, turned toward the courtroom, attempting to once again make eye contact with Shelby. The bailiff, however, had moved in behind Betty, trying to help her from her chair in order to remove the cuffs and shackles. Betty pushed at the bailiff, determined to let Shelby know her intentions. Shelby saw everything as Betty flashed a huge grin and she was escorted out of the courtroom. She again mouthed the words: "You're mine, bitch."

"This court is adjourned and the jury is dismissed," the judge announced. "The State of Utah thanks you for your time."

Shelby sat numb in disbelief as the bailiff shut the door behind Betty.

"It'll be alright, girl," Sandy said, placing her hand on Shelby's arm. "That bitch deserves a Texas trial anyway. The Lone Star State doesn't take kindly to killers, even ones who don't complete the attempt. She'll get what's coming to her down there."

"I know. I just wish they'd keep her locked up until then. You know she's not going to stick around and wait to get picked up again."

Eddy offered his hand to Shelby, but she chose to remain seated for a while, trying to gather her thoughts. "Thanks, Eddy," she said. "I'll be there in a minute. I'll meet you both at the cars."

Shelby sat in silence, contemplating everything Betty had done to her over the last two years. The case should have been open and shut based on the emails Ted's widow Annabel had given Jack. *How is it possible that after all the horrible things Betty has inflicted on me, she's being let out of jail completely unpunished?* Shelby wondered. What petrified her were Betty's own words, which proved she wasn't done terrorizing Shelby. Shelby quickly wiped away the tears welling up in her eyes. *Crying isn't going to help. The only way to beat Betty is to stay one step ahead of her,* she resolved.

"Hey, how ya doing, girl?" Sandy called as Shelby approached their car.

"I'm okay. I need to get to the motel and change my flight reservations. I want to go home today. In a perverted kind of way Jack will be glad I'm finished up here so soon. He's been really upset with me for staying in the trucking business. Now he'll have one more reason to use against me to quit."

"Are you saying Jack wants you to stop driving a truck? Well, that's not going to happen. Is it?"

Shelby wanted to stay with trucking, but Jack was making it harder for her with every passing day. It seemed the longer she continued to drive the more upset he got with her. She knew things were going to get even worse once he learned that Betty was out.

Eddy placed a comforting hand on her arm. "Do you really think that Jack wants you to stop driving? He's probably just concerned with your safety, Shelby. I know I'd feel the same way if my wife had gone through all you have experienced at the hands of Betty. Don't worry too much about it. I'm sure he'll calm down about things, especially when Texas gets a hold of Betty."

"Thanks, Eddy. I sure hope you're right."

"Well, he better not expect me to give up my gator without a fight," Sandy muttered.

Betty's lawyer interrupted their laughter to Sandy's response "Are you Eddy?" he asked.

"Yes…why?"

The lawyer moved his briefcase from one hand to the other and took a folded piece of paper out from under his arm and handed it to Eddy. "Betty requested I give this to you. When she gets back to Texas, her new lawyer will be contacting you with a legal request. I told Betty that this letter isn't going to work, but she insisted that I give it to you anyway."

Eddy took the letter, opened it, and began reading it as the lawyer left the lobby.

"What does the bitch want now?" asked Sandy, leaning toward Eddy to try to see the letter. "She better not think she's getting her job back."

Eddy rolled his eyes and handed her the letter. "That's exactly what she wants."

"Seriously?" Sandy grabbed the letter from Eddy and stared at it. "What is she—insane?" She read the letter and abruptly handed it back to Eddy. "Yeah, right. Not while I still work for ESCC. Can she really do this, Eddy?"

Eddy took the letter, folded it up, and then placed it in his shirt pocket. "I doubt it, but I'll check with ESCC's legal department when we get back to make sure. I'm pretty sure this is just a ploy on Betty's part."

"Yeah. She's probably just trying to get a rise out of us."

"Don't forget, she still has charges pending in Texas," said Eddy. "I really doubt she'll head down there of her own free will or, for that matter, stay here as the judge requested. She's just being her normal evil self, trying to show us she's still controlling things. Or at least she *thinks* she is."

Shelby knew underestimating Betty was a mistake, but she didn't say anything. She was tired of talking about Betty, and especially of thinking about her. "I've got to go, guys. I need to change my flight and pack. Plus, that drive to Salt Lake Airport is several miles away. I hope I can still get a flight out today. Are you guys flying back today, too?"

"No, I think we'll stay the night in Salt Lake and try to get out tomorrow. I'm pretty sure Speedy can handle things one more day."

Back at the motel a few hours later, Shelby hugged Sandy and shook hands with Eddy. "I'll see ya back in Texas."

As Shelby got into her rental car and headed for the airport, Sandy called out, "See ya soon, Shelby. And don't forget to tell Jack I'm not giving up my gator."

Shelby waved back, not wanting to think about Jack's response to the outcome of the trial.

◊◊◊

Betty took a deep breath of fresh air and examined the little bit of money that she'd had when she was arrested. There wasn't enough to make it very far. Her cell phone had been turned off because she couldn't make her payments while she was in jail. With a sigh, she decided that her best option to get out of town was to find a trucker.

She looked around and decided to head in a westerly direction. She wanted to avoid the public as much as possible, especially since everyone would probably recognize her from photos that had been in the local paper. She did not want any kind of exposure right now. She walked briskly through the evening shadows of the trees along the streets. *I have to get out of this godforsaken town,* she thought.

CHAPTER TWO

The weather was chilly but Betty's blood was pumping as she rubbed her arms and walked down the streets as dusk fell. Her coat went missing months ago during her arrest but she figured she'd get someone to loan her one once she found a ride out of town. After several blocks, she finally spotted a store where some eighteen-wheelers were parked in the back parking lot. She went into the store, purchased a soda, and then walked around the store, checking out the merchandise. She tried to avoid face-to-face contact with anyone while she kept an eye out for a driver of one of the trucks parked out back.

It didn't take long for Betty to find what she was looking for. The door jingled open and the clerk happily greeted the young man as he walked through the door. "Hey, Billy. Thought you caught a load and were headed to Salt Lake?"

The young man walked to the counter and leaned on it, flirting with the pretty little brunette standing at the register. "Yeah, but it's on hold for a little while so thought I'd come back in here and see if I could talk you into going out with me after you get off work tonight."

The clerk blushed at the invitation. "Oh, that would be fun, Billy. But I don't get off until eleven."

"Not a problem," he answered, grinning. "I'll just get me a nap and wait in my truck for you. We'll have to take your car if you don't mind, since my truck's too big for most of the parking lots around here."

"Okay, sure. I'll come out to your truck when I get off."

"Sounds like a plan."

Betty practically gagged at the display of puppy love at the counter. But this love-struck fool was just what she was looking for…maybe more.

With his head in the clouds she could get more than just a ride—she'd get his truck if she worked it right.

Betty hung back and hid as best she could in the shadows, trying to see which truck was Billy's. Betty watched as Billy unlocked and entered a white and black KW truck with an empty flatbed trailer. She found a smelly but secluded spot behind a large trash dumpster where she felt she could hold out and still keep an eye on her prey without drawing any attention.

She looked around her hiding spot, hoping to find something she could use to help convince Billy that she needed to borrow his truck for a while. She really wasn't concerned with whether he would willingly let her use the truck or not—she knew he wouldn't—but she needed something to help her make sure he wouldn't be a problem when she took it. She reached down and picked up a piece of pipe that was lying next to the building. *This should work nicely in convincing young Billy that he needs to give me his truck. Of course, I'll be nice and let him have a few seconds to decide.* Betty laughed to herself as she lifted the pipe into the air and inspected the strength and structure of the weapon she'd chosen for her chore. She tapped it several times into the palm of her hand. *Yes, very nice.*

Betty knew she would need to give Billy some time to fall asleep. Spending time in a small, dank cell had trained her to remain still in an uncomfortable space. She hid behind the trashcans for nearly an hour before she decided to approach Billy's truck. She hoped she would be able to overtake the groggy driver. She moved out of her hiding space, carrying the piece of pipe in her hand. She moved as inconspicuously as possible toward the white KW. She was cold now that it was completely dark and her belly growled from hunger, making her even more determined to get Billy's truck with or without his consent. She went directly to the passenger's side of the truck—not only because it was somewhat less exposed—but because she figured she'd have a greater advantage over Billy if she didn't have to deal with the steering wheel. She would hold on to him as long as she could—at least until she got out of town.

Betty placed the pipe next to the truck, out of sight of the driver but within her reach. She knocked quietly but purposefully on the passenger's side door and stood still, waiting for an answer. It took Billy several knocks and a little time to respond, but he finally pulled the curtain back. Seeing that the female at the bottom of his truck wasn't the young woman he was expecting or even anyone he knew, he frowned. "What do you want? I'm trying to sleep here."

Betty put on her sad look and begged. "Please, sir, I'm out of money and I just need a few dollars to get a place to sleep for the night. Can you help me, please?"

Billy wasn't in the mood to deal with a panhandler, but he sighed and reached for his wallet anyway as he opened the passenger side door. "Look," he said, "I can't give you much, but…" Before he could finish his sentence, Betty had placed the piece of pipe into his chest and pushed him as hard as she could back into his truck, pinning him against the steering wheel. With almost supernatural strength, Betty was on top of Billy, swinging the pipe at him with all her might. The first blow from the pipe sent Billy reeling backward. In a state of semi-consciousness, Billy struggled to catch his breath as he tried to block the blows.

Betty clenched her hands tightly around the pipe and swung it at Billy again with all the anger she'd built up while in prison. With each word, Betty swung harder and harder: "I WANT YOUR TRUCK, AND YOU'RE GIVING IT TO ME WHETHER YOU WANT TO OR NOT!" Blow after blow left Billy defenseless against the attack.

Within a few moments, Billy went limp in his driver's seat. His head was now pressed next to the seat sideways as blood oozed from the side of his mouth through his partially opened lips. His eyes closed to the darkness of the truck he once called home. The wallet he'd clutched in his hand fell to the floorboard from his now lifeless fingers. The truck was drenched with his blood and resembled a stockyard slaughterhouse.

Betty took a few deep breaths after her last hard swing of the pipe to Billy's head and fell into the passenger's seat of her victim's truck, truly exhausted for the first time in weeks. She'd managed to accomplish what she'd set out to do, although it had been a lot harder than she'd anticipated. Blood was everywhere. Betty knew this parking lot was not the place to clean things up since the clerk would be coming out soon for her date. Betty had to get going.

The rush of adrenaline that had just flooded her veins abated and Betty let the pipe she was holding fall to the floor. She stared at Billy's face and then looked away and grabbed his heavy limp body. Since he wasn't wearing a shirt, she had to pull him out of the driver's seat by his slippery blood-covered arms and head. Unable to get a tight grip on Billy's body made pulling him out of the seat extremely difficult, but soon Betty was able to roll Billy out of the driver's seat and onto the floor of the sleeper. He was now face down with one arm under his body and the other arm awkwardly thrown over his back.

Betty coldly stepped over Billy's body and plopped into the driver's seat. "There, you son of a bitch," she whispered under her breath. "You shouldn't have made me do that to you. Now you just stay there until I find a nice quiet place to let you out."

She found some paper towels in the sleeper and began wiping at the blood on her hands along with some of the blood that had splattered on the steering wheel. Betty was still trying to calm her breathing as she took down the sleep curtain and callously threw the blood-stained wad of material over Billy's back. She checked out the parking lot through the windshield to see if anyone had observed the suspicious activities that had just occurred in her corner of the lot. "Good," she said aloud. "It looks like everyone is still minding their own business…just the way I like it."

Next she had to get the truck out of the parking lot without much attention. She released the air brakes and, leaving the lights off, moved the truck slowly around the store to the opposite side where it appeared to be less bright. She hoped no one in or outside the store would notice the truck's departure.

Betty passed the city limits and was several miles down the highway toward Salt Lake when she finally relaxed. She pulled out the pack of smokes she'd shoplifted from the store. She puffed on a cigarette like it was oxygen for her lungs. Then she sat back and rolled the big rig down the two-lane highway. She had missed the serene feelings that came over her when she was sitting up high in a big rig, rolling at the top end of the gears and cruising down the highway in the dark of night with only her headlights visible. Betty had grown up in a truck after her mother left her father. She rode with him until he unexpectedly died of a heart attack in a truck stop one day when she was thirteen years old. CPS came and took her from her daddy's truck and handed her over to a foster family that had been more concerned with the monthly check than taking care of her. She ran away when she turned fifteen…returning to the highway.

At the time, Betty had nothing of value but her body, so she quickly learned how to use it to get a place to sleep, food, rides to the next truck terminals and, eventually, money. She'd meet several nice truckers who, after figuring out how young she was, tried to get her to give up the road. Some even offered their homes as safe havens. Offers that were too late for a youngster who was by then completely stripped of any self-respect and had only one goal in mind for her life. She couldn't wait until her twenty-first birthday, when she'd be eligible to get her CDL driver's license. She saved every dime she could and took lessons in truck parking lots from trucker friends. Betty forced herself to continue toward her goal no matter what she had to do, including sleeping with some of the most horrible-smelling, bald and overweight drivers she'd ever met.

The night before her twenty-first birthday, Betty found herself one state away from the terminal she'd been using as a home base. She'd been riding with a fat cow of a driver who had used and abused her for the two days. She was hoping the pig was going to pull over soon so she could get out and find another ride. More than anything else, she wanted to take a bath, since all she could smell on herself was his stink. She hadn't made much money off of him either, but he wasn't smart enough to keep his wallet hidden, so she knew before departing this rig she was cleaning the bastard out. She was determined to spend her birthday alone in a motel room before she went to take her test.

Her chance to get out of the pig's truck came when he needed to relieve himself at a truck stop near the state border. Betty quickly gathered her backpack and the cash out of the man's wallet after he disappeared into the store. She'd done this more than a few thousand times, so slipping out of sight behind the trucks parked for the night and hiding out until the angry driver left wasn't anything out of the ordinary. The hard part was always avoiding the cops, whom he'd undoubtedly call to report the stolen money. At first she thought his wallet was stuffed with one-dollar bills, and then she looked at the wad of bills in her hand—it was over a thousand dollars in one hundred dollar bills. That was when she knew for sure she could survive on the road by herself. "I'll never have to fuck another fat pig again."

Betty gazed through the dark night and located a spot off the side of the road that looked secluded enough to get rid of Billy's body. She maneuvered the truck off the road and placed it as close as she could to the edge near the brush. She didn't want to have to pull him any further than necessary out of the truck to hide his body. She turned off the lights on the truck and put on the air brakes before getting out of the driver's seat.

She looked down at Billy's body on the floor and reached for his arm behind his back and pulled at it backward, causing his body to roll over and onto her feet. "Great." She kicked at Billy's back as she pulled one foot out and then another. "Dammit! My only pair of shoes, too." She'd lost a lot of muscle tone while in jail, and although Billy wasn't that big, her lack of strength made his removal difficult and time-consuming. Blood from Billy's body got on Betty's face, hands, and in her hair as she fumbled and fell with him from the sleeper area to the passenger seat. "Dammit, boy. You're heavy." Betty worked Billy's body up into the seat and then opened the passenger's side door, letting a cold breeze flow through the cab to dry some of the blood that had gotten on her face. She fell into the driver's seat, exhausted from lugging Billy's body from the floor. "Okay," she muttered. "Just a little further and you'll be out of here."

She opened the driver's side door, got out, and went to the passenger's side of the truck. She pulled at Billy's arms until she caused his body to fall like a bowling ball from the seat onto her chest. With Billy's body now pressed up against her, Betty let go of her hold on the truck handle near the door and swung her body back out of the way at the same time she pushed Billy away from her chest. The bloody body of her victim rolled from one step to another and landed with his face in the dirt and his legs still clinging to the last step. With one hard kick, Betty moved the rest of Billy's body to the ground and jumped from the step to the ground next to the even more battered body.

With callous disregard, she grabbed his arms and dragged Billy face-down about twenty feet from the truck toward a large patch of bushes. His body was slippery from the blood, but Betty knew that she had to hide Billy's body if she didn't want him to be discovered right away. "There," she said, shoving him under the bushes. "Maybe your sweet little girlfriend will find you here and cry over you." Betty left Billy's body in a mass of weeds, dirt, and blood without thinking twice about it.

Betty wiped at the blood on her hands and face. She climbed up into the truck and cleaned up the best she could in the dark. She did not want to stay in that spot too long and decided it was time to head toward Salt Lake.

CHAPTER THREE

Shelby had landed in West Texas just as it was getting dark. She'd called Jack from on the way to the airport in Salt Lake, but after their conversation, she wasn't sure if he was going to be at home to meet her. He'd made it perfectly clear that with Betty getting out of jail, Shelby needed to quit driving and go back to teaching. Shelby, of course, had refused. He'd hung up on her and would not take any further calls from her for the rest of the day. She was having a hard time understanding Jack's current obsession with her going back to teaching. Shelby loved being out on the open road and wondered if their relationship would survive her desire to be a trucker.

Jack had calmed down a bit as he reached the airport to pick up Shelby. He'd thought about sending Steven to get his mother, but knew that he and Shelby needed to deal with the problems they were having. Jack pulled into the parking lot of the airport and spotted his wife standing next to the curb with her pull-along bag. He stopped next to the curb and reached over the seat to open the door from the driver's side without getting out of the truck to help her with her bag. Shelby was so offended by Jack's behavior that she turned and headed back to the terminal. "What the hell is your problem?" he called after her, but she didn't seem to hear him. Jack sat in the truck, fuming.

Shelby found a seat near baggage claim and took out her cell phone to call Steven. She got Steven's voice mail and left him a message. She sat in silence in the airport, her anger with her husband mounting. Shelby called Steven once more.

Jack walked through the sliding doors and spotted his wife talking on her cell phone. "What the hell was that all about, Shelby?" he asked as he approached her.

Shelby continued with her message to Steven and refused to respond to Jack's question.

"Well?"

Shelby finished her message, hung up, and continued to ignore her husband.

Jack sat down next to Shelby. "You know, if I don't get back to the truck they're going to tow it."

"Then go. Steven will pick me up."

"Come on, we can talk about this on the way home."

Shelby's eyes welled up with tears, and she quickly turned from Jack, not wanting to give him the satisfaction of knowing he'd made her cry. "Steven is coming," she muttered. "Just leave. I don't want to talk to you right now."

He decided that maybe they really did need time to cool off before talking. "Fine," he said, rising to his feet. "We'll continue this conversation at home."

"Jack," she said, clenching her fists tightly on her lap, "If this conversation is about my driving, you can either live with it or get out. I'm done feeling bad about loving my work. I have never been anything but supportive when it came to your job, and now it's your turn to be supportive of mine."

Jack shook his head as he turned his back on Shelby and walked to his truck. *Am I really ready to throw our marriage and family away over her career? Is she?* As he pulled away from the airport, Jack hated thinking about the painful scenarios.

Shelby sat in the airport terminal in tears, wondering if she was being too stubborn about the whole trucking issue. Her cell phone rang. "I'll be there in a little while," Steven explained. "How come Dad's not picking you up?"

"Your father and I are not seeing eye to eye over my career." She took a deep breath. "So I need you to come get me, please."

"Gotcha, Mom. "I'll be there soon."

◊◊◊

On her way to Salt Lake, Betty decided the safest thing to do was to ditch the truck she'd stolen as soon as possible. She didn't know how long it would be before Billy's body was discovered or how long it would take the cops to figure out his truck was missing. As she pulled into an empty space near the rear of the truck stop in Salt Lake, her intended destination, she announced, "Mission accomplished."

Her first order of business was to get cleaned up and get rid of any evidence in the truck that might lead to her. Then she had to find herself some money. It was still dark, so she had a few hours to accomplish her objectives. Then she'd sleep in the truck for a little while before finding a new ride in the morning. She wanted to head straight for Texas where she would bide her time and wait for just the right moment before taking care of little Miss Barbie. That however probably wasn't the most plausible scenario until things cooled down.

Betty rubbed at the dry blood on her face and hands again, realizing that before she went into the truck stop for a shower, she needed to get rid of the blood on herself and the truck. She found more paper towels, a spray bottle of glass cleaner, and some bottled water. After wiping at different areas of the truck that had blood splatter it was obvious that she was going to need more supplies to clean up all the blood.

She rummaged through Billy's personal things and happened upon his wallet that he'd dropped in the floorboard. She removed the cash and credit cards. Betty figured if she limited her credit card usage to necessities and sold what she could of Billy's valuable stuff to long haul drivers, she would limit the possibility of someone identifying her. It was the simplest way to get more cash. She also knew that she would have to catch the eye of some lonely trucker tomorrow for a ride, so she was going to have to clean up and put on a little makeup.

Betty found a pair of Billy's jeans and a t-shirt, which were too big but would work for the time being. There was a ditty bag for a shower in the closet, which she took along with a pair of his boxers. She stripped off her clothes and wiped as much blood off of her body as possible before going into the truck stop for a shower. Betty used Billy's point card that she'd found in his wallet to pay for the shower. No one seemed to pay any attention to her, which was just what she wanted.

Betty scrubbed every inch of her body and washed her hair in the shower, and then got out and wrapped herself in a towel. She found a brush for her hair and Billy's toothbrush in his ditty bag. Using his toothbrush seemed a little weird, but as she began brushing her teeth she figured it was one less thing she would have to purchase.

After her shower, Betty took the garbage bag she'd taken from the trashcan in the shower room for gathering her bloody clothes and other bloody items from the truck. She'd picked out some food, bleach, make-up, a backpack, a jacket and some clothing that fit. The spaced out young man at the sales counter hardly looked at her. She swiped Billy's credit card as the clerk stuffed her items in a couple of bags. She headed back to Billy's truck. It was late and she needed some sleep. *I'll try and sell some of Billy's things and maybe even make contact with a possible ride out of town when I wake up.*

Betty thought about how to sell Billy's stuff without attracting anyone to his truck. She watched several truckers enter the store and had an idea. She walked over to the store and approached a young female clerk who had just started her shift. "Is there a pawn shop around?" Betty asked, making sure the guys gathered around the coffee pots heard her. "My daughter had complications with her baby's delivery. They won't let her take my grandson home until the hospital bill is paid."

A man with dark curly hair and a thick mustache approached her. "What are you trying to sell?" he asked.

"I've got a television, refrigerator, microwave, stereo system, CB, truck chrome, snow chains, tools, video movies, music, and some books."

"Aren't you going to need that stuff?"

She motioned for him to step away from the group. He followed her outside to the side of the building. "May I be honest with you?" she asked.

"Of course."

"The truck is my son of a bitch son-in-law's. He deserted my daughter, didn't even take her to the hospital. I'm selling his stuff, but he can't know. I'll give you a good deal. I just need some cash so I can get to my daughter."

He followed her to the truck. "Wait here," she said. I don't want my son-in-law to get wind that anyone else has been in his truck. He may tell the cops I stole it, which is a lie, but I don't trust the prick. I'll bring the stuff out to you."

The man knew Betty was full of shit, but didn't care; he would have no trouble fencing the items. Betty drove away from the truck stop with several hundred dollars in her pocket.

Next, she would have to get rid of the truck. She thought about abandoning it, but there were still blood splatters from Billy and even if she could wipe off all of her fingerprints, even a missed hair follicle would reveal her DNA. She needed the truck to disappear. *Like Ted*, she thought. Her former co-worker had careened his truck over a cliff in the mountains, which fell noiselessly, crumpled, and then burst into flames at the bottom of the canyon. She just needed to find the right spot in the Wasatch or Quirch Mountain Range. Unlike Ted, she would need to exit the truck before it fell over the side of the mountain.

Betty pulled off the highway when she saw the exit with a truck stop. She parked in back and then went inside and purchased a Utah roadmap. She went back to Billy's truck, studied the map and devised a plan. She found a route that would keep her off the highway but with roads wide enough to accommodate the rig. She saw that the western side of the Wasatch Range was interspersed with a number of valleys. The map key indicated the range dropped sharply to the valleys on that side.

Betty climbed the mountain roads until she found a spot that was mostly secluded, but close enough to a town that she could hitchhike once she jumped from the truck. She had one chance to time it just right, accelerate the truck to the shoulder, open her driver's door, step out onto the steps and then jump before it plunged through the guardrail and down into the canyon.

◊◊◊

Shelby and Jack had not spoken a word after Steven dropped her at home from the airport. For the first time since they were married, Jack took a pillow and blanket and slept on the couch. As Shelby lay crying in the big cold bed, she knew her relationship with Jack was in serious trouble. She loved Jack but she wasn't giving up driving—at least, she hoped she wouldn't have to.

The next morning wasn't much better as the couple sat in silence at the breakfast table. Jack read the paper and Steven was busy on his laptop.

"Steven," Jack said, "Please leave your mother and me alone for a while." Steven gathered his stuff and left the room. "Shelby, we need to talk about what is going on with us," Jack said.

Shelby brought the toast she'd just finished making to the table and sat across from Jack.

Jack took a deep breath, "I don't want you out there anymore, Shelby," he began, gearing himself up for a long argument. "It's too dangerous, and I miss having you here."

Shelby shook her head. "I might give up the job with ESCC so that Betty can't find me," she said. "But, I'm not going to stop driving. I like it. I like the freedom and the adventure. Can't you understand that? Can't you see how happy it makes me?"

"So what do you think you could get besides sand hauling?"

"I've been thinking that maybe I could go to work for Jayne's trucking company."

"Doesn't her company specialize in long hauling?"

"Yes…primarily, but she has dedicational stuff, so…I could get something that would be on a set schedule and be home on specific days."

"Okay," he said and let out a long sigh. "At least I'd know when you'd be home."

Shelby smiled engagingly at her husband. "Really? Would you really be happier with me if I took something like that instead?"

Jack chewed on his toast as he thought. "Yeah, I guess so. What choice do I have?"

Shelby was thankful for the compromise. "Okay. I'll talk to Jayne today."

Jack got up from the table and kissed his wife stiffly on her forehead. "Let me know what Jayne says and what you plan to do." Shelby reached for a hug, but Jack walked away and out the front door for work, leaving her to wonder if their relationship would ever be the same.

Jayne was happy to hear from Shelby and had her set up in a new truck with a cross-country produce schedule within a couple of weeks.

Shelby hated leaving her friends at ESCC, but her marriage had to take priority. Their relationship was still rocky, but now that Shelby was on a regular schedule and home more, Jack didn't seem as upset.

◊◊◊

After finishing his long haul, Jimmy had gone to see his girlfriend before heading back to pick up his next load. He squinted when he saw a figure hitchhiking. He eased over to the shoulder.

Betty kept walking, pretending she didn't notice him. Jimmy rolled down his window and shouted at her, "Hey, lady, it's not safe walking out here alone. If you'd like a ride, I'd be happy to assist."

Betty didn't care for the man's looks, but a ride was a ride, and she wasn't in any position to be picky. "That would be great," she said, putting on a big fake smile.

He reached over and opened the passenger side door. Betty climbed in. "Where you headed?" he asked.

"Bakersfield."

"Well, I'm scheduled in the opposite direction. Let's get to the yard. I'm sure we can find a driver headed that way. I've got to ask…what you doin' out here?"

"My old man. We were headed to California, to start over. We had a fight and he threw me out of the car. I got a job lined up, but I need to get there."

"Tough break. We'll find you a ride headed that way."

"Great," said Betty.

Betty was in the dispatch office sipping coffee when Jimmy entered with a man who looked even seedier than he did. "Betty, this is Bean. He's headed to Barstow and can take you at least that far."

"I don't have much money," Betty gave the driver a wink, letting him know she might be interested in more than just a ride.

The driver smiled, obviously catching her drift. "Don't worry about the money," he said with a sleazy smile. "I'm sure we can work something out."

The driver pointed toward a bright yellow Pete in the parking lot. "My truck's over there."

They were on their way within the hour.

Betty wasn't thrilled about having to have sex with this man but she would get rid of him soon enough. Betty had grown up on the highway and had learned after her father died how to get what she needed from the men on the road. But she had never quite gotten used to the constant blabbering that some truckers did when they had company. When she was trucking alone, she could always turn the radio off if a driver babbled on and on, but it was hard to turn someone off when you were in the same truck. Betty knew she had to shut this guy up if she wanted to hold onto her sanity until they got to California.

Once Bean crossed the California state line on Highway 15, Betty couldn't take it any longer. "Hey, Bean, why don't you take a nap and let me drive for a little while?"

"You drive?"

"As a kid, I used to go out with my dad. I love to drive, and I know exactly where we're headed."

Bean looked uncertain. He clearly wasn't keen on the idea of a woman behind the wheel of his 459 Peter Cat, but Betty could tell he was tempted by the idea of a nap. "You sure you can handle this baby of mine?" he asked. "She's all I got, and she's pretty powerful. Maybe we could take a nap together?"

"Let's save that for when we get to Barstow, then we can spend the whole night together before I have to leave," Betty forced herself to say, although she wanted to slap the crap out of the pig. "Besides, you'll just be right there in the sleeper if I need your help."

"Alright. Let's see what ya got, little lady."

As Betty drove down the road in peace, with Bean snoring in the sleeper, she turned the CB up slightly, hoping to get some "bear" information. Driving in California was always slow, but with good intelligence, Betty knew she'd be able to make up some time. Barstow was only a couple of hours away through the mountains with another couple of hours into Bakersfield, California.

◊◊◊

The day after Betty rolled out of Utah with Bean, a couple of kids on four-wheel off-road vehicles discovered Billy's body. The state police sent the body to the coroner and cordoned off the area as a crime scene.

"I think I've seen that kid hanging out at the truck stop in Duchesne," a trooper told his colleagues. "I'm not sure, but I think he's friends with one of the clerks who works there. Maybe she can give us a little information about who he is and why someone would have done this to him."

The lead detective responded, "Go check it out, Leroy, and let me know what you find."

CHAPTER FOUR

Betty was glad when she finally rolled the truck into the truck stop in Barstow. "Hey, Bean, I'm stopping at the truck stop for a quick bathroom break, but I'm still feeling great so I'll finish her out to Bakersfield so you can rest."

"Okay," he mumbled and went back to drooling in his sleep. Betty hoped Bean would stay passed out, since she was only supposed to be getting a lift to Barstow where Bean was supposed to be dropping his load.

Betty hurried into the store, bought a prepaid cell phone, and made a call to her old boyfriend in Bakersfield. "Hey, Joey! It's me, Betty," she crooned.

"What ya want now, Betty?" he asked, obviously not thrilled to hear her voice.

"Well," she sighed. "I'm coming to town, and I'd really like to see you."

"And who do you want me to try to kill for you this time?"

"Oh, baby, that's old news!" She laughed. "I want to see you and make things up to you."

"Yeah, right. I heard you were in jail. So what? You running from the cops or something?"

"Baby, you are such a kidder. I was in jail on some technicality, but they let me out. I admit I've been a wild child, but I want to start my life over with you. You've got to admit we've got good chemistry between us."

Joey's libido overruled his brain. "Okay…I'm going to give you one more chance, but if you fuck me over again, we're finished for good."

"Thank you, darling. I should be at Butch's in about two hours."

"Two hours? How'd you get to California?"

"I got a ride with a driver out of Salt Lake."

"Salt Lake? Why aren't you in your own truck?"

"That jail thing? It was for hauling violations. Those assholes at ESCC fired me."

"Okay…give me a call when you get to Butch's."

◊◊◊

Leroy reached the truck stop and showed his badge at the counter to the young woman behind the counter. "Officer Leroy Summers. May I have a word with you, ma'am?"

"Sure," she said, her voice trembling a little. "Have I done something?"

"No, ma'am. Just asking some questions about a young man who may have been hanging around here lately."

"A lot of guys hang out around here. Has someone done something wrong?"

He extracted one of the Polaroid pictures of Billy taken at the scene. "We're just trying to identify a body. I have a picture of him; he's in really bad shape. I don't want to upset you, but we're trying to identify him."

Jessie nodded and came around the counter. She almost gagged when she looked at the picture. "Oh my God, it's Billy." Leroy caught her before she collapsed onto the floor and helped her over to a chair. She began to sob.

"I'm sorry, ma'am. I know this is difficult, but I need you to tell me what you know so we can find out who did this to him."

As Leroy tried to comfort and coax Jessie, his partner Officer Trapper entered the store after showing Polaroids to folks in the parking lot. He stood silently next to Leroy, took his notebook out of his pocket and made notes as Jessie spoke.

"You said his name is Billy?"

"Yes, Billy Watson. Now I understand why he wasn't here last night. We had a date. I thought he stood me up." She began weeping again. "I was so angry at him…I didn't know…"

Leroy gave her a few moments to compose herself. "So he drove a truck? What did it look like?"

"It was a big white rig with a flat trailer on the back."

"Do you know if he owned the truck or if he worked for a company?"

"He worked for some company out of Texas called Lightning Transporters or something like that."

"Do you remember anything else?"

Jessica thought for a minute. "He mentioned something about KW, but I never really knew what that meant."

"Was that in reference to his truck?"

"Yes, he called it his KW."

"Did Billy live around here, or in Texas?"

"Well, I think he lived with his folks in north Texas somewhere. He always talked about the farmlands near his folks' place in Amarillo. He liked it there and talked about maybe buying a little piece of land outside of town."

Trapper interrupted. "So you think he got called to deliver a load?"

"I don't know." Tears continued to roll down her cheeks. "We had plans to go out last night after I got off. I was supposed to go out back to his truck and pick him up in my car. But I saw him pull out around ten thirty without saying goodbye…he didn't even have his lights on when he pulled out. I thought he was just in a hurry or something and that he would call me later… but he never did." Jessie wiped her eyes.

"Did he ever mention to you about picking up hitchhikers or giving rides to anyone?" Trapper asked.

"No, Billy wasn't one to do that, I don't think. He was really picky about his truck and having a stranger in it for a ride just doesn't sound like him."

"What else can you tell me about last night, before you saw him leave in his truck?"

"He was in here, I guess, around seven or eight." Jessie took a deep breath through her sobs. "I really liked him. I can't believe someone killed him."

"Was there anyone in here last night that was different or who you've never seen before?"

Jessie thought for a few minutes. "Yeah, there was a strange lady in here last night. She was real skinny and had short blondish-brown hair. She bought a soda and hung around looking at stuff for a while and then she just left. I think it was shortly after Billy left."

"How's that?" Leroy asked.

"Well, after he left, I heard the bell over the door and I thought maybe he was coming back in to see me. But it was that lady, leaving." Jessie turned in her seat and talked to her coworker behind the counter. "Maggie, do you remember that skinny lady? The one you thought stole the cigarettes you put on the counter for Mr. Paul?"

"Yeah, she went by the counter and then out the door. I think she took them, alright."

"Did she get in a car, or was she walking?" Trapper asked.

"I'm not sure. We got kind of busy, and I just didn't pay much attention I guess," Jessie said.

Trapper and Leroy looked at each other and Trapper put his notebook away. "Thanks for your time, Jessie. If we have any further questions, how can we get ahold of you?"

Jessie reached in her pocket and took out a pen and then grabbed a napkin from the counter and wrote down her name and number on it. "Here. Please let me know what you find out."

"Yes, ma'am. We'll let you know."

Leroy and Trapper walked out into the parking lot. "What do you think, Leroy?" asked Trapper.

"I think we need to find that woman Jessie mentioned. Do you think it's a coincidence that a strange woman shows up here the same day that trucker woman was released from county lock-up after her murder case was declared a mistrial?"

Trapper scratched his head. "No way. That woman has to be halfway out of the state by now."

"Yeah, in Billy's truck. Let's find out what time she was released and get a picture we can show Jessie."

◊◊◊

Betty eased the truck into the fuel isle at Butch's in Bakersfield. She put the truck in park and looked back at the sleeper. Bean was snoring. She reached for her things, careful not to wake him, and quietly climbed out of the truck.

She walked away quickly with her bags and headed toward another truck stop just across the street. After she slipped around the building, she used her cell phone to call Joey. "Hey, I'm here, but I'm at the stop across from Butch's. Come get me, baby. I need you."

"On my way, darlin'."

CHAPTER FIVE

Shelby liked everything about her new job with Jayne Edwards. She was making good money and was making new friends; she was now a member of Women in Trucking. The only drawback was she was gone even more than before, which irritated Jack. *I don't know why she even bothers coming home,* he often thought. *It's obvious she loves the road more than me.*

Jack knew he had two choices: sit around stewing about his absent wife or take up something that gave him pleasure. It didn't take him long to hook up with his old riding buddies. They usually met at the local bars to drink and play pool. Several were divorced and others had their own domestic issues. Their conversation focused on booze, bikes, and sports. Being among old buddies made him feel twenty years younger. With his kids grown and his wife driving across the country, he was beginning to enjoy his newfound freedom. After a few weeks, he had escalated from one or two beers in a couple of hours to consuming several beers over the course of many hours.

One night, if he hadn't been tired and a little afraid of what he was thinking, he might have stayed until closing. The cute little lady at the bar had caught his eye. He was willing to dance with her, but thought that might have opened up a door he wasn't sure he wanted to go through—at least not yet anyway. "I gotta go, guys," Jack announced, ignoring their protests.

When Jack left the bar and walked over to his bike, he noticed he was not the only one to have come through the door. "Need some company?" the cute gal who had been at the bar asked. "I love motorcycles and I really like this motorcycle rider."

Jack was flattered. Part of his body wanted to take this cute gal home. "Thanks," he said. "But, I better not tonight. I got work in the morning and well, the old ball and chain might have some objections to my keeping company with another woman."

"Oh, I didn't know you were married. Sorry."

"For now. Maybe another time, sugar."

"I don't need an angry wife after me. If you guys don't work out, look me up." She handed Jack a piece of paper with her number on it and then kissed him on the cheek. "See ya later, handsome."

Jack took the piece of paper and reached for her hand. "You can count on it."

She sashayed by him so that Jack had no doubt about what she really wanted from him. "I'll be waiting for a call."

As Jack was watching her walk to her late model Honda sedan, his phone rang. Shelby's name popped up on the caller ID. "Shit." He shoved the phone back into his pocket and started his bike. "Not now, Shelby." He patted his shirt pocket to make sure the gal's number was still there. He pulled out of the parking lot. He wasn't sure he was going to call her, but the idea became more tempting the longer he rode towards home.

Why didn't he answer? Shelby wondered. *He needs to answer even when we're fighting. He's acting like a spoiled brat.* She was on the Nevada/California border and had hoped to talk to him before going to bed. Part of her wanted to avoid any more conflict, but she knew if they stopped communicating things were only going to get worse. "Where can he be at this hour?" She wondered aloud as she changed into her pajamas. "Maybe he went to bed early." Shelby hoped she was right as she lay her head down on her pillow and drifted off to sleep.

◊◊◊

The information Jessie had provided to the police was enough for them to put a profile together about him, including details about his truck. They contacted his employer and discovered he had a company credit card and requested the bank put a trace on charges over the last several weeks. They went to the store that posted the last transaction, with a copy of the receipt and Betty's picture.

Based on the date and time stamp, the manager motioned them to the clerk who had been on duty. Trapper showed the young man Betty's picture. "Is this the person who made the purchases on this receipt?" he asked.

"Yeah, I think so," the kid replied.

"Did you ask her for identification?"

Afraid he was going to get into trouble for not asking for ID he said, "She gave me the credit card and I ran it before I realized it had a man's name on it. When I questioned her about it, she said it was her boyfriend's and that he was asleep in their truck. She pointed to it in the parking lot."

"And you believed her?" Leroy asked.

"Yeah, I mean…,"

"Never mind, describe the truck."

The clerk gave him the same description that Jessica had given them.

The two officers showed Betty's picture around the parking lot.

"Yeah, I remember a couple of weeks ago she was looking to pawn some stuff."

"Did she say why she needed the money?"

"Maybe, she seemed in a hurry. Julio stepped in. He sells all kinds of shit from the back of his truck. When I see him, I just walk away."

"I don't know about you," Leroy said to Trapper, "but I'm convinced that killer Betty Burton somehow made it from Duchesne to this truck stop in Salt Lake, after hijacking Billy."

◊◊◊

"Why are you here instead of over at Butch's Truck Stop?" Joey asked Betty as she climbed into his pickup truck.

Before answering, she leaned over and gave him a deep, passionate kiss. "No reason." Betty looked over at the fuel island at Butch's where Bean's truck was still parked, which meant Bean still didn't know she was gone—at least for now. "Come on, let's get out of here," she said, "I really want to get back to your place."

Betty spent the next few days satisfying Joey's every desire. She had food, a roof over her head and plenty of sex, but what she needed was money. She wanted to disappear before the cops connected Billy's killing to her. But before that, she still had a score to settle…little Miss Barbie was going to die.

◊◊◊

"Joey…," Betty said one night as he lay on the bed, panting from their strenuous lovemaking. "I do appreciate all you are doing for me…but I feel bad… I'd like to make some money of my own so I don't feel like a kept woman."

"Wow, you really have changed. Don't worry, darlin', you're giving me all a man could want."

"I'm serious. I want to go shopping, get some nice things…with my own money."

"Okay, I'll ask around."

◊◊◊

"Guess what, darlin'?" Joey called as he walked through the door after work a few days later. "I talked with my boss today, and he's going to see if he can get you a job as a driver. Isn't that great?"

"That sounds great! But to be honest, I was thinking maybe I should give driving a rest for a while and try something different. You know, something that wouldn't take me away from the house and you so much. Even if I do get a job with you at your company, we'd be on different routes and probably different shifts. What good would that be if we never got to see each other?"

Joey looked at Betty, something in her voice sounded strange. "Yeah, maybe you're right…." He slouched to the sofa and turned on the TV.

Betty went to the refrigerator and got a beer for each of them. "Don't be like that," she said, handing him the beer. "You know I just want to spend time with you. I was thinking of maybe waiting tables at the truck stop."

Joey thought about the idea. Since he ate lunch in that restaurant every day, he'd be able to see her and keep an eye on her. "Okay, I like that idea. But I gotta admit—I'm a little concerned you'll hook up with some trucker and take off on me again."

"Not a chance." Betty snuggled up to him and laid her head on his chest. "I like being here with you."

◊◊◊

Shelby hadn't talked with Jack in two days. Every time she called the house either the answering machine picked up or Steven answered. All he knew was his dad was out but didn't know where. His cell phone went right to voice mail. Shelby had a sudden desire to go home, but she was headed out of California toward Washington State with a load to deliver. As she hit the highway, she tried Jack's cell phone one more time. "Come on, Jack. Stop being a baby and answer the phone."

"Hello?"

Shelby let out a sigh of relief. "Jack, where have you been? I've been trying to call you for the last two days."

"I've been busy," he sniped. "You know, doing my job."

"Jack stop acting like this and talk things out with me. Ignoring me isn't going to fix anything. It's just going to make things worse."

"Look, Shelby. We are never going to come to a compromise on this because there isn't one. I want you home and you want the road. End of discussion. You do your thing; I'll do mine. If and when you get tired of the road and if there's anything left of our relationship, we'll deal with it then. Right now I'm busy at my job. I'm going out with my friends tonight. Maybe we can talk things over when you get home in a few weeks."

"Out with your friends?" she spat. "What? You've decided to party because I won't give in to you? You're acting like a child."

"I have work to do. I've gotta go." He hung up without saying goodbye.

"What an asshole!" Shelby shouted. "I'm not taking this anymore." When she was done on the West Coast she'd head back to Texas and stay there until the issue with Jack was settled once and for all.

◊◊◊

Betty filled out the application at the truck stop and then put it in her pocket. She sipped at the iced tea she'd ordered, thinking about how she was going to get the job without a paper trail. "Can I get you anything else?" the waitress asked, reaching for Betty's glass. "I can give Larry your application, if you like?"

Betty took her glass back from the waitress. "No, but can you have Larry come out here so I can talk to him for a minute? I sure would appreciate it, hon."

"I can see if he's busy."

Betty sat sipping her tea. Staying with Joey Altman had benefited her in a few ways. She had been able to buy hair dye and conditioner, so her hair shined a lovely chestnut brown. The sumptuous dinners she cooked helped fill her body out in the right places, and based on their evening romps, she could still convince any red-blooded male to do whatever she wanted.

A tall, thirty-something man with pocked skin and oily hair approached her. "Hi, I'm Larry, the manager," he said. "Jenny said you wanted to talk to me."

Betty leaned forward, showing a bit of cleavage as Larry took a seat across from her in the booth. "Yes, sir. Nice to meet you. My name is Betty."

"What can I do for you?"

"Well, this is kind of embarrassing, but I had a traffic accident…and a couple warrants for my arrest…hit and run…failure to appear…minor stuff and well…I really need a job. One that I can stay under the wire, if you know what I mean?"

"Yeah, I understand," said the manager, smiling slowly. "Been there myself, but I really can't do anything like that here. It's all corporate-controlled."

"Yeah, but I would be willing to just work for tips. I won't take the pay and maybe we can work something else out on the side if you'll do me this favor." Her lips formed a perfect pout and she looked up at him through her dark eyelashes. She twisted a strand of hair around her finger.

Larry leaned back in his chair, and observed the cougar in front of him. He reached out and touched Betty's hand. "Welcome aboard, Betty. I think we are going to have fun working together. You start tomorrow at eight a.m. sharp."

Betty patted Larry's hand. "Thank you, Larry."

"Be on time." He leaned forward and whispered, "Just remember, the first sign of trouble from you and you're gone."

"I promise you won't be disappointed."

On her way back to Joey's, Betty stopped and bought Joey's favorite beer. When she arrived back at his place, she fixed him dinner.

"Smells great," Joey said. What are we celebrating?"

"I got a job today. Waiting tables at the truck stop during the day."

"Good for you," he said and headed to the living room. "Bring me a plate out here. I want to watch the game," Joey said and turned on the TV.

I'm going to enjoy fucking Larry, Betty thought.

◊◊◊

"I'm sorry Brandi, but I have to go home," Shelby explained to the exasperated dispatcher. "It's an emergency. If you can get me a load out of Washington, Oregon or California going to Texas, I'll load it. I just want you to know I'm headed home with or without a load."

"I'll do what I can but with such short notice it's going to be hard. Jayne isn't going to like this. Can I ask what the emergency is?"

"It's my husband…he's not well right now."

"Okay. I'll call ya back in a couple hours."

Brandi called her in less than twenty minutes. "Be in L.A. in the morning and get a load headed for Dallas."

"Thanks Brandi, I owe you one."

"You're welcome. Let me know how your husband is doing."

Shelby tried to call Jack with the news she was headed home, but he wasn't taking her calls. Frustrated, she tried Steven.

"No, Mom. Dad's not here. I haven't seen him much at all this week. He's been hanging out with Uncle Tuck and Ralph. I know 'cause they called here yesterday for him. Oh yeah, and some lady called last weekend for him. When I told her he wasn't home she said she thought she might be looking for a different Jack."

"Don't tell your father, but I'm going to be coming through on my way to Dallas. I'm going to find out just what the hell he's up to."

"I don't like all the fighting you guys have been doing lately. Please don't put me in the middle."

"I'm sorry. It's been really hard for me as well. Your father is just being stubborn…and I'm being stubborn, too. Maybe if I come home, your hard-headed parents can work it out."

"I hope so, Mom. Love ya."

"Me too, baby. I'll be home in about three days."

Shelby had a little trouble with a tire when she got near Bakersfield. "Hey, lady driver," said a voice through the grainy speakers. "Just thought you might like to know you got a flat on your inside rear back tandem."

"Yeah, thanks for the information, driver. I realized it a few miles back and I'm taking it on into Bakersfield to get fixed."

"Hope everything is alright. This is John Boy if you need any help."

"Thanks, John Boy. This is Barbie, I'll be okay once I get to the truck stop."

"Okay, Barbie. Be careful."

"Same to you."

CHAPTER SIX

It was taking forever for the mechanics to fix her tire. She phoned Brandi, but the call went straight to voice mail. "Hey, Brandi, I know it's early and so I just want you to know I got a flat and I'm having it fixed in Bakersfield. I should make my pickup before noon sometime but I'm going to be late." Shelby hung up the phone and told the repair guys she was going into the truck stop for some breakfast. "Call me on my cell when my truck's ready."

It was close to 6:00 a.m. as Shelby entered the restaurant. The place was bustling with early morning customers. She found a seat at the truckers' counter and waited for a waitress to notice. "Can I get you some coffee this morning?" The waitress put a menu in front of Shelby and reached for a cup from under the counter.

"Yes, please, and a couple of eggs over easy and some dry whole wheat toast."

◊◊◊

Betty left for work early. She let Joey sleep in since he didn't have to work today. She walked through the door of the restaurant, put on an apron, and headed to the back of the room. "Hey, gang, what section of tables do I get this morning?" Today Betty was friendly, but the other waitresses considered her to be a Jekyll and Hyde. They knew not to cross her and kept their distance. Sheila was the wait staff supervisor, and most of the time she stood her ground with Betty, but today she didn't seem in the mood for a fight so she gave Betty a really good section.

"You can have section five," Sheila told her. "But you'll need to help cover the truckers' counter."

"No problem. Thanks."

Betty looked over her section and then over the counter area. *I'll be dammed.* She stepped back into the pantry and couldn't believe her luck as she looked around the corner again at Shelby sitting at the counter. She almost burst out laughing but was interrupted by another waitress. "Betty, you have a table of four."

"Yeah, okay." Betty quickly went to work but did everything she could to keep an eye on Shelby while not letting Shelby see her.

"Betty, you have a customer at the counter."

Betty noticed it was one of her regulars but didn't want to blow her cover. "Sandy, can you cover that one for me? I'm a little busy."

"Okay, but he requested you."

"Yeah, I know, but I really need to finish with these people back here. I'll be up there soon."

Sandy rolled her eyes. "Okay."

Betty took care of her customers and went to the storage room in the rear of the kitchen. She remembered seeing some rat poison next to the wall and decided she was going to do her best to get it into Shelby's food.

"Perfect." Betty reached down and picked up the poison. "This might not kill you Shelby, but you are definitely going to be sick as a dog." Betty dumped some of the poison into a napkin she'd hid in her pocket before leaving the storage room. She went to the food counter. "Hey, Harvey, the lady at the counter needs her food. What did she order?"

"Oh, I think hers is that scrambled eggs and toast."

"Okay, well, can I have it before she has a cow?"

"Yeah, sure. It's down there at the end."

Betty took the plate down and added some of the poison to the eggs and then when Harvey wasn't looking, she replaced the plate back under the heat lamp and took a different plate out to one of her customers. "Thanks, Harvey."

"You got it, Betty."

Shelby sat reading a local paper that had been left on the counter. "Here ya go, ma'am. Is there anything else I can get for you this morning?"

"Maybe some honey if you have some please," answered Shelby.

"Alright, be right back."

While the waitress was gone, the man sitting next to Shelby spoke up. "Not too many people remember how wonderful honey is on toast. I even put it in my coffee."

Shelby wasn't really interested in a conversation with anyone, but the man was older and seemed nice enough. "Yeah, I love honey," she said just to be friendly. "And it's so much better for you than sugar. Being a driver we don't get much exercise and so I know if I don't watch it I'll end up with a butt the size of Texas."

The man and Shelby were laughing when the waitress came back with Shelby's honey and the man's food. "There ya are, ma'am, and there's your eggs, sir." Both Shelby and the man took their items and thanked the waitress.

Betty watched from her side of the room, hoping that soon enough Shelby would be feeling sick or doubling over in pain. *Come on, bitch. Eat your eggs all up.*

The man who was sitting next to Shelby covered his scrambled eggs in salsa and salt and pepper before taking his first bite. Shelby dabbed at the yoke of her eggs with her honey toast and drank some coffee. The two drivers enjoyed their meals in quiet until the man began to rub his stomach.

"Man, I feel terrible," he said, groaning.

Shelby looked at the driver and noticed that he'd turned white as a sheet. "Are you okay, mister?" Shelby watched as the man tried to get up from his seat and then fell to the floor. Shelby yelled for the waitress. "Call an ambulance now! I think this man is having a heart attack or something."

The waitress covered her mouth and ran to make the call. "Oh my God."

Shelby had CPR training, which she could administer in case the man became unresponsive, but he was simply clutching his stomach. "It hurts so bad. Get me some help, please! I knew those eggs tasted funny." Shelby did her best to keep the man comfortable while they waited for the ambulance. The man was beginning to have trouble breathing so Shelby did all she could to keep him calm.

"Please everyone, move back. The ambulance is on the way," Larry called out.

Betty hadn't seen exactly what had happened, but not seeing Shelby at the counter made her believe that her plan had worked and that Shelby was the one on the floor. She went back to her customers and tried to pretend nothing was going on until one of them returned to the table. "Poor old guy, they think he had a heart attack or something. That lady driver over there's doing a great job keeping him calm, though."

Shit, Betty thought in disbelief.

Shelby stayed with the man until he was taken away in the ambulance. She got his name and handle. He was from Texas also and she promised him she'd look him up when he got back home.

As the ambulance pulled out, Shelby turned to go back into the restaurant. A policeman stopped her at the door. "Excuse me, ma'am. Can you tell me anything about the man or what happened?"

"I have no idea what happened. We were just sitting there enjoying our breakfast and all of a sudden he turned white and fell to the floor. I know he's from Texas and he's a truck driver, but not much more than that. I hope he'll be alright."

"It may just be food poisoning or something."

"All he had was scrambled eggs and toast. I had eggs and toast and I'm fine."

The officer held the door for Shelby. "I'm sure everything will be alright."

The bustling room went quiet when the policeman entered. He went to talk with Larry who was standing next to the register. Shelby's phone rang several times during the entire episode, but she ignored it while caring for the man. She went to the counter, laid a couple dollars down, and checked her phone. There were calls from the repair shop as well as Brandi. She picked up the check and went to the register to pay it. She placed her ticket on the counter. Larry took the ticket. "No need, ma'am. It's on the house. Thank you so much for helping that man. Was he a friend of yours?"

Shelby was touched by the generosity. "Thank you. No, I just talked with him for the first time this morning."

"Well, thank you for saving his life."

"Not sure I did that, but you're welcome."

Betty was furious that her little plan had not worked. When the break-fast service resumed she slammed plates down in front of customers and fought with co-workers. "Get the hell out of the way! Can't you see that I'm working here?"

Before long, Larry asked her to come to the back office. "Look, I'm not sure what is up with you today, but I suggest you either change the attitude or go home for the day."

Betty was tired of men telling her what to do. "Okay, I think you're right. I'm not feeling really well. Maybe it was those eggs I ate a little while ago." Betty took her apron off and headed toward the front door. *I know you walked out of here, Barbie, but I'm going to find out where you're headed and settle things once and for all.*

◊◊◊

Even with all the mishaps, Shelby made it into L.A. before noon. She got her load and headed towards Texas. Road construction slowed her progress and she found it difficult to stay awake when she was tired and the traffic moved at a snail's pace. She was halfway to Indio when she finally decided that it was time to call Jack again. It was almost three in California, almost five in Texas, and that meant Jack would be getting ready to leave work. She let the phone ring several times and was about to hang up before it went to voice mail when Jack answered. "Hello?"

His voice sounded strangely cheerful, and Shelby could hear lots of loud background noise. "Jack?" she said, a little confused.

Jack realized that he'd answered his cell phone to the one person he really didn't want to talk to in front of his friends. He'd been drinking since four and was beginning to feel a little buzzed. He held the phone away from his mouth and covered it with his hand, but his fingers were around the top but not the speaker. "It's the old ball and chain calling from California or wherever. Let me see what she wants and then we can continue with what's really important. The beer and the women!" The whole table broke out in a cheer. "Hey, Shelby. What's up?"

Shelby wanted to chew him out, but swallowed her anger. She didn't want to lose the opportunity to speak with him. "Well, I was wondering if we could talk about a few things. Is this a good time?"

"No, not really. I'm out with the guys and I'm having a great time. Can we talk about this stuff whenever you decide to come home again?"

Shelby cringed. She knew trying to talk to Jack while he was drinking was a bad idea. *Maybe if I let him have some fun, he'll be in a better mood when I get home*, she reasoned. "Fine, Jack," she said. "I'll be home soon. Promise me we can sit down and try and work these things out between us when I get there?"

"Sure, Shelby, when you get home. See ya."

He just hung up without saying goodbye or that he loves me. That's happening too often, Shelby thought.

As soon as he ended the call, Jack turned off his phone and put it in his pocket. He went over to one of the girls sitting at the bar. "May I have this dance, please?"

"Sure," she answered with a sly smile.

Jack and the girl danced several times and then joined his friends again. "Wow, I'm getting old. I used to dance all night, now I'm tired after two dances."

"How's Shelby doing, Jack?" his friend Tucker asked.

Jack blew the question off with a wave of his hand. "Who knows?"

Tucker raised his eyebrows. "You're sure Shelby would like you dancing with all those women, Jack? What about your heart? Don't you think maybe you should be taking it a little slower with the beer and dancing? Sure wouldn't want to see my old buddy lying on the ground fighting for his life again."

"Frankly, Tuck, it's none of your business. And I really don't care what Shelby thinks. She's never home and my heart is stronger than ever. Butt out."

Tucker lifted his beer in the air and toasted his friend in a truce. "Good enough, my friend."

One of the girls from the bar came over and grabbed Jack by the hand for another dance. He happily joined her on the floor. After the dance, he went back to the table, fell into his chair, and drank some beer. "Man, that girl is going to wear me out."

Tammy, the girl Jack had gotten friendly with the other night in the bar, came through the door just as Jack finished off his beer. He slammed his bottle on the table and smiled at her as she passed Jack and his friends. Tammy smiled a seductive smile and took a seat on a barstool. She ordered herself a beer just as Jack found his way to the barstool next to her. "I'll get that, Mac." Jack laid a twenty on the counter and whispered in Tammy's ear. "You look beautiful tonight."

"Thanks, Jack."

"You remembered my name."

"Kind of hard to forget a handsome man like you, Jack."

Mac placed the beers they had ordered in front of the couple and gave Jack his change. "Thanks, Mac." Jack sipped at his and then said, "I haven't seen you in a while. Where have you been?"

"I've been away on business. I'm a buyer for a clothing distributor and I go to a lot of style shows around the country."

"Oh. So you're away from home a lot, too?"

"No, not really. I travel maybe once a month for about four days."

"That's not too bad. My wife is gone all the time. She drives a big eighteen-wheel truck all over the country. She spends more time with that truck than with me, so I guess she likes it."

"So, I gather you're still with her? That's why you haven't called me yet?"

"Yeah, but trust me, things are not going well. I'm not sure what's going to happen. Hey, can we change the subject? Better yet—how about a dance?"

"Sure."

Jack took Tammy out on the floor and danced with her for several songs, including a very romantic slow one. The conversation and companionship between Tammy and Jack was a nice distraction for Jack. Shelby never crossed his mind. At closing time, Jack came back to reality and realized that he and Tammy were the only ones left in the bar. Jack's friends had apparently left earlier, and Jack had been so into Tammy he hadn't even noticed. "Wow. Everyone's gone," he said. "Maybe we better get out of here."

"Yeah, you could be right." Tammy gathered her things. They left arm in arm.

In the parking lot, Jack knew he was going to have to make a serious decision about just how far he was going to go with Tammy. He walked her toward her car and decided that he better keep things platonic for a while. He didn't know if he was ready to cheat on Shelby…yet. He found it difficult to resist the temptation of going home with Tammy when she planted a deep passionate kiss on his lips.

"Not ready to take me to bed yet, are you, Jack?"

Jack shook as he fought the urge to kiss the beautiful woman before him.

"That's okay, I can wait. I rather like the fact you aren't a cheater. Not too many honorable men like you around these days." She got in her car and rolled down the window. "You have my number and my offer is still open when you finally finish things with your wife. I'll be at Buckeye's Friday for band night. I usually make it here, like tonight, for lady's night. I hope I see you again, Jack."

Jack touched Tammy's cheek and let her drive out of the parking lot. "You can count on it. I'll be here." Jack walked to his bike and sat on it for a while, thinking about his life and what he really wanted.

He realized he was speeding down the street on his bike and accelerated when his saw Tammy's rear bumper. He honked his horn at her. Tammy pulled her car to the side of the road and opened her car door just in time for Jack to reach down and plant a deep passionate kiss on her. "Jack, what's going on?"

"I don't know, Tammy, but I know I want to be with you and I want to spend the night with you. I'm not sure what's happened to my marriage, but frankly, I don't care at this point."

"Are you sure, Jack? Are you sure it's not just the alcohol talking? I don't want to be a one-night stand or someone you're using to get even with your wife."

"I know. I don't want that either and I can't promise you anything. I don't know what is going to happen, but right now I want to make love to you and the rest of it we can deal with tomorrow."

Tammy kissed him and then pushed him out of her car door. "Follow me, big boy."

Jack went back to his bike, not caring what he was doing or what the consequences of his actions were going to be in the morning.

◊◊◊

Betty walked into the tire shop and went straight to one of the garage workers working on a truck. "Hey, I need to ask you a question. You got a minute?"

The man turned toward Betty and wiped some of the grease from his hands. "I got a minute, but you're not supposed to be in here, doll-face."

"I just need to know if a blonde woman was in here and if you know where she might be headed."

"Yes, but you're still not supposed to be in here, so why don't we step outside?"

"Fine, but I'm in a hurry." Betty let him go ahead of her and picked up the wrench he'd left on the floor and shoved it in her jacket.

Betty and the man went out to the parking lot. Betty looked at him like a damsel in distress. "Yeah, there was a blonde in here earlier with a flat tire that we fixed for her. She was a little late picking it up though. Heard she was helping some man in the restaurant that had a heart attack or something."

"Where the hell was she headed?"

"I think she said she was headed to L.A. and then back to Texas."

"What kind of trailer was she pulling? Was it a sand hauler?"

"No, she was pulling a reefer for Interstate Produce."

"Maybe we can go into the back office and..." Betty was gone before the man could finish his request.

Betty had known from the beginning that she wasn't going to stay in Bakersfield long, but she hadn't expected to run into Shelby so soon. "Damn, the bitch went to a different company," she muttered to herself. "Bet she was afraid I'd find her. Guess what, Barbie? You found me, and now I'm on my way to finish you." Betty shook out her hair and hiked up her skirt. She went back to the truck stop, trolling for a driver who would take her to L.A. in exchange for some sexual favor. She found her mark in no time.

Betty climbed into the cab of a flatbed driver headed to L.A. "Thanks ,man, I really appreciate the lift. Do you know where Interstate Produce usually loads or unloads in L.A.? I have a job waiting for me down there if I can hook up with my co-driver in time. Stupid girl forgot to let me know where to meet her."

"No, I don't roll in that circle," answered the driver, "but I suppose we can reach out over the radio and locate those loading spots."

"Great idea. Thanks."

Betty worked the CB the entire way over to Grapevine and on into downtown L.A. until she finally located someone who knew some of the loading docks for Interstate Produce. "Thanks, driver. I sure appreciate the help."

"No problem. I'm glad you found out the information you needed, but I got to stop over here at the next available spot and let you out. I have to make my own load times."

"Okay," she said through gritted teeth. "But can you stop somewhere so I can use the restroom?"

"Sure. I need to use the restroom myself. Sorry I can't help you out further but I really need to do my job."

"I understand," she said, as they both headed to the restrooms. "Hey, how about I give you something sweet for the ride?"

"It's got to be a quickie." Betty took the man by the hand into the women's restroom, knowing that it had less traffic than the men's toilet. She lured him with kisses and heavy petting into a stall.

He was no longer moving when Betty left the stall with his wallet in her purse. She quickly turned the lock on the door. There was a janitor's closet next to the bathroom. She looked in, saw the bright yellow out of order sign, and put it on the door. She walked casually through the truck stop and over to the man's truck.

She drove to the next exit where there was an outlet mall. She parked at the far south end of the expansive mall. She walked all the way to the east side. She found a drug store, purchased hair dye, scissors, a gray sweatshirt and black leggings, and three chocolate bars, using the cash she found in the stolen wallet.

She studied the directory and saw there was a movie theater at the far north end, across the street from the outlet mall. She ate two of the chocolate bars as she crossed the street and walked over to the movie theater, then bought a ticket for the first movie. Once the theater opened, she skipped the movie and went into the bathroom where she stripped, chopped off her hair, dyed it and changed clothes.

She slipped into the movie as her hair dried and took a nap while the film played. She woke up as the credits were rolling. She took the plastic bag that held the empty packaging and her waitress clothes and dumped it in the large trash can outside the theater. She crossed the street, went to the west side of the mall, found an early model pickup truck parked at the end of a row, used a stolen credit to get in, reached under the dashboard and found the right wires. The engine roared to life.

CHAPTER SEVEN

Jack woke up with Tammy in his arms. He was in her apartment and in her bed. She was asleep as he lay there and thought through what he'd just done—not only to Tammy but also to Shelby. He felt a little guilty as he wondered how he was going to manage both women. He was angry with Shelby. He doubted their marriage would survive, but he wasn't sure he was ready to give up on it completely. The beautiful woman in his arms was exactly what the doctor ordered. She made him feel young and virile. He wasn't looking to give her up right now either. *Am I the kind of man who can handle a wife and a lover? Maybe.* He hoped, if he was lucky, Shelby wouldn't find out about Tammy and Tammy would want to keep the chemistry they had discovered between them.

Tammy woke up and reached her arms around Jack's neck. "Hey, handsome," she said in a husky voice. "You were wonderful last night. Do you want some breakfast?"

Jack kissed Tammy and moved to his side so he could see her lying naked on her back in front of him. "Maybe if you're on the menu." Jack ran his fingers over her breasts and down her tummy until Tammy giggled from the tickle.

"Okay, but we'll be late for work if we indulge in too much honey on our toast."

Jack laughed and pulled Tammy on top of him. "Give me some of that honey."

Tammy leaned forward and kissed Jack as he moved to let her have all she wanted of him.

◊◊◊

Betty finally gave up on the fifth loading facility—like the others; it was closed. She figured that Shelby was probably out of L.A. by now. "I'm going to find that bitch, whatever it takes," she vowed.

As she headed out of L.A. and down the highway toward Riverside, Betty felt free for the first time since getting out of jail. She was a redhead in a nondescript pickup truck. She knew she was going to have to change license plates soon and ditch the cell phone since Joey Altman had been blowing hers up all day. She didn't care; she was on her way back home.

It didn't take Betty long to figure out Shelby was no longer in California. She knew her nemesis still lived in Texas, so decided to head toward Odessa. With the nondescript pickup truck and a bandanna under a ball cap, Betty could have been easily taken for a male driving down the road. She was sure she was a step or two ahead of the cops, but the cash she had lifted from the man's wallet was running low. She knew if she gussied herself up, she could make a few quick bucks from truck stop Johns.

◊◊◊

It took Shelby a couple more days to get home. It was early evening when she finally pulled her truck up in front of the house. Jack's truck was not in the driveway and no lights were on in the house. *Strange,* Shelby thought.

Shelby entered the house, "I'm home," she announced. Steven didn't answer; he either had a date or was working overtime. *Maybe Jack got held up at work, too,* she thought as she pulled out her cell phone.

"Hello?" Jack answered. She heard a cheerfulness in his voice again and hoped he was done being angry with her.

"Hey, Jack. I'm home," she said. The background noise she heard was indicative of a bar, but still, she had to ask. "Where are you?"

"I'm out with the guys," he answered. "I'll be home late, so you go ahead and rest and we'll talk in the morning, okay?"

"Okay, Jack," she said, hesitantly. "Are you sure you don't want me to come down and join you for a little while?"

"No…no, you rest. I know you've been putting in a lot of hours on the road. In fact, I didn't think you were going to be home for a couple months."

"I decided I needed to come back home so we could talk."

"Well…that's fine. I've got to go…we'll talk tomorrow. See ya in the morning."

"Who was that, Jack?" Tammy asked.

"Shelby's home."

"Oh, so I guess you won't be staying with me tonight, huh?" she pouted.

Jack got off his stool and took Tammy by the hand. "Not all night. That would be too obvious. But after this dance I think we need to go to your place."

"Okay," Tammy smiled.

Ralph and Tucker saw the two slip out the door. "Hope Shelby doesn't find out what Romeo's been up to," Tucker said. "She'll cut his nuts off and feed them to that gal."

"You got that right. Wouldn't want to be in his shoes when she finds out."

Shelby did have suspicions but did not want her thoughts to run wild. She decided to get a bite to eat and watch some TV before going to bed. It felt strange being alone in her house as she walked from one room to another. She watched the news and a bit of some late night show. She was headed to bed when Steven pulled in the driveway.

"Hey, baby boy. I'm home," she said when he walked through the door.

Steven hugged his mother. "Sorry, Mom. Just here for a quick change of clothes. I'm off to Amanda's house. Dad's out again, I see."

Shelby nodded sadly. "Yeah, I guess he needs to be with his buddies for a while."

"I guess, but they sure do party a lot. He's been gone almost all week."

"You mean he's been out drinking every night?"

"I don't know for sure. I sure haven't seen much of him lately. His office called here Thursday morning looking for him. Guess he missed work or something."

"What? Why didn't he answer the phone?"

"Like I said, he hasn't been here much. Sorry, Mom. Amanda's waiting." Steven went to his room.

"Oh no!" Shelby sat down hard on the sofa. Her stomach churned. She took a deep breath. *No way. Jack would never do that to me. We have always worked our problems out. He loves me.* Tears welled up in her eyes as she thought about what her husband might be doing. *What should I do? Follow him? Spy on him? Trust him? Let it all go and hope he isn't cheating?* She finally decided not to jump to any conclusions or let her imagination get the better of her. *I'm sure he has a logical explanation for not coming home and for missing work,* she tried to convince herself.

Shelby got up and went to the bedroom. She laid her head on her pillow and tried to fall asleep, but sleep wouldn't come. She heard Steven leave and listened for hours for Jack to pull in the driveway. It was almost four in the morning when his pickup finally arrived. Shelby felt a combination of relief and anger. She pretended to be asleep when Jack snuck into their room. Jack dropped his clothes into the hamper and went straight to the shower without even kissing her, which was his usual custom.

Shelby knew then that something was up. However, she wasn't going to act like she suspected anything. She'd do her best to keep things to herself until she got the goods on Jack. If he was, in fact, having an affair, she'd make them both sorry.

The next morning, Shelby tried to act normal as she fixed them breakfast. "Honey, is it a good time to talk now?" she asked as they ate breakfast.

Jack was slightly hungover, but wasn't going to admit it. At first, he was going to blow her off, but realized it would be in his best interest to make peace with his wife. "Okay, honey," he said. "I'm sorry I've been such an ass about your job lately. I won't say anything more about your job. I'm disappointed that you're not home very much, but I understand you love your job. What would make me happy is if you let me know when you are going to be home so we can plan some quality time together."

Something in Jack's voice made Shelby suspicious. "Why the sudden change in attitude, Jack?"

"I thought you wanted me to back off, Shelby? Now you want me to be upset about the job?" He was frustrated. *How do other guys balance a wife and a mistress?* he wondered. *I have to stay calm.*

Shelby took a deep breath. "No. Your…I don't know…ambivalence about my job is such a dramatic change. It's just not like you to change your mind like this, but I'm grateful you're okay with my driving. Thank you."

Shelby went to kiss Jack, but he jumped up from the table. "You're welcome. I've got to get to the office."

Shelby was shocked. Jack had never refused a kiss under any circumstances. She sat down and sipped at her coffee. She was now convinced Jack was up to something, and she was determined to find out what. Her first order of business was to call Jayne to see if she could be assigned to Texas only routes. "Hey, Jayne. Can I come in and talk to you for a few minutes?"

"Sure, Shelby. Come on into the office. How is Jack doing? Dispatch told me you had an emergency."

"Yeah, he's okay for now, but I need to talk to you about Jack." Shelby remained intentionally vague, letting Jayne believe Jack's problems were physical.

"No problem, Shelby. I'll see you soon."

Before going to see Jayne and preparing to head for Dallas, Shelby went to their bedroom and looked through Jack's things for any clues as to his strange behavior. Pieces of scrap paper with telephone numbers scribbled on them were strewn across his dresser. She found a blank piece of paper and jotted some of the numbers down. She tried to convince herself that these numbers were work related, but decided to call a few of them anyway. Nothing else seemed out of the norm except for the perfume smell on his shirt from last night. *If he danced with someone at the bar, that might explain the smell. But why was he dancing and how close did he get to his partner?* The evidence she was really looking for most likely resided on his cell phone. But Shelby knew that was going to be hard to get since Jack hardly ever let his phone out of his sight.

Shelby felt sure that up until this point Jack had been faithful. She figured he was going through some sort of midlife crisis, which didn't excuse his behavior, but he wasn't a natural liar. If he was playing around, she'd catch him…eventually.

Jack loved her, but didn't always appreciate how savvy she was. He thought she was idealistic, someone who didn't look at things for how they were, but as she wanted them to be. Maybe it was Jack who wasn't the realist. Maybe he couldn't see that Shelby knew the truth when she saw it.

◊◊◊

"Wow. Someone did a number on this dude."

Two L.A. police officers looked over the body of the man that was lying face down in the restroom. They had been called to the scene a few hours earlier, but were still waiting for the coroner to arrive so they could have the body removed. Homicide detectives were scanning the area for evidence while the uniformed police officers kept the public at bay. One of the detectives, Brad Stevenson, found the wrench and informed his supervisor. "Lieutenant Tripp, I think I located the possible murder weapon." The Lieutenant eyed the evidence without touching it. "Bag it for forensics and try not to touch the handle. Maybe we can get a print match."

Lieutenant Tripp conferred with another of his unit members as they searched the crime scene. "Did you get anything from the attendant inside the store or from any of the customers? What about the man who found him in the bathroom?"

"Not much, Joe. No one remembers hearing or seeing anything."

"Any ideas other than robbery?"

"Nope, that seems to be the only motive. With his wallet gone, we won't even have an ID until we take his fingerprints. And even then if he's just some poor unlucky soul, without his prints on file somewhere, we won't know who he is 'til someone comes looking for him."

Joe sighed. "Well, let's get this scene finished and get him out of here."

◊◊◊

Shelby was ready to get back on the road. She made one call before she left, and was relieved when Jack answered. "Hey, Jack. If everything is okay between us, I'm going to go ahead and take my load to Dallas now. There are some loads out there they want me to take east if you're okay with that."

"Sure, sounds like a good run," Jack's tone was blasé. "Have fun and be careful."

Shelby noticed there was no term of endearment…no honey…no baby. "Okay, see ya later." Shelby was now convinced Jack was having an affair. It was true she was headed east, but not to the East Coast, she would be back in Texas in no time, but wasn't about to let him know that.

"Alright. See ya." Jack was relieved. With Shelby back out on the road, he could spend more time with Tammy and not have to worry about his wife. As soon as he got off the phone with Shelby, he called Tammy. "Hey, what's up, beautiful?"

"Not much, baby. Just working."

"Shelby left for another trip. You want to get together tonight?"

"Sure, but I have to work late, so why don't I just meet you at my place around eight. We can have a late dinner and watch a movie or something."

"Sounds great. Miss you."

CHAPTER EIGHT

Betty was not a sentimental person; still she looked forward to being in her own home with her own stuff. She parked the pickup around the back of an abandoned restaurant, then she slipped out of the truck, pulled up her collar, and pulled the bill down as far as she could over her face. It was dusk and she was hard to see as she walked along the side of the road.

When she reached her house, she was relieved no one was squatting in it. The place was run over with weeds and grass.

She reached for her keys, which luckily had been returned to her, and unlocked the front door. It was apparent that the cops had been there, tossing her place looking for evidence to send to Utah to incriminate her, but to her amazement, everything seemed to be just as she'd left it; no one had broken in and taken anything. There was no electricity and she couldn't see very well in the dark, but she would take care of that as soon as she could. A putrid stench came from the kitchen. She figured some critter had crawled under the refrigerator or oven and died. "I'll deal with that tomorrow," she muttered as she made her way back to the bedroom.

As she removed her clothing, the man's wallet fell out of her pocket. She picked it up and remembered the credit cards. She hoped she could use one tomorrow to get her utilities turned back on. She really wanted to take a shower, but she would have to wait. Dust flew when she pulled back the comforter but she didn't care. She was home, and right now, nothing else mattered.

◊◊◊

Shelby reached Dallas and met up with some of her buddies at the truck stop. Several truckers sat at the counter, drinking coffee when Shelby walked in.

"Where ya been hiding, Barbie? Come to join us for coffee?" Knight Wolf called out.

Shelby joined the others at the counter. "Oh, been running a lot of stuff to the West Coast. Having some trouble with the hubby, so I'm going to try and keep it a little closer to home for a while."

"Trouble on the home front makes things a lot harder on the road."

"Yeah, but I think I'm going to solve the problem soon or at least find out who the problem might be."

"Oh, one of those problems?" Doo Little, another trucker, asked. "Blonde, redhead, or brunette?"

"Not sure yet, but I'm fixing to find out."

After coffee, Shelby went back to her truck and called Jack without taking notice of the time. When he didn't answer, she wasn't surprised. She placed another call.

"Hello?"

"Steven, this is Mom. Is Dad at home?"

Steven sounded groggy. "I don't know, Mom. It's three in the morning. Did you call his cell phone?"

"Yes, and he didn't answer. Can you please check and see if he's home?"

"Sure," Steven groaned. "What's wrong, Mom? You okay? Are you in trouble?"

"Everything is fine, honey. I'm just worried about your dad and all the partying he's been doing lately. When he didn't answer his cell, I got worried he might have gotten in an accident or something."

Steven pushed open a door and announced. "He's not home from the bar yet. The bed is still made." He heard Shelby sigh. "I'll text you when he gets in; you let me know if you reach him beforehand."

"Okay, honey. Go back to sleep. I'm sorry I woke you up."

Shelby sat back in her seat and thought for a few minutes, willing herself to remain calm. She did not want Jack to know she suspected infidelity. Shelby had developed the practice when she was teaching, making lists to organize her thoughts for her lesson plans. She needed a plan now. She grabbed a notepad and pen and began jotting down some observations, such as the time and dates of phone calls not answered and comments Steven had made about Jack not being home. When she was done writing, she scanned the list and knew what she had to do.

Her heart ached at the realization that her husband was with someone else. She wondered what was wrong with her and why he couldn't give her the same support she'd always given him. Tears filled her eyes as she lay down in her sleeper. "Jack is an asshole for making me look like a fool," she mumbled, "but when I get done with him, he'll see who the real fool is and…" Just then Steven texted her: *Dad's home.* She texted her thanks back and added: "Home 4:30 a.m." to her list.

◊◊◊

Betty pretended she was the trucker's wife when she called the utility company on her cell phone the next morning. She told them they had purchased the house and wanted the utilities turned on immediately. She paid the deposit with one of the trucker's credit cards and they promised to send someone out that afternoon.

With the utilities turned on, Betty's next issue was transportation. Her truck and car had been impounded when she was arrested and it would cost a fortune to pay the tow yard to get them out. Besides, she didn't want anyone to know she was back. She walked out of the house and went over to the dilapidated carport. Leaves and branches covered the tarp, totally camouflaging the car underneath. It took Betty almost an hour to clear the debris and tarp off the 1984 Chevy Camaro, a classic eighties car. The once fire engine red car was dull, and it was difficult to tell the paint from the rust. It had been Ted's project car, which he kept at Betty's so that his wife Annabel would not know about it. "What did I ever see in that pussy?" Betty asked herself. "At least I have the sucker's car." Ted had replaced most of the hoses and had tuned up the motor. Betty went to the front of the car, bent down, and reached up under the front driver's side wheel well. Sure enough, the spare key was right where Ted had left it the last time he was at her house. She yanked open the driver's side door and got into the musty car. She placed the key in the ignition, but the engine would not turn over. The battery was dead.

She hoped the utility company was sending a man over to get her lights back on. She needed a favor: a jump for a jump.

◊◊◊

Shelby had not gotten much sleep, but she needed to get on the road. The voice of Knight Wolf came through the radio as soon as she hit the highway. "Be careful, Barbie. If that thing with the hubby doesn't work out, you know I'm always available."

Shelby rolled her eyes. "Behave yourself, Knight Wolf. You know your old lady would kick your ass."

"Got that right, Barbie," he laughed. "Stay safe."

Shelby wished that Jack knew what other men thought about her. *Maybe then he wouldn't take our marriage for granted.*

Her delivery in Dallas was quick, and she was within an hour of her next load when she called Jack.

"Hello?"

Shelby hadn't expected him to answer. "Hi," she said, startled. "Just checking on you. I tried to call you last night but you didn't answer."

"I was pretty tired last night. Guess I didn't hear the phone."

"Really? Did you go out last night?"

"For a little while. But I was home pretty early."

"I see."

"Why?"

"No reason. Just asking. I've been worried that you might be spending too much time at the bars, but I guess I'm worrying for nothing."

"Yeah, I got it under control."

"Okay then, I won't worry."

"So when you coming home?"

"Oh not for a while. Headed east right now."

"Okay, be careful."

"Alright. Talk to you later, Jack."

That conversation was one of the coldest Shelby had ever had with her husband. She forced herself to put it out of her thoughts as she drove to her pickup point. The load was headed right back to West Texas, but she'd already decided she wasn't telling anyone she'd be in the area. She planned to find out just what Jack was up to. She drove as fast as she could without getting pulled over.

Shelby pulled into the War Truck Stop at 1:30 a.m. She parked the truck and called a cab to check out the first bar where Jack might be hanging out. As the cab pulled up, she wasn't surprised when she saw Jack's bike in the parking lot. She handed an extra twenty-dollar bill over to the cabbie and asked if they could sit there for a while. She wanted to see where Jack went after the place closed. Before long, Jack and several of his buddies came out and got on their bikes to go home. A couple of girls came out after the guys but they got in a car and left together.

Jack sat on his bike for a little while before leaving. He was talking on his cell phone with someone. Shelby wondered who he could possibly be talking to that late at night, and from his body language, it didn't look like business. Jack hung up and pulled out of the parking lot. Shelby asked the cabbie to follow him for a little while. When she was sure he was headed home, she asked the cabbie to take her back to her truck. She paid the cabbie, got into her truck, pulled out her cell phone and called Jack.

"Hello?" he answered.

"Just checking in to see how my guys are doing," she said, trying to sound casual.

"We're fine, Shelby. What's with all the checkups?"

"I miss you, that's all. Can't I call and talk to my husband?"

"It's late, I'm in bed. Shouldn't you be in bed too?"

"I am in bed, Jack. I just wanted to talk to you."

"Well, call me tomorrow. I'm tired."

"Okay, I love you."

When Jack didn't respond in kind, she hung up and crawled into the sleeper, hoping things wouldn't look so bleak when she got up in a few hours.

◊◊◊

Betty went through the trucker's wallet, trying to figure out which cards she could use without causing suspicion. She came across a slip of paper with his PIN scribbled on it, giving her access to cash. She decided to go to the convenience store near the ESCC yard and pulse some money. As she drove passed her old trucking company's yard, things appeared pretty quiet. She still wanted to track down Shelby. She got her cash, bought a six-pack of beer and drove back to her house to devise a plan.

When Betty got back to her house, she was surprised to find that a pickup was in her driveway. She studied the pickup closely before entering the drive and saw lawn mowing equipment in the back. She parked at the curb, grabbed her six-pack and walked cautiously toward the pickup. Two men got out and walked toward her.

"Can I help you?" she asked.

"We just noticed you moved into this old house and wondered if you would like someone to clean up the yard?"

"Well, how much would you charge me?"

"A hundred and fifty bucks. We'll do front and back and clear out all the trash."

Betty thought carefully about the offer. She would like having a clean yard, but worried if the change would be too drastic, and tip off the cops. "Here's the thing, my husband and I are getting divorced. I don't want him to have the house. I'll pay you in cash, but if the cops or anyone else comes by, you have to tell them it's your place."

"Okay, we can do that if you throw in some beer."

"You got it. Be here in the morning around seven."

◊◊◊

Jack was at work when Tammy called him the next morning. "Hi, sweetheart. How is your trip going?"

"Oh, it's alright," she answered. "I should be home Friday. Wish I was coming home tonight instead of being in this cold-ass hotel by myself. I could use a little Jack."

"I wish you were here so I could give you a little Jack."

"So you really do miss me?"

"Of course. It was really a drag at the bar last night without you, and I had to sleep alone."

"I'll be home soon, baby. Hey, is your wife still out of town?"

"Yeah, she should be gone for a while I think. Why?"

"Well, maybe you should take me out to dinner and to your house for a change."

Jack liked his relationship with her the way it was. Taking her home would only complicate things. "Tammy, you know I can't take you to my house," he said. "My son still lives at home, and too many people know me in this town. Someone would be sure to mention our having dinner to Shelby."

"What about the fact that you dance with me at the bar and you don't hide leaving with me?"

"That's different, Tammy. Those are my biker friends, and there's a code of silence between us."

"Oh, so I guess I'm just your fuck buddy."

"It's not like that, Tammy, and you know it. It's complicated. I can't wait for you to get home. Maybe we can plan a trip out of town sometime soon."

"That sounds like a reasonable compromise. I can't wait to see you."

◊◊◊

Betty got into her car as soon as the lawn crew arrived. "Hey, I have a few things I need to do in town," she told the boys. "The beer is in the refrigerator and you get paid when I get back if the yard is looking good. Remember, if anyone shows up, you guys live here."

"Got it."

Betty pulled into the truck stop and was suddenly distracted by a refrigerator truck that had just pulled out in front of her. The driver was blonde and looked a whole lot like Shelby. "No way," she muttered to herself. "I couldn't possibly be so lucky." Betty turned her car around and began to follow Shelby. *Where is she headed?* Betty wondered.

The Camaro was not registered and had stolen license plates. Although she had received her wallet back when she was released from prison, her driver's license was suspended. She knew she had to be careful about cops. Still, she was determined not to let Shelby out of her sight. Shelby drove several miles north to a small town. She pulled into a local grocery store and backed her truck into the unloading dock at the back of the store. Betty pulled into the front of the store, waiting for Shelby to finish her delivery.

While her truck was being unloaded, Shelby called dispatch for her next load. She learned she was headed to South Texas to pick up a load of fruit, which had to be in El Paso by Saturday. She decided she'd return to the truck stop to get fuel and take a shower before heading south. With luck, she'd be able to make it back to the house by Friday. *I bet Jack is seeing his girlfriend on the weekends. If I make it back in time, maybe I can find out for sure. If I don't catch him doing anything, then I'll believe he's just going through some midlife crisis phase.* She drove back to the truck stop determined to find out one way or another.

Betty followed Shelby back to the truck stop, parked her car two rows down and surveyed her prey. "What's with the shower bag, Shelby?" she whispered. In her experience, when a woman used a public shower, instead of going home, that meant marital problems. She got out of the Camaro and strolled over to the truck stop. She followed Shelby as close as she dared without being spotted and then went into the restaurant and got a glass of iced tea while Shelby took her shower. She had been away from her house for a couple of hours. She needed to get back because she didn't trust the lawn boys not to rob her blind. Just as she was about to leave, Shelby appeared and stopped in the lobby to talk with a friend. Betty got up and paid for her drink, and walked slowly behind Shelby and her friend, trying to overhear their conversation.

Shelby gave the man a hug before they walked out to the parking lot. "It is so good to see you, Bull Frog. How's your wife? It's been so long since I've seen any of my friends from my sand-hauling days."

"Wanda is great," answered Bull Frog.

"Is she still trucking?"

"No. She just got tired of the road. She missed being home."

"I understand. I've been feeling that way a little myself lately."

"So what are you doing these days?"

"Produce mainly. Today I'm headed to South Texas for a load of fruit to El Paso. It isn't due there till Saturday, so I think I'll come home on Friday and surprise Jack."

Betty slipped out the door and headed to her car, pleased she had some intel on Shelby. She got into her car, lit a cigarette and inhaled deeply. She had Little Miss Barbie in her sights and enough time to devise the perfect plan.

CHAPTER NINE

Jack was getting ready to leave work and phoned Tammy before he headed out.

"What are we doing tonight?" she asked.

"I thought we could have some dinner before heading over to the bar. Okay if I shower at your place?"

"Sure. Then I'll fix us something. See ya in a bit."

Jack was glad that Tammy had—at least for now—given up on wanting to go out someplace in public other than the bar. He wasn't sure how he was going to handle her if she continued to insist on them being seen together.

Once he arrived at her house, they enjoyed their dinner and a few rounds in the sack before taking a shower together. Then they headed to the bar on his bike.

◊◊◊

It was a little past three on Friday afternoon when Shelby returned to the War Truck Stop. She had refrained from calling Jack for a couple of days because he seemed so perturbed when she did. Her plan was to take a nap and then get something to eat. Once she was sure Jack was out of the house, she'd take a cab home and change clothes before getting on her bike and heading over to the bar.

Betty had arrived at Shelby's house just before noon. She had broken into the ESCC employee database back when both she and Shelby were working for the trucking firm. She had been confident that Shelby still lived in the same house. After three hours staking out Shelby's house, Betty was getting frustrated that Shelby hadn't appeared. Her husband had come home at lunchtime and had an overnight bag with him when he left. Her son had also returned to the house, but did not stay long. Betty remembered that Shelby had showered at the War Truck Stop, which made her think that is where Shelby was now. She turned the Camaro around and headed there to see if she could find Shelby.

It was easy to spot Shelby's truck as soon as she pulled into the parking lot. "I'm not sure why you're staying at the truck stop Ms. Thing, but I'm so glad you're here. What I have planned will be much easier to pull off here anyway." Betty parked at the rear of the lot and walked past the parked trucks to the restaurant. It was too light out to do anything yet. She decided to check and see if Shelby was in the truck stop or in her truck.

Inside the truck stop Betty checked out the restrooms, drivers' lounge, and restaurant. When she didn't see any sign of Shelby, she went to the counter and asked the clerk if her friend might be taking a shower. She described Shelby and when she was sure that Shelby wasn't in the store anywhere, she bought a soda and went back to her car. "This is going to work out even better than I expected." Betty sipped her drink and sat in her car, waiting for it to get dark.

Trucks moved in and out by the dozens, parking in every available spot and making their own spots when no more slots were left. The only place left to park was an overflow dirt lot behind the parking lot. Darkness fell over the parking lot as Shelby slept and Betty waited.

Shelby woke up, pulled back the curtain, and realized she'd overslept. She was anxious to get to her house, but she wanted something to eat first and needed to freshen up. She gathered her things and went into the truck stop.

Betty saw Shelby emerge from her truck with her shower bag. "Good. I need you gone long enough to give your truck a little special attention." Betty didn't get out of her car until she was sure Shelby was out of sight. She estimated how long it would take Shelby to take a shower and change. She would have to work fast.

Betty opened the trunk and took out the small gas can and rags she'd brought from home and placed them into what looked like a shower bag. She scurried across the parking lot toward Shelby's truck and checked to see if the driver of the truck on the passenger side of Shelby's truck was in the driver's seat or if the sleep cover was in the window. She breathed a sigh of relief when she saw the sleep cover was over the window. She slowly moved back to the deck between Shelby's truck and trailer where the refrigerated unit, the reefer, was located. She pulled herself up onto the deck and took the rags out of the shower bag and shoved several of them into the unit's openings. She took the gas out and soaked the ends of the rags and then got down and found a comfortable spot to hide.

◊◊◊

Shelby stood in the shower and let the hot water relax her. *God, Jack. I hope I'm wrong about what I think you're up to and that when I get to the bar you're just drinking with your buddies and shooting pool.* It killed her to think that the man she loved so much might be sharing himself with someone else—a gift he'd promised to her when they got married years ago. She finished her shower and headed back to her truck.

Betty waited for a few moments for Shelby to get settled in. She moved into position, struck a match on the heel of her boot, and lit the tips of each of the rags. She jumped down and walked quickly back to her car, anxious to see the fireworks.

Shelby was moving out of her parking space when she smelled smoke. At first, she thought it was her imagination, but when she saw smoke in her mirrors, she knew she was in trouble. A loud pop confirmed where the smoke was coming from. She quickly got on the radio. "THIS IS BARBIE. MY REEFER TRAILER IS ON FIRE! I NEED HELP NOW! CALL 911 WHILE I TRY TO GET THIS TRAILER AWAY FROM THE OTHER TRUCKS AROUND ME!"

"Barbie this is Southpaw. Where are you?"

"I'M PULLING OUT OF THE FRONT LINE NOW, BUT I'M NOT SURE WHERE TO TAKE THIS THING TO GET IT AWAY FROM THE OTHER TRUCKS!"

"Okay, girl, pull around to the back. Several of us will meet you there so we can unhook the trailer. Maybe we can at least save the tractor."

"HURRY, GUYS. THIS THING IS BURNING FAST, AND WITH THE AIR I'M ADDING TO IT TRYING TO GET BACK THERE, IT'S ONLY GETTING HOTTER!"

"Gotcha, girl. We're on our way."

Betty laughed when she saw Shelby pull her truck out of her parking space. "Go ahead, Shelby, give it some more oxygen so it will burn like hell." Her laughter suddenly turned to anger as she watched several drivers exit their trucks and head toward the open field to the rear of the truck stop. "Oh hell no. You guys aren't going to help this bitch out this time." Betty started her car and headed in the direction of about five of the drivers who were running across the parking lot. She hit the accelerator and pointed her car directly at them.

"LIGHTFOOT, LOOK OUT! THAT CAR IS COMING DIRECTLY AT US!"

Lightfoot and Dark Man dodged behind a nearby truck. Sandman took a dive to the payment, just barely rolling out of the way as Betty sped out of the parking lot. "What the hell was that crazy bitch thinking? She could have killed one of us."

"I think that was the idea. Come on, let's go help Barbie." When they reached the open field, they found Shelby and several other drivers using her fire extinguisher to try to clear the fire away enough to get ahold of the fifth wheel handle.

"It's still too hot, Southpaw," called Shelby. "Wait!"

Shelby handed her fire extinguisher to Southpaw and opened her storage compartment. "Here, let me see if I can pull it with this fifth wheel pull bar."

Lightfoot took hold of the bar. "Give it to me, Shelby. You get in that truck and get ready to pull away when we can get you unhooked."

Sandman and Double L each took a side, reaching for the airlines as Southpaw sprayed the lines and fifth wheel with the extinguisher.

"Okay, guys. On the count of three, let's see if we can get this baby separated."

"What about the landing gear?"

"Alabama Kid turned it down as much as he could, but the fire is engulfing the trailer too quickly now. Let's get this baby apart before that reefer blows, okay? One, two, three—GO!"

Everyone did their part as Shelby put her truck in gear and pulled the tractor out from under the trailer, which was now almost one-quarter of the way engulfed in flames. "GET BACK!" someone yelled as the trailer came out from under the truck and landed hard on the half lowered landing gear.

The fire department entered the lot with lights and sirens and quickly took over the situation. Shelby and the other truckers stood by her tractor a few yards away and watched as the fire was put out. "Dammit, girl, what the hell happened to your trailer?"

"I have no idea, Southpaw," she answered, her eyes tear-filled. "I was pulling out and smelled smoke. I looked out the mirror and the reefer was on fire. All I could think about was getting the hell out of there so that none of the other trucks caught on fire."

"Well, that's not all the excitement that went on in this place tonight," Dark Man and Lightfoot confirmed.

Shelby was confused. "What?"

"Some crazy person tried to run us over as we were headed this way."

"No way."

"Yep. Looked like a crazy bitch, but who knows—might have been one of those skinny pot heads."

"Oh my God. Wait…could you tell who was driving? Was it a woman with mousy brown hair? Real skinny?"

"Don't know, Barbie. Didn't have time enough to get a good look."

"I was too busy trying to save my truck-driving ass."

"I think that crazy bitch might have found me, and she might be after me again."

"What? The one that tried to kill you in Utah?"

"Yeah."

"There's no way that bitch would ever bring herself back to Texas. She's crazy but not stupid."

"Yeah, maybe you're right…still…"

It took the fire department a couple of hours to extinguish the fire completely and talk with everyone involved. Shelby explained what happened and how with Southpaw's advice she had brought the trailer to the field.

"That was good thinking. You might want to contact your trucking company. You've lost the trailer for sure, and probably most of the cargo."

"I already put a phone call into dispatch and the supervisor is supposed to call back soon. Do you have any idea how it started?"

"Yeah, but I want to have my investigators look at it more closely in the morning before I finish my report. I'll have my guys keep an eye on it for a little while, but I have all the information I need for now. This is my card. Be sure to call me when you know what your company plans to do with the trailer."

Shelby took the card and shook the fire chief's hand. "Thank you. I will."

Shelby received a text from the trucking company advising her to report in on Monday to fill out paperwork and see about getting back out on the road.

Shelby and the truckers walked toward her truck. "Thanks, guys. I appreciate all the help. God, I wonder how that thing caught on fire? I've heard of that happening, but I thought it was older more worn-out models."

Double L found a stick and scooped up a piece of cloth with it. "We need to make sure the inspectors see this," he said.

"What's that?"

"I pulled it out of the reefer on the passenger side when I went over to undo the air line. I think this is what might have started, or at least helped to start, the fire."

"You might have caught a rag or towel on the reefer and it just caught on fire," Southpaw said.

"Well, it smells like it was soaked in gasoline," Double L countered.

Southpaw saw the look on Shelby's face and knew he had to assure her it wasn't what she was thinking. "No way, Barbie. It was just an accident."

"I hope you're right," she said as she headed to the driver's side door of her truck. She still intended to go home and then to find out what was going on with Jack. Part of her wanted to call him and tell him everything that had just happened, but she knew it would probably only cause problems, so she decided to just keep it to herself.

Shelby arrived home at around midnight and, just as she suspected, Jack was not there, nor was Steven. The house felt quiet and lonely. She took another shower to get rid of the smoke smell that was still in her hair and on her skin. After her shower she tried to watch a little TV, hoping that Jack would come home, but he never showed up.

Steven came home around 3:00 a.m. "Hey, Mom. What are you doing here?"

"Oh, I had a little problem tonight with my trailer. I'm sure they'll have a new one ready for me on Monday. Do you know where your father is tonight?"

Steven shrugged. "Not a clue, Mom. He's probably where he always is—out with his biker friends."

"That's what I figured. I guess I'll go to bed."

"He'll be here in the morning, I'm sure."

Shelby gave Steven a kiss goodnight and went to her bedroom. She lay in bed, wide awake, waiting to hear Jack's truck pull in—but it never did.

The next morning, Shelby stood at the counter, drinking coffee. Her stomach was in knots, knowing that Jack had stayed out all night. She wanted to know where he'd spent the night—in her heart she was convinced it was with another woman. She tried to convince herself he would never do that to her…but the evidence seemed clear.

"Hey, Mom. Dad still asleep?" Steven asked as he stepped into the kitchen and poured himself a cup of coffee.

"No, he never came home."

"Oh! Did you call Ralph or Tucker?"

"No, not yet. It's still early. I wouldn't want to wake them if they had an all-night party somewhere. I'll check with them later. You off to work?"

"Yeah. I better get going or I'm going to be late."

"Okay. Have a great day."

Saturdays were her usual cleaning days back when she was teaching school. Shelby decided the house could use a good once-over and hoped that cleaning would take her mind off Jack. By 6:00 p.m., Shelby had deep-cleaned her house, but instead of taking her mind off Jack, she spent the day obsessing about where he was. She was afraid if she didn't find out soon, she was going to lose her mind. She went to the bedroom and selected a pair of her most stylish tight jeans and matched it to a low-cut t-shirt. Shelby carefully applied her makeup, making herself look like she was twenty years younger—a knockout. *If Jack is fooling around, at least he'll see what he's losing*, she thought.

It was 8:00 p.m. by the time Shelby pulled her bike out of Jack's shop behind their house and warmed the little pink and white rocket up for a ride. She loved the bike that Jack had built just for her. It was fast, and she loved the way it felt whenever she rode it. Tonight she wasn't going to wear her leathers—just her helmet.

By the time she arrived at the bar, Shelby was resolved that nothing was going to restrict her from kicking some ass if she was right about Jack. She pulled into the parking lot, but didn't see Jack's bike. She wanted to go inside, but decided she'd park her bike out of site on the side of the building and wait to see if he showed up.

By 9:30 p.m., Jack still hadn't arrived. *Maybe I've got this all wrong*, Shelby thought. *Maybe he was in an accident last night and is in the hospital.* Just as she was about to leave, everything that she'd feared came true as Jack and Tammy rolled up into the parking lot on Jack's bike. Shelby's heart sunk as she watched Jack help Tammy off his bike and kiss her with a kiss that she'd always thought was hers alone. She wanted to jump out right then and let him know that she'd caught him, but the anger inside of her was stronger now than the hurt. Instead, she would let the couple go inside and have a couple drinks and maybe a couple dances before bursting their bubble—or worse.

Shelby took deep breaths, trying to calm her racing heart. It took her almost twenty minutes to gather her resolve. She entered the bar and let her eyes adjust to the dimness of the room. She scanned the room and made eye contact with Tucker and Ralph. Ralph tilted his head toward the bar. Shelby turned her attention to the bar and saw the two lovers sitting close together.

She walked towards them with her fists clinched. Jack had his back to the door and Tammy was concentrating too hard on Jack's eyes to notice Shelby standing next to them at the bar. "Don't you think you need to buy your wife a drink, Jack?"

Jack's arm dropped down from around Tammy's waist as he turned to face Shelby. "Shelby, what are you doing here?"

"Oh, I don't know, Jack. I came back early last night to surprise you. But you never came home." Shelby looked at Tammy trying to hide behind Jack. "I see what kept you out all night and all day Jack, but God only knows why? She's uglier than an old hen sitting on a stump covered with chicken shit. No wait, that's you, Jack. You're the shit!"

Jack's face turned red as he tried to diffuse the situation. "Can't we talk about this outside or at home, baby? It isn't what you think."

Shelby laughed. "What I think is that I'm going to kick your ass." She swung her fist and cold-cocked Jack in the mouth. As he tried to gain his balance, Shelby took off after Tammy, who was attempting to run toward the bathroom. "Not so fast, bitch!" she called. "It's time you met Jack's better half." Shelby pulled Tammy by the hair and dragged her to the floor. She straddled the woman and pounded her in the face. Tammy was defenseless against Shelby's strength and anger. Jack gathered himself and looked to his buddies for help, but both of them turned away. They had tried to warn Jack about what Shelby would do, but he hadn't listened.

Jack ran to rescue Tammy from Shelby's clutches, but got another hook in the face as she continued to pummel his girlfriend. Ralph and Tucker realized after a few minutes they were going to have to do something fast or the whole place was going to be crawling with cops. Tucker and Ralph grabbed Shelby and pulled her off Tammy.

"Let me go you bastards! You knew all along he was making a fool out of me and you let him. LET ME GO! I'M GOING TO MAKE THAT BITCH WISH SHE'D NEVER MET JACK AND GLAD SHE'S ONLY MET ME ONCE!"

Ralph pulled Shelby outside who by this time was crying as much as she was fighting. "Shelby, calm down before you get yourself thrown in jail."

Shelby fell into Ralph's arms and cried. "How could he do this, Ralph? How could you guys let him do this and not tell me?"

Ralph did his best to comfort Shelby. It got worse when Jack came out of the bar; his nose was bleeding. "Shelby, you shouldn't have done that. Tammy is really hurt."

Shelby turned on him. "You think I give a fuck that your little whore is hurt? Fuck you, Jack! Stay away from my house, and stay the fuck away from me. I WANT A DIVORCE, YOU SON OF A BITCH!"

"Look, Shelby, I'm sorry. It just happened. You were gone all the time. It's nothing, just a fling. I love you."

Shelby got in Jack's face. "FUCK YOU! THIS ISN'T ABOUT MY JOB. THIS IS ABOUT YOUR BEING A DICK! GO BACK INSIDE AND TAKE CARE OF YOUR LITTLE BITCH! MY ATTORNEY WILL BE IN TOUCH WITH YOU MONDAY!"

Shelby went to her bike and started it up. Jack tried to follow but Ralph held him back. "SHELBY!" shouted Jack.

"Let her go, Jack. Nothing you can do now but let her go."

He followed Ralph back into the bar to check on Tammy. Tammy was bleeding from cuts and scratches on her face and arms. Her nose was broken and her eyes were black. The bartender had given her an ice pack and a wet rag.

"I'm sorry, baby," Jack pleaded.

Tammy dropped the icepack and slapped Jack in the face. "SORRY! YOU LET HER BEAT ON ME, YOU SON OF A BITCH!" She turned to the bartender. "Call me a cab," she demanded.

Jack made his way over to his friends, humiliated. "May I crash at your place 'til I get this thing fixed?"

"Yeah, I don't think Kelly will mind."

◊◊◊

With a headache the size of Texas, Shelby pulled herself out of bed. She'd come home last night in tears and mad as hell. After putting her bike away, all she could remember was pulling out the tequila bottle from the bar. The rest of her night was a blur except for the one and only phone call she accepted from Jack. Without letting him speak, she made it perfectly clear that coming near her or the house would be a big mistake. She told him his belongings would be outside on the porch in the morning—everything else would be divided up in court.

Shelby went into the kitchen and swallowed four aspirin with a cup of black coffee. Shelby sat at her table in disbelief. *My marriage is over and my trailer is in ashes. What the hell am I going to do with the rest of my life?*

Steven walked into the kitchen and interrupted her thoughts. "Hey, Mom. How are you feeling this morning?" he asked as he poured himself a cup of coffee.

"Not well," she muttered.

"I figured as much. When I got home last night you were in pretty bad shape. So did you really kick Dad out of the house? Did he really have an affair?"

"Yes, and yes."

"I never saw that coming. What are ya going to do now?"

"I have no idea, sweetie, but I am taking some time off to figure it out."

"Well, I got a promotion at work so I can help out some."

"Oh, I appreciate that, but you need to keep working on college. Besides, I've worked pretty hard these last few years and most everything we have is paid off, so I think I can manage things alone."

"Okay, but I'm here for you." Steven kissed his mom's forehead.

Moments after Steven left for work, Shelby's cell phone rang. She followed the sound of the ringing and found her cell phone buried under throw pillows in the living room. She pulled it out and checked the ID—it was her office. She really didn't want to deal with anything this morning, but her job was on the line so she answered it. "Hello?" she said nervously.

"Shelby, this is Brandi. We have a new trailer for you to pick up on Monday. The other trailer will be picked up by a towing company. The fire department decided they wanted to do some further investigation."

"Okay. Can you tell me what they think happened?"

"No, not really, but something looked suspicious and they wanted to make sure it wasn't sabotage before turning it over to the insurance guys."

"Sabotage? What a weekend. My truck is almost blown up and my husband has a new girlfriend."

"What?"

"Never mind. I'm just blowing off steam. Please have Jayne call me when she gets a chance?"

"Sure."

"Thanks, Brandi. Talk to you later."

Shelby hadn't meant to mention her problems with Jack to the dispatcher and was glad Brandi hadn't really heard what she'd said. She hoped Jayne would let her have a few days off until she could figure out what she was going to do. She sat back in her easy chair and looked around the living room at all the things that she and Jack had gathered together over the years. It made her realize just how alone she was in her own home. She closed her eyes and hoped that her eyelids would help ease the pain in her head and keep her from seeing all the memories that existed around the house.

Exhaustion took over and an hour later, she was awakened by the doorbell. She went to the door and found Jack standing there. "I thought you were going to have my stuff on the porch?"

"Yeah, well, I had a little trouble sleeping last night. Can't imagine why."

"Look, Shelby, I'm not going to stand here and fight with you. Just give me some of my stuff or I'll come in and get it so I can leave."

Shelby opened the door and let Jack in. "Be my guest. You've managed to destroy everything else we have, so why not take the house apart, too?"

"Whatever." Jack walked into the house and went to their bedroom. Shelby decided she didn't care what he got and went back to the living room. She was surprised Jack wasn't trying harder to come home, especially after the number of "I'm sorry, Shelbys," she'd heard last night. She figured he and Tammy must have made up and he wasn't out in the cold. *It really doesn't matter to me anymore*, she thought as she covered her eyes with her arm and waited for him to finish and leave her in peace.

In the bedroom, Jack gathered what he could for his first load. He had hoped that Shelby would have followed him to the bedroom, although he'd acted like he didn't want her too. Guilt was the least of his worries. He loved

Shelby no matter what, and this mess he'd made was killing him. He couldn't believe he'd not only just fucked up his life, but his life with the only woman he ever loved or would ever love. As he pulled things out of the closet and drawers, he wondered what he was going to do without her. *I've been selfish and stupid. I've treated her badly. How am I ever going to fix this thing?* He wanted Shelby back, he wanted his life back. As he continued to get his stuff together, he decided not to take everything since he still had hopes of coming home.

His first load out didn't even cause Shelby to flinch and the second load made her hope he was finished. The liquor had numbed her feeling as she sat unconcerned with Jack's presence. *He obviously has no remorse for his actions. I'm going to give him exactly what he wants—his freedom. I still love Jack, but he doesn't love me anymore. His actions are proof. Now I just have to figure out how to tell my heart to stop hurting.*

Jack moved two more loads out of the house and then without saying anything, closed the front door and left. He had wanted to stay and talk but knew that there was no use to even try right now. *I'll give her some time. Maybe before everything is completely gone between us, I'll find the right words to say to her to get her to take me back.* He felt sick as he looked at his home in the rearview mirror, knowing that everything he loved was back there in that little three-bedroom ranch and he'd just destroyed it.

Shelby finally removed her arm from off her face and got out of her easy chair. She walked to the bedroom and saw the empty space in the closet that once was filled with Jack's things. She walked into the closet and fell to her knees on top of a dirty shirt he'd left on the floor. She curled up into a fetal position and wept. *How can this be happening? Why did I let him leave? Why wasn't I enough? Why is my job so important to me?* The questions and tears flooded her mind as she lay on the floor with his shirt in her arms.

CHAPTER TEN

Betty still couldn't believe it, once again, Shelby had been rescued. "What do I have to do to get rid of that bitch?" She wanted her dead—it was worth any risk she had to take. She decided she needed a plan. *Getting this done might take some time.* She needed to know Shelby's routine so she could catch her when she least expected it. The detailed surveillance would require more than one set of eyes. She needed an accomplice or two. Ted was dead and Shelby had made her poison to the local truckers. She thought about it for a while and decided to reach out to the lawn guys.

"Hey, Pedro. I was wondering if you and your buddy might want to earn some extra money?"

"The name is Pete, but yes, we are interested in making some money."

"The job I have isn't mowing, but it pays well."

"What is it?"

"I want you to keep an eye on someone for me and let me know what she's doing.

"All we have to do is watch her?"

"Yes, report to me her every move. When she moves you tell me and you follow her until I tell you not to. I'll pay you by the hour and cover your meals and fuel."

"When do we start?"

◊◊◊

"Hello?" Shelby croaked into the phone.

"Shelby, this is Jayne. I got a message you needed to talk with me? You weren't sleeping were you?"

"Oh, I'm just not feeling very well. I was wondering if it would be okay to take some personal time off. I'm having some marriage issues, and I need to get a lawyer besides taking care of some other things. I know this is short notice, but I really need the time if you can spare me for a few days."

"Sure, take all the time you need. I'm sorry you're having troubles."

"It will be okay once I give Jack his freedom. Oh, did you hear from the fire department about the trailer?"

"Not yet. They should let me know something soon."

"Well, let me know. I should be ready to roll by next week."

"Okay, kiddo. If there's anything I can do for you just let me know."

"Thanks, Jayne."

Shelby hung up her cell phone and pulled herself up off the floor. She needed to put the hurt aside and focus. She couldn't let Jack or anyone else bring her down. She took a shower, got dressed, and got to work putting the rest of Jack's personal things together in boxes and put them in the garage until he asked for them.

◊◊◊

"Look, Tammy, I told you from the beginning I was married."

"Yes, but you gave me the impression you weren't happy with her and planned on getting a divorce."

"I have been upset with her, but I never said I wanted a divorce."

"So what we had between us was nothing more than sex?"

"I don't know what it is, but it isn't working for me."

"You bastard, you let that bitch hit me on purpose!"

"Don't be ridiculous! I would never have let her hit you if I could have stopped her. Don't call her a bitch either, we did this—not her."

"No, Jack. *You* did this!"

"You're right. I did do this! Now I'm not doing it anymore. Goodbye, Tammy."

"Good riddance, Jack!"

Jack was relieved things were over with Tammy. She had become too possessive. He didn't know if he would be able to fix things with Shelby, but at least he wasn't going to have to deal with Tammy anymore. He would give Shelby some time and then see what he could do about repairing the damage he'd done to their marriage. He headed back to Ralph's house.

Ralph came out of the house and handed Jack a beer. "You okay, buddy?"

"No, not really. I have managed to really fuck things up. I don't know what my problem is. I love Shelby, but this truck driving job of hers has been driving me crazy."

Ralph's wife joined them on the porch. "You should be proud of her for doing something that most women don't get to do. At least she's not sitting at home on her ass, spending all your money," Kelly said.

"I know, but I liked it when she was at home and teaching school."

"That should be her decision, not yours. Shouldn't you consider her feelings more than your own?"

"You're right. It's probably too late now anyway. She wouldn't even look at me when I was at the house today."

"Give her some time. You guys have been together forever. She'll come around."

◊◊◊

Shelby was not certain how she wanted to proceed. She wasn't ready for divorce, but thought a separation might give her the time and space to figure out her next step. She was in front of her computer, Googling divorce lawyers when her cell phone rang. The ID showed it was Jack. She hesitated and then answered. "Hello?"

"Hey, Shelby, this is Jack. I was wondering if I could come by tonight and talk to Steven and you?"

"I don't know, Jack. Steven's upset…and I really need some time."

"I know. I don't want to talk about getting back together or anything, I just want to tell both of you how sorry I am."

"Oh hell, Jack, just leave it alone for a while…there is still a lot of pain."

"I would if I could, but I can't. I fucked up and I want my family back."

"Little late for that, don't you think? Besides what about Tammy? I'm working on filing for a separation as soon as…"

"So soon?" Jack interrupted. "I think we should talk first."

"Talk about what? The fact is you were fucking someone else. You made your bed and now you don't want to sleep in it? Or maybe you do but you want my bed too? Trust me, Jack, that will never happen."

Jack knew he was going to have to grovel, but couldn't find the right words. "Look, Shelby, she's gone. I'm done with her, and I'm sorry I ever got involved with her. I'm staying with Ralph and Kelly. I really want to fix this mess I've made. Please, at least let me talk to Steven."

"I can't stop you from talking with Steven; he's a grown man. Do whatever you want, but leave me out of it. I just want you to stay away from me for a while so I can figure this shit out."

"Is it okay if I come by the house tonight to see Steven?"

"Why call me? He has his own cell phone. He can speak for himself."

◊◊◊

"What you're saying doesn't make sense. She should be out on the road by now," Betty said to Peter.

"I'm telling you, she hasn't left her house all day."

"That is strange. Keep an eye on her tonight and let me know if she or anyone comes or goes from her house."

"We did see a guy who we assumed was her husband. Looks like he may be in the doghouse. He drove up, went inside and carried clothes and shit to his pickup. Since he wasn't using a suitcase, we figured he was being kicked to the curb."

"Why are you just telling me this now?"

"You told us to watch the lady."

"You morons. Go watch her house and tell me everything that goes on there."

"Okay, boss."

As the men headed out, Peter turned and handed Betty a red card. "Oh, wait, I almost forgot. This was on the door when we got here tonight."

Betty took the card and looked at it.

"Did you see who left it?"

"It looks like it's from the electric company. Did you forget to pay the light bill?"

"Get the fuck out of here."

Betty called the electric company to complain about the threat they left to cut off her service. She was told the credit card she had used for the deposit was suspended, creating a past due balance. She assured them it was a mistake by the bank and would get them their damn money.

Right now Betty had bigger fish to fry. She needed to find out what was going on with Shelby and her husband.

◊◊◊

Tammy sat at the bar nursing a beer. She'd stopped at the bar after work hoping to run into Jack. She had done her best to cover her bruises with makeup but those who had been there that night knew what had happened. "I'd be too embarrassed to come back here after that beat down," the waitress told the bartender.

Tammy motioned to the bartender. "Have you seen Jack in here lately?" she asked.

"I haven't seen him. Have you asked his buddies over there?" he asked, pointing to their usual table.

She was working up the courage to approach them and ordered another beer. She remained at the bar, milling over in her head what she would say to Jack if he walked through the door. She missed him and hoped they could work things out. After a few more beers, Tammy was gaining the nerve to approach Jack's friends when a woman with short red hair came in and sat at the bar. Tammy avoided making eye contact with her. Something about her seemed off. Tammy ordered another beer and chugged it down, hoping for the buzz she needed to face Jack's friends.

"Boy, I wish I could drink a beer that fast. They say the faster you drink them the faster the buzz comes on. Is that true?" Betty said.

Tammy didn't respond.

"Oh, well, I'm kind of a lightweight anyway. Kind of quiet in here tonight, isn't it?"

Tammy ignored the woman, stood up, ordered another beer, picked it up from the bar and walked toward the table where Ralph, Tucker, and Slider were seated. "Excuse me, gentleman, but I was wondering if you've seen Jack tonight? I really need to speak with him and return some of his things."

Slider spoke up. "No, ma'am. I haven't seen him in several days. But if I do, I promise to pass along your message."

"Do you think he'll be coming in tonight?"

"I'm pretty sure he's going to be staying away from here for a while."

"Why?"

Betty heard Tammy mention Jack and cocked her head, trying to hear what was being said. Although she could not make out all the words, the woman's body language indicated distress. Betty was also sure she had seen some kind of bruises under the woman's makeup. Betty sipped at her beer and tried to listen to the table talk from the bar, uncertain if the Jack mentioned was Shelby's husband.

"Well, please tell Jack he needs to call me right away. It is very important," Tammy announced.

"Okay, we'll let him know if we see him."

Tammy stumbled back to her spot at the bar. "Fuck Jack Mathews," Tammy said, laying her head on top of her arms perched on the bar.

Betty moved next to Tammy. "Hey. I'm not trying to be nosy or anything, but you look like you could use a friend to talk to."

Tammy lifted her head slightly off the bar and took another drink of her beer. She didn't really want to talk, but maybe if she did she would feel better.

"Sounds like you have man troubles? Been there, done that."

"Yeah, that son of a bitch used me and then threw me away. Bad thing is I think I love him." Tears flowed from Tammy's eyes. She took a gulp of her beer.

Betty pulled a tissue from her pocket and handed it to Tammy as she patted her gently on the back. "I know what you're going through. Men are assholes. My ex was married and said he didn't want to be with his wife, but then the minute I turn my back he's right back with her. I couldn't believe I fell for him."

"My guy isn't even going back to his wife. She found out we were seeing each other and now he's trying to get back with her. She's a real bitch, too. Look what she did to me." Tammy showed Betty her bruises. "I should have had her thrown in jail, but Jack told me not to."

"Jack? I know a couple Jacks. Is he from around here?"

"Yeah, he's in the oil business. Been here for years. That wife of his is some kind of truck driver or something. She must be an imbecile if she's a truck driver. That's why I don't understand why Jack doesn't want to be with me. I'm smart and funny and kind of pretty without the bruises. I just don't get it. I would have made him a great wife."

"Sure, but most men don't know a good thing even if it's right in front of them."

"You're right. Men are just blind to everything good."

"What was his last name?"

"Mathews."

Bingo! Betty thought. *If I work this right, I may be able to get this woman to help me get even with Jack and Shelby.* Betty patted Tammy on the back and bought her another beer. "Well, I don't know if I know your Jack or not, but it sounds like maybe you would like to get back at this guy."

"Oh, I don't know about that. I just want him back."

"Are you sure? I mean, look at all the pain you're in. Do you really want some guy in your life who would throw you away in a heartbeat over some bitch who can't possibly be as intelligent as you?"

Tammy gave that some thought. "Probably not. But how do you get rid of the pain in your heart?"

"Find another man who's better. Listen to me, honey, men are just as expendable as they think we are. The trick is to always remember that and stay one step ahead of them. I know you made the mistake this time of letting your heart get involved, but next time, just use the guy for what you want and don't let your feelings get in the way."

"Yeah. I'm pissed. I want to get back at Jack and his bitch wife."

Betty had to force herself to not grin. "Well, getting even can sometimes get messy and dangerous. Are you sure you can handle that kind of thing?" Betty could tell the alcohol had control over Tammy, which made her putty in Betty's hands. She just needed to push a little harder. "On the other hand, it feels good to stand up for yourself."

"Yeah, I'm ready. I really want to get his wife and if I do, then maybe Jack will want me back. Is that possible without getting into too much trouble?"

"Here's my number," Betty said, scrawling her phone number on a crumpled receipt from her pocket. "Call me when you've had a chance to sober up and maybe we can talk again. I'd be happy to help you get even with those two for hurting you. By the way, you never did tell me what happened to you anyway." Tammy began from the beginning and told Betty everything that had happened between Jack and her. Betty was pleased to learn that Shelby and Jack were apart because that would make getting to Shelby easier. "So where is Jack now?" she asked.

"I don't know. Probably back home with that bitch, I guess."

"Oh, I doubt that."

"You think they aren't together?"

"I'm pretty sure of it. No woman would want a man in her house who's just cheated on her."

"Yeah, you're right, but where could he be?"

Betty looked toward the table where Jack's friends were sitting. "Probably with one of those guys."

"Really? But they said…"

"Honey, men lie. Never forget that."

◊◊◊

The Utah Highway Patrol were called to the site of the mangled, burned out remains of a big rig that had careened off a ridge in the Wasatch Mountains. It was apparent that no one had survived the crash. There were no human remains anywhere.

When Petersen heard about the crash he became suspicious. *What are the chances that two big rigs fall off the side of a mountain within months of each other, when it's been more than a decade since something like that's happened*? He was still pissed that a mistrial had been called on the Burton case. He knew Polk wanted to retry her, but the bitch had disappeared.

He contacted the officers on the site. "Stay put until I get there and call for the recovery dog unit."

"There's nothing here to recover, Sarge. Everything is burnt to a crisp."

"It doesn't make any sense. The driver didn't just disappear." *Or did she?*

He remembered a report that had come over the wire about the body of a murder victim dumped in the woods. Officer Leroy Jenkins was the lead investigator. Petersen got his number and gave him a call. After a brief conversation, both lawmen were convinced that the crashed truck and the dead trucker on the side of the road had something to do with Betty Burton. As soon as Petersen hung up, his computer lit up with a report that another trucker's body was found in a bathroom in L.A. He saw Brad Stevenson's name in the report and called him immediately.

CHAPTER ELEVEN

Jack reached Steven on his cell phone. "I was wondering if you'd go to dinner tonight with me so we can talk."

"Can't. I have to work, and then I'm going out with my girlfriend. What do you want to talk to me about? Shouldn't you be talking to Mom?"

"I just want to let you know I'm sorry, son."

"I know, Dad, but I'm really busy right now and I don't think I'm the one you need to be apologizing to. Hey, if you want to have lunch tomorrow, I can meet you after class."

"Great. I'll call you in the morning and we'll pick a place. I love you."

"Love you, too, Dad. Hey, I don't know if you know or not, but Jack and Mark are both going to be here this weekend. Mark is bringing his new girlfriend home from North Carolina. She's a Marine, and from what Mark says, she's a really good Marine."

"I hope your mom will let me come to the house and see them."

"Maybe. I don't think she told Mark anything, but I mentioned some of it to Jack Jr."

"Okay, my boy. I'll see ya tomorrow. Love ya."

"Love ya, too."

◊◊◊

Shelby had managed to make coffee and get dressed, but she didn't feel like doing much of anything. When her cell phone rang, she looked at the ID and then said out loud, "Look, Jack. I'm not interested in talking right now." She answered it anyway. "Hello?"

"I just thought I would call and see if I could come by and talk to you."

"There is nothing to talk about, Jack."

"Come on, Shelby. We need to talk. If not for ourselves, for the boys."

"The boys weren't your concern when you were with Tammy, were they?"

"Look, I didn't call to fight—just talk. Besides, Steven told me Mark was coming home this weekend and I really want to come over and see him. Why didn't you tell me he was coming in?"

"I just found out this morning. I was going to tell you, but you already know so I guess I didn't need to."

"May I come over?"

"I guess so. But I haven't told Mark anything about our pending separation so I guess you better be the one to break that news."

"Okay, what time would be good for me to come over?"

"Sometime around eleven—that way you and Jack Jr. can start the grill. I suggest you meet Mark and his girl at the airport Saturday morning at ten, maybe you can talk to him a little about what's going on before he gets to the house."

"Okay, I will. Hey, I know this doesn't matter to you right now, and I know you won't believe me, but I love you."

"Yeah, okay." When Shelby hung up she felt a little better, but she wasn't sure exactly why. *Is it because Jack is coming over Saturday or because he's not with Tammy anymore? Is it because he still loves me? Why am I even thinking about the son of a bitch?* Shelby began to hum as she started cleaning Mark's room.

◊◊◊

Tammy couldn't help herself. She was sitting outside the bar again, hoping to see Jack. She tried calling and again got his voice mail. He hadn't taken a call from her all week. "Damn you, Jack! Why can't you see that we need to be together?" She threw her phone into her purse and got out of her car. "Well, if I see you in here, maybe we can talk. If not, I can try to get drunk enough to not feel the pain."

Tammy pulled her bar stool up to the bar and surveyed the room. No Jack and none of Jack's friends. She rummaged through her purse and took out her wallet. As she pulled out some cash to pay for the beer, a receipt with a number on it fell onto the bar. She paid the barmaid, picked up the napkin and looked at the number. She suddenly remembered that it was from that woman she'd met a few days ago. She sipped her beer and thought about their discussion. Although she'd been pretty wasted, she remembered most of their conversation. *Maybe I should give this gal a call and get some suggestions on how to make sure Jack Mathews gets what he deserves.*

◊◊◊

Betty needed money and fast. She needed her lights turned back on and she needed cash to pay Pete for his surveillance. Just as she was devising a plan, her cell phone rang.

"Hey, this is Tammy from the bar. I don't know if you remember me…"

"Of course, I remember you," she said, her voice filled with syrupy sweetness.

"Well, you told me to give you a call if I decided that I wanted to get back at Jack. I'm ready to make that bastard pay."

"Let's meet for lunch tomorrow."

"Do you really think you can help me come up with something to make him pay for what he and his wife did to me?"

"You can count on it. I'll call you in the morning and set everything up." When she hung up, Betty rubbed her hands together, anticipating her good fortune. Not only would she use this woman to help her get Shelby, after seeing how the gal was dressed and what she drove, she knew Tammy was the source for her much-needed cash.

◊◊◊

Betty was sitting in the restaurant, waiting for Tammy. When she saw her walk through the door wearing a pink cashmere sweater over light tan wool slacks and carrying a Hermes bag. She smiled broadly and stood up to greet her new "best friend."

"Hey, Tammy, how are you?"

Tammy smiled and shook Betty's hand. "Hanging in there. How are you?"

"Good. I'm glad you called. I see you remember at least some of our talk."

"Yes. Are you sure we can make him hurt as bad as I do?"

"Of course we can. I don't want to say too much in a public space, maybe we can chat a little about your relationship with him and then we can go over to your house and get to the nitty gritty."

Tammy wasn't sure she wanted Betty at her house, but her desire to get even with Jack was overruling all logic. "You're not thinking of physical harm are you…or anything illegal? I just want him to hurt like I am…to know what it feels like to be used."

"Well, his wife caused you physical harm, which is illegal, and now he wants to get back with that bitch, what about an eye for an eye?"

"I know...but…"

"Look, I have a plan to deal with both Jack and his wife. We'll go to your house and discuss it. If you're not interested that's okay, I'll drop it."

After lunch, Betty followed Tammy to her condo. Tammy offered Betty a seat in the living room, put her purse down by the sofa, and went into the kitchen to get them some iced tea. Betty scanned the room. *Tammy definitely has money to spare*, she thought. The easiest thing would be to snatch her wallet out of her purse, but Tammy would suspect her immediately when she noticed it was missing. She noticed a small, antique writing desk in the corner of the room. It was obvious from the papers on top that this is where she sat to pay her bills, if she could get Tammy out of the room long enough, maybe she could steal her checkbook.

Tammy returned to the living room with a pitcher of tea and two frosted glasses on a silver tray. She placed it on the coffee table in front of the sofa and said, "Go ahead and pour yourself a glass, I need to go pee."

Betty quickly poured herself a glass and when she heard the lock turn on the bathroom door she hurried over to the desk, opened the center drawer and saw the checkbook. She lifted it and had it in her purse within seconds. "This is really good tea," she said when Tammy returned to the living room.

"Thanks," Tammy said, and poured herself a glass. She sat down in a beige upholstered armchair adorned with gold-leaf flowers and sipped at her tea. She put her glass back on the tray and asked, "So what's your plan? What would I have to do?"

"For now, I just want information about what they are doing and where they are. Later on there might be something else. That means just keeping an eye on them for the time being."

"Okay, but Jack won't talk to me, and although I know he's staying with one of his friends, I don't know which one or where."

"You know where he works, right?"

"Yeah, he told me that much about himself."

"Well, take off a little early one day after work and follow him when he leaves his job. Just spend some time watching what he does and keep me informed."

"That sounds easy enough, but what about his wife? I've never been to their house and other than knowing that she drives a big truck I really don't know much about her."

"Don't worry about her right now. Just concentrate on Jack. If everything works out, I think we can get even with those two really soon."

"Okay. I want to help, especially if I can get back at Jack."

"I'm going to help you any way I can. I may need to get some supplies to do my part. Neither of us want to be using our credit cards for this. Do you have any cash?"

"Cash? You want me to give you money?"

"It's not for me. Look at it this way, if you had to hire a private investigator it would cost you thousands of dollars. I'm not asking for that, just a few hundred bucks to get some things."

"Okay...," Tammy said with trepidation. She went to her purse and took out her wallet. "I only have $235 in cash. I can write you a check?"

"Oh no, $225 should be fine for now. I'll let you know if I need more." She got up, took the cash from Tammy, shook her hand, and left.

◊◊◊

Jack had gone to the airport to pick up Mark and his girlfriend. Shelby didn't understand why she had butterflies in her stomach or why she was so concerned with how she looked as she primped in front of the mirror. She tried hard to convince herself that it was just to make sure Jack realized what he'd given up. Deep inside she knew as she put on the last of her makeup that it was more than that—she did care what Jack thought. She put her powder brush down. "Knock it off, Shelby! He cheated on you…you don't trust him anymore…it's just a family dinner." She left her room and went to get a drink. She needed something to calm her nerves before everyone showed up.

Shelby sipped at her drink, thinking about how she was going to behave around Jack as she walked to the kitchen to finish prepping for dinner. Still in her own thoughts, Mark and Jack, along with Mark's girlfriend, entered the house. Mark hugged his mother. "I'm so glad you're home, son."

"Mom, this is my girl, Lacy." Shelby gave the thin woman a short hug. "So good to meet you," she told her, and pointed at their bags. "Mark, your room is ready. Why don't you take her things there? Jack Jr. and the kids should be here soon."

"Okay, Mom." Mark grabbed the bags. He and Lacy disappeared down the hall.

Jack whispered. "I didn't get a chance to talk with Mark. I didn't know if I should around Lacy."

Shelby smirked, taking her empty glass of ice back to the bar for a refill. "Figures. I'm not telling him, so you'd better."

Before she could finish filling her glass Jack Jr. and his family came through the door, making the house full of noise and laughter. Shelby loved it when the grand babies were over and the house was filled with the sounds of children. She missed her boys being young and even missed the children she used to teach at school. "Mawma! Mawma!" the grand babies yelled as Shelby stepped out of the bar and opened her arms for a hug. They scurried back and forth between Jack and Shelby. When they ran back to Jack he would tickle them and then grab them and hoist them into the air as they giggled, just as he had done with his own sons. Shelby loved that about Jack—he was a great father and grandfather.

Jack, Shelby, and their family had a nice dinner. Shelby tried to focus on how pleasant it was to have her family around the dinner table and not on Jack's infidelity. They let Mark drive the conversation as he and Lacy told them about their lives. When dinner was over Jack decided it was time to let Mark and Jack Jr. know what was going on between Shelby and him. Lacy and Junior's wife offered to help Shelby clean up in the kitchen. Jack took this as his cue to invite Mark and Jack Jr. to the back porch. Steven, already well aware of the topic, took the kids out front to play tag.

"Mark, Junior, I need to talk to you about something, but I didn't know if you wanted me to tell you in front of the girls. It's about your mother and me."

"What is it?" Mark asked.

Jack had prepared a speech, but the words would not come. After several deep breaths, he just spit out the truth.

"Oh hell, Dad. What were you thinking?" Mark asked, more in shock than anger. "You love Mom, and I know she still loves you. What are you guys doing? What about our family? Man, this is not what I wanted Lacy to see when I brought her home. I want to marry this girl, Dad."

Jack tried to reassure Mark, but it was difficult since he could not say for certain what going to happen between Shelby and him. "We still both love each other and I'm hoping in time she'll forgive me and we can work through this mess. Right now she just needs space. I'm still going to be here for her as much as she'll let me. I wanted you to hear everything from me since it is entirely my fault."

"Man, I need a beer," Mark said.

"Me, too," Junior said.

Jack reached into the cooler and pulled one out for each of his sons.

"Now I'm not sure I want to get married," Mark said. I figured if I could have a marriage like yours and Mom's it would be worth getting tied down. Now that even you guys are having problems, I don't know if I want to try it."

"Look, son. Marriage is great. I know if you ask Lacy to marry you, you guys will be fine. Truth is, no one is perfect. I really messed things up and I've got to fix them. I just hope your mom will give me a second chance."

"Man, Dad. Was this girl really worth this?" Junior asked. "I heard a little of this from Steven a few days ago, but I didn't know it was this bad."

"No, son. She wasn't. It was stupid."

They went back into the house and joined the women in the kitchen. "Mom, it's getting late and we need to get the kids home for bed," Junior said. "The food was great and I'm glad to see that you and Dad are at least talking." He gave her a hug and a kiss.

"Oh thanks, baby. It is getting late. You'd better get your family home."

As soon as they left, Steven announced that he, Mark, and Lacy were going to catch up with some friends over drinks.

"Okay," Shelby said. "Have fun."

Jack looked at the dishes in the drying rack. "Here, let me dry," he offered gently.

They worked side by side. Jack reached for a dish on the counter at the same time Shelby did, causing them to be in each other's personal space. Jack moved in and kissed Shelby. Shelby returned the kiss but then turned away, realizing that she wasn't supposed to be kissing someone she was angry with.

Jack pulled her back and touched her chin, forcing her to look into his eyes. "You look beautiful tonight, Shelby Mathews, and I love you and I don't care how long it takes me, I'm going to get you back."

Jack and Shelby continued to clean the kitchen together in silence. Shelby couldn't help it, no matter how hard she tried she couldn't stop loving Jack and she loved having him in the kitchen with her. She wondered if she should ask him to stay the night. Before she could ask Jack put down his towel and started toward the living room door.

Shelby wiped her hands with the towel and followed him.

Jack took her hands and kissed her cheek. "Thank you for today. It was great."

As she watched, Jack walked out the door, Shelby was tempted to pull him back into the house but she knew she would probably regret it later. She did not know if she would ever be able to trust him again. She was glad Jack had taken the initiative to leave before things got out of hand. Still, she missed him in their bed that night.

CHAPTER TWELVE

Tammy tossed and turned all night. She was so conflicted. One moment she wanted Jack back and the next she wanted to rip him apart. She sat up in bed when her cell phone rang. She reached for it, hoping it was Jack, but it was Betty. "Hey, I drove passed Shelby's house last night. Looks like they were having some kind of family reunion. Jack was there, their kids, and grandkids, too. One big happy family."

Tammy felt anger course through her blood. "Bastard. He must think I'm some kind of easy lay. I'm way better than that bitch ass wife of his."

"Are you ready to make him pay for treating you like a cheap piece of ass?"

"Fuckin' A," Tammy replied.

"Good, try and follow him today," Betty said.

Tammy slammed her apartment door shut and went to her car. She knew where Jack worked, and she was going to see him.

◊◊◊

Jack was the happiest he had been at work in a long time. He knew it was because of the time he had spent with Shelby and his family. After dinner on Saturday, Steven had called Sunday morning to say that Mark, Lacy, Shelby, and he were taking their motorcycles out for an afternoon ride. He asked Jack if he wanted to join them. He'd hoped contacting him was Shelby's idea, but it didn't matter. He had the chance to spend the day with her doing something they both loved. Shelby was one hell of a woman when it came to riding. Jack laughed as he thought about the races that he'd had with her over the weekend and the ones he let her win…at least he thought he had let her win.

Whatever prompted me to stray? Shelby is the only woman I could ever want…the only woman I could ever love. She's the glue that holds our family together. He felt horrible that he'd been so stubborn about her job. If she could only understand how much he missed her when she was out on the road. He didn't care about that anymore. He wanted her back on her terms.

Jack's thoughts were interrupted by a voice over the intercom. "Jack, there's some woman in the front office demanding to speak with you. She isn't very pleasant. Should I call security?"

Jack got up from his desk, and when he rounded the corner, his heart sank. Tammy ran toward him but was suddenly stopped by two security guards.

Jack walked toward her and motioned for the two men to let her go. "Thanks, guys. I got this." Tammy jerked her arms away from the two men and reached for Jack. Jack grabbed her by the arm and pushed her toward the front door, then pulled her to her car. "What the hell are you doing here?" He whispered in her ear. "This is where I work. Coming here is not okay."

Tammy pulled her arm away from Jack, but he reached for it again. He needed her gone, not in the middle of his office parking lot threatening to make a scene. He tried to get her to get into her car. "Look, Tammy. I told you, I'm getting back with Shelby. What we had was nice, but it's over."

Tammy jerked away as soon as Jack opened her car door and began hitting Jack in the arm and face. "You bastard. You think you can just use me and throw me away like that? I have news for you, Jack Mathews. I'll get you for this. No one uses me and dumps me!" Tammy slapped Jack hard and then got in her car. She started it and almost backed over Jack as her tires screeched out of the parking lot.

Jack stood in the parking lot, wiping the sweat from his forehead. He was glad to see her leave but was a little concerned with her threat. Several employees who had been watching the confrontation from the front steps approached Jack. "Everything okay?"

Jack turned and started walking toward the building. "Yeah, just a crazy mistake." Jack was the division manager, his bosses worked out of the corporate offices in Oklahoma City. He doubted they would get word of Tammy's surprise visit. He was, however, worried about Shelby finding out. The best he could do was make light of the incident. As he walked back into the building he said, "Don't ever think the grass is greener boys. Women can be mean as hell when they don't get what they want."

The women groaned but the men just nodded their heads in agreement. Everyone laughed and headed back to work. Jack hadn't told too many people about his indiscretion. There was some gossip about an affair, but none of the people he worked with had ever met Tammy. Jack stopped by his secretary's desk. "Sorry about that. If that woman ever comes in here again, please call the police and have her removed."

◊◊◊

Shelby had enjoyed her weekend with her family, but was itching to get back to work. She'd called dispatch and received her assignment to pick up a load out of El Paso and head toward Washington State. This assignment meant being away from home for a week, but she was looking forward to the time away so she could think and get her head around what was going on with Jack and her. The one good thing about her situation with Jack, although she knew good wasn't the right word, was that she had been so preoccupied with their problems she did not have time to think about Betty and her release from jail.

◊◊◊

Betty was frustrated and angry as she pulled her car out onto Interstate 20. *The Camaro, with its damn four-cylinder Iron Duke, was almost as weak as Ted*, Betty thought. *Why couldn't he have had at least a V-6?* The old car was fine for getting around town, but not being in a truck meant it would be difficult to keep up with Shelby. She was determined not to let Shelby out of her sight. With any luck, not only would she get a ride from a trucker, she hoped she'd get the perfect opportunity to get rid of Shelby somewhere along the highway. Betty had managed to rig up her old CB in her car and knew that in time it would come in handy in keeping tabs on Shelby too.

Betty's cell phone rang. It was Tammy. "I've been sitting outside this bastard's office since this morning!" Tammy burst out. "I managed to get to talk to him but as usual, he blew me off like I was nothing. I hate him, Betty. He's such a pig. I'm going to find out where he's staying, just like you suggested. I'm ready to do anything to get revenge on that asshole."

"That's good, Tammy. It's important that you don't get too emotional. Stay cool. Just wait 'til he gets off work and then follow him to wherever he's staying. Having that information will be a big help. You can rest assured I have wonderful plans for that man and if things work out, I'll let you help."

"Good. I wanna see the bastard squirm."

"He will, trust me. Gotta go."

Betty looked at her gas gauge. "Shit." She wondered how long it would be before Shelby pulled over for a break because she was running low on fuel. Her phone rang again. "What?" she bellowed.

It was Peter. "Betty, the cops were here today."

"What did you tell them?" she asked nervously.

"Nothing. We told them we were renting the place, a friend hooked us up and we didn't know the owner."

"Did they believe you?"

"Yeah, I think so. They walked around the outside of the house and over to the carport. They asked what happened to the car that had been there."

"What did you tell them?"

"I said I never saw no car."

"Good. Did they leave you alone or are they still checking on the place?"

"No one's come to the place, I seen a couple of patrol cars cruising the street a couple of times."

"Just don't do or say anything stupid. I'm sure they'll go away."

"Okay, Betty, but we are out of beer. When you gonna be back?"

"I'll BE BACK WHEN I GET BACK."

"Okay, we'll just wait on the beer. What these cops want with you anyway?"

"Don't worry about it. Just watch my house if you want to get paid."

Betty hung up and slammed her hand against the steering wheel. "MORONS! I'm surrounded by fucking morons." Betty knew that someone was looking for her. She wasn't sure which agency, but someone smart had figured things out a little too quickly. She was determined more than ever to settle things with Shelby—and fast.

Betty was glad when she looked up from her temper tantrum and saw that Shelby was getting off at the next exit. It was around noon, so she figured Shelby wanted to get something to eat. Betty needed fuel, but decided that she needed a truck more. She drove past the entrance of the truck stop and pulled the Camaro off the road and maneuvered it behind a stand of cedar trees. She removed the stolen license plates and slipped them into her over-sized bag. Then she hiked back to the truck stop. She saw that Shelby had pulled her truck through the fuel island, which meant that Betty wouldn't have a lot of time to find a ride.

Betty decided she'd have to go into the truck stop if she was going to get any information on where Shelby might be headed. Truckers always talked with each other about their loads and destinations while waiting in lines, so there was a pretty good chance she could find out something if she listened. She moved through the store and caught a glimpse of Shelby standing in line to get a sandwich. She reached into her bag and pulled out a ball cap, moving the brim down low to shield her eyes. She turned up the collar of her shirt. She moved closer but still did her best to avoid Shelby. One thing she knew about Shelby was that guys flocked to her like flies to horse shit. She waited until a guy sauntered over to Shelby and started talking to her. Betty stood with her back to the man, out of Shelby's line of vision, but closed enough to overhear their conversation.

"Yeah, I'm headed to Washington…the state, not D.C." Shelby laughed.

"You definitely want that clarified before you hit the road," the man said.

"Especially when you're hauling fruit," Shelby said.

"Well, be careful out there, Barbie."

"You too, Fiddler," Shelby said with a wink. She paid for her sandwich and drink, and headed back to her truck.

Betty kept a close eye on the driver as Shelby left the store then she cut in front of another man behind Fiddler. "Hey."

"Oh, don't get your panties in a bunch, he's my husband," Betty growled at the man she'd cut in front of.

The man backed down as Fiddler turned to her, winked and then placed his order. "Well…my wife and I will have…." The man looked square at Betty and smiled. "Honey, what do you want?"

Betty was surprised by the trucker's willingness to play along. "You know…the small number two with mayo please."

The man turned to the cashier. "Make that two. My wife and I think a lot alike."

Betty quickly pulled money from her pocket and tried to pay for her sandwich, but Fiddler refused and bought the sandwich for her. They walked over to the condiment station for extra mayonnaise packets.

"Thank you for the sandwich," she told him, smiling, "But you didn't need to pay for it. I have money."

"I know, but I should take care of my wife, don't ya think?"

The two laughed as they walked out to the parking lot.

The man walked toward the line of trucks parked at the side of the fuel island. Betty knew from experience that most of these trucks were shut down for breaks. She moved casually with Fiddler toward his truck, hoping to get a glimpse of Shelby's rig. As they reached his rig, Betty stuck out her hand. "My name's Betty. Thanks for the sandwich."

"My name is Kenny, but everyone calls me Fiddler."

"Sorry for all that in there. I was just in a hurry and didn't want to wait in line. I figured that little blonde lady in front of you earlier was your wife."

The man chuckled. "No, she was a looker and all, but a little high maintenance for my taste."

"It did look like she was flirting with you. That's why I thought you were together."

"No. She's a driver, believe it or not. She's headed to Eloy, Arizona. I just came in from there and she was asking me about a posted detour."

Is this guy a trucker or my angel? Betty wondered. *Free lunch, the information I needed and no sex required. I must be doing something right.*

Betty cocked her head to the side and looked up at Fiddler through her eyelashes. "It's been a pleasure meeting you, Fiddler," she said. "My handle was Cheeks when I was on the road. So, am I more to your taste?"

"You could say that. Determined, bold, smart, and beautiful, but not the Barbie-doll type."

Betty giggled and kicked at the gravel in the lot. "So are you married?"

"Nope, never had the time for all that marriage stuff, being a truck driver. The only woman I'd want to commit to would be one who'd want to go on the road with me. There aren't many of them around. I've never had the fortune to meet one, anyway."

"Oh, you might be surprised."

Betty reached into her pocket and pulled out a gas receipt and a pen. "Look, I'm in a hurry right now, but I like you and I would like to get to know you. Trust me when I say this, but I never give my cell phone out to any man. I'm a female trucker, never been married, and for me to say, 'I like you,' is rare. You've caught my interest and I've been around truckers my whole life. You, sir, have just done what no man alive has ever done, floored this little female driver. Give me a call if you're still interested." Betty handed the man the paper. "Thanks for the sandwich, hubby."

Fiddler took the slip of paper and watched as Betty walked around to the backside of the store and disappeared. He looked at the number, put it in his pocket, and got into his own truck. He didn't need to think about it any further—this strange, mysterious woman intrigued him.

Eloy was about an hour south of Phoenix. Betty could do what Shelby could not: drive straight through without taking a break. She was going to push the Camaro as hard as she could. She went into the store, bought energy shots and remembering a news story about a lady astronaut, some adult diapers. Heading back to her Camaro she lifted another set of license plates, filled up her tank, and hit the highway.

◊◊◊

After L.A. Detective Stevenson finished his call with Utah State Police Officer Sgt. Arnold Petersen, he compared the information he had on his case with the murder case in Duchesne again. It was clear from the forensic evidence collected in both cases that Betty Burton was the prime suspect in both murders. He then contacted the police departments in Salt Lake City and some of the surrounding agencies between the two cities asking if there had been any sighting of this vicious killer. She was under the radar and the consensus was that she could be anywhere in the country. After conferring with the FBI an APB was sent out to all law enforcement agencies across the U.S.

The only trail was the credit card receipts. When one of the cards revealed she had used it to get her lights turned on, Stevenson had to laugh at the irony. "I'll be damned. That bitch actually went home. I guess she's not that clever after all." Stevenson was confused because Betty was still wanted in Texas for attempted murder. He figured there was no way she could be stupid enough to pursue Shelby Mathews, the woman she had tried to kill. But Betty was a psychopath and he'd dealt with stranger things in his line of work. One thing was for sure, he would never get used to the fact that people were crazy.

He contacted local law enforcement in Odessa, Texas and asked them to check out her house.

The cops called back a couple of hours later. Detective Stevenson was disappointed when he learned Betty was not at her house. They did not have a warrant to go inside, but the two men who were there said they had been renting the place and had no idea where the owner lived. When they asked Pedro (Peter) where he sent the rent check, he informed them that he was staying there in exchange for fixing up the place. Clearly he was not holding up his end of the bargain.

The cops had walked around the property and saw the tarp in the carport. When he asked the renters about Betty's car, they said they had never seen a vehicle on the property. Her car was impounded and had recently been auctioned off. Pedro (Peter) said Betty had never contacted him about her vehicle.

Stevenson asked them to show her picture around town and let him know if anyone had seen Betty in the past few days. The credit card information indicated that she had been there, but where was she now? He did not want to alarm Shelby Mathews and decided not to contact her yet with his suspicions. Betty had definitely been in Bakersfield, California and Stevenson was going to make that piece of shit boyfriend of hers tell him everything he knew about the whereabouts of Betty Burton.

CHAPTER THIRTEEN

Shelby's trip through New Mexico and Arizona was smooth and fast. She was so happy to be back out on the road. Since she was early, she decided to roll her big rig into the parking lot at the big truck stop in Eloy Arizona, where she could wash the dirt off both her and the truck. Afterwards she'd get a nice warm meal in the restaurant and then go to sleep for the night. The truck wash wasn't busy so it didn't take long to clean up the rig; then she found a quiet place to park near the rear of the parking lot. Normally she wouldn't park that far back from the front, but she knew within a couple hours the place would be swarming with sleepy, hungry, and smelly drivers. She knew that parking further back would be more suited to getting some sleep.

◊◊◊

Betty had made it to Eloy in record time. There were a few close calls on the highway when she saw highway patrol with their radar guns, but whenever she saw them, she'd move back over to the right-hand lane. She figured the suckers in the fancy sports cars would get stopped before the tin can she was riding in, whose looks belied how fast it could go. The downside was that it got terrible mileage and by the time she pulled into the truck stop in Eloy, all the cash she had gotten from Tammy was gone. She hoped she'd be able to use some of Tammy's checks at one of the check cashing places.

Betty parked the Camaro around the side of the truck stop in a dark corner of the lot. She knew an attractive woman walking in a truck stop parking lot during the day was pretty safe but at night it was best to get where you're going and stay there. Usually, the only ones walking around without a place to go were "commercials." Betty could tell from the flashing lights some of these truckers wanted to know what she was selling. She didn't care about any of those horny bastards. *I've had my fill of them cocksuckers.* She wasn't going back to hooking unless she had no other choice. She'd do what she had to get into trucks, if need be, but she wasn't going to let any man use her body again. *Except maybe Fiddler.*

A picture of the man ran through Betty's mind as she walked up and down the rows of trucks. She couldn't put her finger on it but Fiddler was different. For the first time in her life a man had gotten under her skin, which gave her a strange feeling. She didn't want anything from him, which was really messing with her head. She always wanted something from everyone.

Her thoughts were interrupted when she spotted Shelby's pretty blue and silver Peter. She sneaked between Shelby's and another truck and looked over Shelby's trailer. Betty thought of her perfect plan as she pulled at the security seal on the door.

◊◊◊

Shelby had finished her shower and had put her things away when her stomach churned. She figured she was just hungry. As Shelby walked toward the restaurant, she stopped by the door and looked toward the parking lot where her truck was parked. She couldn't see her truck but she had that strange feeling in her stomach again. *Stop being paranoid, Shelby,* she thought to herself and stepped into the restaurant.

◊◊◊

Betty's heart was racing as she walked briskly to the Camaro. She felt exhilarated when she thought about what she had planned for Shelby. Before she could finish the job, she needed to find a place to hide out for a while. She got in the car and put the key in the ignition but the car would not start. As she got out trying to figure out how she could score some gasoline, a man approached her from the shadows.

"Excusess meee laady, but I wass wonnderin' if ya can help me find my truck?"

104

Betty backed away from the man, but he was so intoxicated that he fell into her, almost knocking her to the ground. "You're an idiot," she said as she pushed him away. "Where's your truck?"

"Ittt'ss rrrighttt ovvvver there." The man slobbered on Betty's face as he pointed and wobbled in the direction of several trucks.

"What kind of truck? What's the color? Who do you drive for?"

"Itt'sss Bbbbluuue. It'ssss riiight there." The man staggered with Betty's help toward a blue freightliner sitting on the front line.

Betty did her best to support the man to the truck. When they got to it she leaned him up against the side. "Wait here." She instructed the man as she quickly ran back to the Camaro and retrieved her things.

"Suuurrre," he slurred.

Betty figured this drunk was the perfect solution to her lodging and transportation issues. The man would be easy to subdue and she'd be closer to Shelby's truck, which meant she could complete her plan without drawing attention to what she was up to.

The man was fumbling through his pockets for his keys when Betty returned. "Here, let me help." Betty put her things down and started rummaging through the man's pockets, easily locating his keys.

The man didn't flinch at Betty's aggression. "Haay, you're kinddaaa cute. Wanna staay with me?"

Betty unlocked the door and started shoving the man into the truck. "That's the plan, big boy." The man smiled at Betty as she continued to push him into his truck. "Get in the bed, big guy. I'll be there in a minute." The driver stumbled over the driver's seat and moved to the sleeper. Betty gathered her things and threw them into the truck.

Betty got into the truck and sat in the driver's seat. She looked around and noticed it was well-used but at least it wasn't filthy. She looked into the sleeper and saw the man fighting to get his pants off. "Okay, baby. Let's get you in bed."

"Yooou take my clothesss off meee and I get youuu neked, too."

Betty made sure the sleeper curtain was closed and then took the pillow from the head of the bed and put it beside her. She got behind the driver who was slouched to the floor and lifted him by the shoulders. "Okay, big boy, help me out." He complied but soon he was flat on his back on the bed, making kissing sounds up at her. "Wouldn't you feel better with this pillow under your head?" she said as she straddled him.

Before he could respond she pushed the pillow over the intoxicated man's face. "That's right, baby. I'm going to help you fall asleep." Betty had to use her entire body to hold the pillow over the man's face as he struggled under the pillow, gasping for air. "Go to sleep, baby. You'll be in a happy place when you wake up, I promise." It took several long struggling minutes for the man to pass. When Betty felt that he was gone, she moved the pillow away from his face, exposing the dead man's blood-red open eyes. She checked for a pulse on his neck to make sure he was gone before getting off his body. "Now you rest for a bit. I have something else I need to do."

Betty climbed off her victim and picked up his pants, checking for his wallet. She found it and was tempted to lift the credit cards, but knew they were a risk. There was $162 cash, which was better than nothing. She put the cash in her pocket. Then she moved to the driver's seat, straightened her hair slightly in the visor mirror, grabbed the trucker's keys and exited the truck. She locked the door and walked to the back of the truck. Shelby's truck was parked on the back row several trucks over to the west. She stealthily moved between the trucks and came in behind the truck from the rear. She hoped Shelby had not returned to her truck yet and noticed what she'd already done.

◊◊◊

Shelby had planned on grabbing some food to take back to her truck to eat. But when she entered the restaurant, she ran into an old friend from her ESCC days, a guy with the handle Tweedy. He invited her to have dinner with him and she accepted. After Tweedy and Shelby talked about her early days on the road, he paid for dinner and they walked out of the truck stop and into the night air in the parking lot. "Thank you so much for dinner," Shelby said, flashing him a genuine smile.

"It was my pleasure," he answered. "I would love to buy you breakfast in the morning if you're going to still be here."

"Oh, that would be wonderful, but I need to get a really early start in the morning. Probably just going to grab a cup of coffee and head out."

"Okay. Well, if you change your mind, I'll save you a seat."

"Thanks. Well, this is me," Shelby said, pointing to her truck. "Thanks again for dinner." Shelby gave Tweedy a kiss on the cheek and went to her door.

Shelby locked her door and moved to her sleeper compartment. She made sure her curtains were in place over the windows before getting ready for bed. She sat on the bed and thought about her day. She'd had plenty of time to think during her uneventful drive. She'd just enjoyed a wonderful dinner with a nice man who'd been kind. She was in her sleeper, feeling wonderful about her day but totally confused about her life. *What am I going to do about Jack?* She knew other men still found her beautiful, and she would never be without companionship, but should she give Jack another shot or move on? Jack had been the love of her life for as long as she could remember. *Would it be foolish of me to take him back after he cheated?*

As Shelby crawled into her bed she knew in her heart she was going to give Jack another chance. She hoped Jack realized what he had with her and would never take her love for granted again.

◊◊◊

Joey Altman sat in the interrogation room of the Bakersfield Police Department. The L.A.P.D. Detective Stevenson had called and asked to have him brought in for questioning. Detective Stevenson drove up from L.A. to question him.

"You're in a heap of trouble, Mr. Altman," Stevenson began. "Harboring a fugitive means hard time. But if you cooperate with us…"

"I told you, I don't know where the bitch is!"

"She was staying with you, right?"

"She called and said she needed a place to stay for a few days. Then she disappeared. She took all my cash with her."

"Why didn't you call the police?"

"Why would I call the cops? I didn't know she was in that much trouble with you guys. She told me she was wanted for traffic violations."

"Well, she left Utah under orders from the judge there not to, and she ended up here with you. Do you have any idea how she left town or with who?"

"Nope. She got a job at the truck stop restaurant while she was here. She used to be a driver. She always had a thing for truckers, would fuck anyone on eighteen wheels. She could have headed out with anyone. She did dye her hair and started wearing make-up. She probably wasn't even waiting tables. Probably was turning tricks. That bitch…I thought she really…"

"Loved you. You're pathetic, Joey. Here's my card. If you hear from her or think of anything else, call me." Stevenson stood up to leave. "One last thing. Do you have any idea where she might be headed?"

Joey shook his head. Stevenson opened the door to the interrogation room. "Texas…I'd bet money she's headed back to Texas. Betty always finishes what she starts. She told me she got fired from her job there."

◊◊◊

Shelby just couldn't sleep. Something was wrong, but she couldn't put her finger on why she'd been feeling weird all day. Unable to shake it, she pulled the covers back and sat on the side of her bed. She stared forward at the glowing gauges on the dashboard. Something caught her eye. The refrigerator unit temperature was too high. She thought the needle was stuck and moved forward and tapped on it. Nothing. Luckily the temperature wasn't at a dangerous level. She figured it would come down as the evening cooled. That weird feeling was still in her stomach so she decided to take a quick walk around her truck and take a look at the reefer.

It was dark and quiet in the parking lot. She knew she was taking a risk being out of her truck but knew she wouldn't be able to sleep until she checked on the trailer. She had a small Mag light and flashed it down the side of her truck. Everything looked okay—then she noticed that the door on the driver's side of her trailer was swaying in the wind. She was sure the door had been sealed shut when she picked up her load earlier in the day. Shelby gasped as she moved toward the rear of her truck. The trailer doors had been opened. As she looked inside the trailer she saw that someone had gone through the freight. The straps were off the pallets and weight and gravity had taken over, several boxes had broken through the plastic wrap and fallen to the floor. She hurried back into her truck and grabbed her cell phone and a larger flashlight. Once she figured out the extent of the damage, she'd have to call the dispatcher and file a report.

Shelby climbed into the trailer. The larger beam of her flashlight exposed the mess that covered the trailer's floor. She knew it was possible that the straps on the freight may have come loose, causing the pallets to tumble over during the drive. But she dismissed that when she examined the straps and saw they had been cut, as were the security straps on the door. She was continuing her inspection when the doors to the trailer suddenly slammed shut and she heard the latches being locked down. Shelby began to panic—she'd just been locked in her own refrigerator trailer.

She pounded on the trailer doors with her flashlight. "Hey, open the doors! I'm in the trailer! Please! I'm in here!" Shelby continued banging and yelling for several minutes, but it was no use. Whoever shut the doors, had left. She pulled her cell phone from her pocket. When she realized she had no signal inside the box, her heart sank. She began to hyperventilate and remembered the vent holes. When she reached for one of them, it was apparent that this situation was no accident. The vents had been sealed off from the outside. Shelby knew she was in trouble and knew who was responsible.

While Shelby banged and screamed, Betty moved back through the parked trucks to the one she'd confiscated from the dead drunk. She shut the curtain to the sleeper where her victim lay. She was pleased with herself as she maneuvered the truck onto the highway and headed east. She knew that Shelby would suffocate in the sealed, unvented trailer. It wouldn't be a quick death, but slow and painful. She'd drive the drunken dead guy's truck to get her back to her car and disappear. It all went off without a hitch.

◊◊◊

Jack was working late to catch up on paperwork he'd been ignoring. He'd tried Shelby's phone several times, but it kept going to voice mail, which worried him. He checked the time: almost ten. He figured she was probably asleep. He got up from his desk and got ready to go home.

Jack pulled his pickup into Ralph's driveway and got out. Just as he reached the door, he spotted a small car parked behind some trees along the dirt road. It was not normal for vehicles to be parked there; he was concerned the driver had car trouble and needed help. He decided to walk back to the road and check it out.

Bright headlights blinded him as he approached the road. Suddenly the car revved its engines and sped past him. Jack jumped back just in time and once the lights were out of his eyes, he recognized the car. It was Tammy. *What is that crazy bitch up to?* Jack wondered. *Why can't she just leave me alone?* Jack knew she wasn't going to be easy to get rid of now. *How am I going to explain this to Shelby?* He regretted hooking up with her. He wondered if it would be possible to get a restraining order to keep her away from him, but he doubted it would work.

◊◊◊

Shelby heard a click, and the cooling unit came on. Along with the closed vents, the temperature in the trailer began to plummet. She shivered and prayed that the fuel would run out quickly and shut down the trailer. She moved around the trailer and ripped plastic wrap off pallets and crates, and began wrapping the material around her so she could stay warm. She didn't know how long she could stand the temperature. She was in a quandary. She needed to move around to stay warm, but she did not want to exert too much energy because of the limited amount of oxygen in the sealed-off trailer. The wrapping around her head was doing a good job of keeping the heat in for now, which meant oxygen depletion was the bigger problem. She quickly formulated a plan.

She climbed on top of the boxes of one pallet, balanced herself and began to throw boxes to the floor. When the top box she was on began to wobble, she moved herself down a step to the space she had just cleared. Maneuvering her petite body like a Cirqu du Soleil performer she removed box after box, until one of the pallets was clear. She jumped in the middle of the boards causing several of them to crack. Using her flashlight as a hammer, she pounded against one of the pallets until one of the slats of wood came free. The board she pulled off had a nail protruding at the end of it.

She put the flashlight on the floor of the trailer and positioned it so the beam would illuminate the vent. Then she climbed onto one pallet that was still erect and wrapped in plastic, pulling up the board with her. Garnering all of her strength, she swung it over her head and like a pinch hitter going for a home run, smashed it against the vent. It worked and air hissed into the trailer.

She curled into a ball between two pallets and calculated the time. She figured she'd been locked in the trailer at around ten-thirty and based on her cell phone had been in the trailer now for about three hours. She had to survive the cold for about four and a half more hours. Then she would try banging and yelling again. She knew staying awake was essential. She began to count seconds, making them into minutes, and minutes into hours to pass the time. She rubbed her fingers and wiggled her toes to keep her blood flowing; she tried hard not to fall asleep.

◊◊◊

Shelby had struggled to stay awake but when she woke up shivering, she realized she'd given way to sleep sometime during the night. At least the fuel had finally run out and now she could feel the trailer warming slightly, although it was still frigid and would be that way for several more hours. She was stiff and didn't have much feeling in her fingers or toes as she attempted to move them. It was dark in the trailer because she'd saved her flashlight batteries. She turned the torch on now to look around again, looking for any way possible to get out.

She moved to the back of the trailer and began pounding on the doors, hoping some of the early morning drivers might hear her. "Please, someone help me! I'm stuck in this trailer!" Shelby yelled. She pounded for several minutes but got no response.

CHAPTER FOURTEEN

Betty was rolling down the highway, basking in her victory, when the dead man's right arm shot out through the sleeper curtain. Betty jumped and then remembered that he was stone cold dead. She pushed it away and decided she needed to find a dark place to dump the body before it started to smell. It was late at night; she was well outside any city or town and felt confident she could dump his body quickly. She pulled off the freeway and onto the service road. She found a dark private road and headed down for a while until she was sure no one could see her truck from the freeway. She pulled the truck over and turned off the lights.

She left the engine running as she turned in the driver's seat and pulled the sleeper curtain back. "You are one big mother," she said. "I told you when you woke up you'd be in a better place." She stood by the sleeper bed, trying to figure out just how she was going to move the man. She decided she'd drag him to the floor and then across the passenger seat. She would have to move him a little at a time.

She climbed onto the bed, put her back against the wall and using all her might, pushed the dead weight onto the floor. She took off his work boots and then took off his belt and wrapped it around his left ankle. She took off her own belt and wrapped it around his right ankle. She opened the passenger's side door and stepped over the man's body and stood with her back to his belted legs. She pulled like an ox dragging a plow behind her. She was only able to move him a few inches at a time. She stopped to rest, and then had an idea. She stepped back over him into the sleeper and got the flask she had seen on the shelf above the headboard. She went back to her victim, squatted down, forced his mouth open and poured the alcohol into his mouth and let it dribble down his chin and onto his chest. This way she would not have to bury him. *A drunk would be found, dead on the side of the road, hit and run… by his own truck.*

Betty felt invigorated by her plan and with superhuman strength pulled at the man's ankles until she was on the ground and his legs and hips were dangling from the door frame. She went over to the driver's side, started the truck and stepped hard on the accelerator. The truck jolted forward and the man fell from the doorway onto the road. Betty left the truck running as she got out, ran over to the body and collected the belts.

Then she climbed into the truck and reached over to close the passenger side door. She sat up straight in the driver's seat, put the vehicle in reverse and ran over the man's body. She turned on her headlights and headed the truck down the road. The tandems on her trailer ran over the man's body again. She felt the bump. "Oops, sorry about that."

Betty drove back to the truck stop, parked the truck in a space in back, and crawled into the sleeper. She was tired from all her accomplishments. She decided to get some sleep before getting gas for the Camaro and heading back home. She knew it wouldn't take the police long to track the truck she was in once they found the man's body because it was a company truck with a GPS tracking device on it. She'd put foil over the tracker stuck in the window, but that wasn't a definite block on the device—just a band-aid for the time being. She didn't care, though. She wanted sleep and wanted to get back to her house.

◊◊◊

When Peter saw three squad cars roll up with lights flashing, he decided he wanted no part of what Betty was into. He woke up his buddy, "We need to get out of here." Before they could gather up their things, there was a knock at the door.

"Police. We have a warrant to search the premises."

Peter sighed and opened the door. The policeman was holding a piece of paper. "Where is Betty Burton?" he demanded.

"I don't know."

"Take a seat, or would you rather we took you two down to the station?"

The lawn keepers decided it was in their best interest to cooperate with the police. They told the cops everything they knew about Betty, the things she asked them to do, the lies she asked them to tell, the electric bill notice and the car she drove. They swore they did not know where she was and promised to let the police know if she tried to contact them.

◊◊◊

Jack woke up from a restless night. He tried Shelby's phone again, but it still went to her voice mail. *Where is she?* he wondered. *Why isn't she answering? Is she still angry and ignoring me? Did something happen to her phone? Is she hurt?* Unable to calm his mind, he called the dispatcher at her trucking company who promised to call him when she checked in after delivering her load, she was still within the schedule window and knew she might be taking her break.

Jack called Steven, Mark, and Jack Jr. to find out if they'd heard from their mother. None of them had. Jack, sick with worry, asked them to call her just in case she was screening his calls. They complied but each reported back that he'd only got her voice mail as well.

"This is crazy! Shelby, where are you?" he muttered.

He began to get ready for work. He moved back in the bedroom after showering and shaving. Once he was dressed he looked out the window that faced the back road. He caught a glimpse of Tammy's bumper and grill.

I need to get that bitch to leave me alone.

◊◊◊

Detective Stevenson could not believe what he was reading on his computer screen. The interstate police database had just posted a brief report of a DOA found on a private road off I10 near Picacho, Arizona. Just after sunrise, a rancher had called the Arizona State Highway Patrol to report a dead drunk found run over on his road. At first, it appeared to be a hit and run. However, when the officers arrived they reported that the dead man had no boots, no belt, and his ankles looked like a garrote had been wrapped around each leg. His wallet did not have any cash, but it did have his credit cards and a CDL.

Stevenson picked up his phone and dialed the FBI field office. "Agent Silverman," he said. "I think we have a serial killer out there, and I'm pretty sure I know who her next victim is."

After his discussion with Silverman, Stevenson called and talked to his boss. Silverman had a task force in place within an hour, and Stevenson was appointed to it. He received his orders and plane tickets.

Agent Silverman met Detective Stevenson, Eloy Police Sergeant Peterson, and Eloy Detective Martinez at the Phoenix Airport. After introductions, the Eloy police detail took them to the police station. In the unit, the officers discussed the murder cases and their suspect, Betty Burton. Since the killing spree covered multiple states and jurisdictions, the FBI headed up the manhunt for Betty Burton. "We've impounded a car we believe might be the one she's been driving, and left word with the store manager that if the owner returns for the vehicle to contact us at once."

"Did anyone remember seeing who was driving the vehicle?"

"No. Should we send them her mug shot?"

"Not yet. Let's check out the car first. She's been a hard one to find, I want to know if this is the car she's been driving. If it is, then she had to have been in this area. We might also find out if she is still here and where she is hiding."

"You believe she's responsible for all the killings?" Martinez asked. "What's her motive and how does the Mathews woman fit in?"

"Well, she was in jail in Utah, awaiting trial on the attempted murder charge of Shelby Mathews. I'm not sure why she wanted to kill her, but psychopaths don't need a reason. The three recent murders all involved truckers and she's been spotted at several truck stops."

"And she used to be a trucker," Utah State Patrol Officer Petersen said. "Our focus should be there."

"Do you know how many truck stops there are just between here and California? Not to mention between Odessa, Texas, and Utah?" Stevenson said. "And she could be headed in any direction right now."

"Should we put out a nationwide alert and have her picture posted at all U.S. truck stops?" Petersen asked.

"That could tip her off," Agent Silverman said. "Let's get a look at her house and see what we can find out from her car."

"So what do you think you'll find in her car?"

Detective Stevenson hesitated. "Don't know, but it's a place to start. Next, I want a look at her house."

"You can't believe she'd head back to Texas? I thought she was smarter than that," Martinez said.

"She may be smart, but she's also fixated on Shelby Mathews," Silverman said. "We should probably put Mrs. Mathews into protective custody."

◊◊◊

Jack went to the police station and asked the desk officer the particulars for filing a restraining order. When he gave his name, the officer picked up the phone, pressed a button and said, "Jack Mathews is here. Do you want to talk to him?" The officer hung up and said to Jack, "Follow me, please." He led Jack to Sergeant Oliver's office.

Jack's heart was racing. "What's wrong?" Jack asked, alarmed.

"Oh, probably nothing, but we've also been trying to get a hold of Shelby," Oliver said. "Do you know where she was headed?"

"Eloy, Arizona. What's this about?"

"Looks like Betty Burton's been causing havoc out there. You never know what that woman will do. A detective from California is going to be here tomorrow. You say Shelby's not taking your calls?"

"I thought it was because she's pissed at me," Jack muttered.

"It may be nothing. Like you said, maybe she's just giving you the cold shoulder. Believe me, I understand. Been there myself. Look, we've got law enforcement from three states on the lookout for Betty Burton. Stay close to home and let me know if she calls."

Jack left and went straight to his office, but he could not concentrate on the work in front of him. He called his three sons and told each of them about Betty and what was going on with their mother. "I know she'll probably be angry at me for checking up on her if nothing is wrong, but I have to make sure she's okay. Please let me know if any of you hear from your mom."

116

◊◊◊

Betty woke up and got ready to head home. She gathered her own belongings and then went through the truck and selected several items she thought would be useful to her. She piled everything on the bed in the sleeper compartment. She got out of the truck and went to the store. She purchased a gas can so she could get fuel for the Camaro, a pack of cigarettes, and a cup of coffee.

After getting coffee and using the restroom Betty walked outside the store toward where she'd parked the Camaro. She lit a cigarette and surveyed the parking lot. Her car was nowhere in sight. She went back into the store and marched up to the clerk at the counter. "Hey, I left my car parked outside your store last night because I was out of gas. Do you know what happened to it?"

"Was that car yours?"

"Yeah. Where is it?"

"The police came and towed it away. Are you in some kind of trouble with the law?" Betty was out the door and halfway to the big truck before the clerk could get the last statement out of her mouth. Betty knew the cops were looking for her. She had to get gone fast. She wondered if those idiot lawn guys had ratted her out. She'd make them pay if they had. At least she had taken care of Shelby, which meant she could disappear where no one would find her.

◊◊◊

"This is Detective Martinez. Yes. Okay, how long ago? Did they see where she went? Okay. Thanks."

"Any news?" Petersen asked.

"That was the manager from the store where we picked up Burton's car. She came back for her vehicle last night. The clerk on duty didn't know she was supposed to tell the manager right away, so Betty has some miles on you guys."

"He's sure it was a female that came for the car?"

"That's what he said."

"Can the clerk make an ID for us?"

"I think so. The manager said the clerk only mentioned the incident to him because the woman took off out of the store in a big hurry."

Silverman interrupted them with more helpful news. "Did you know that hair dye doesn't impact DNA? It can also make your hair fall out. Strands of Betty's hair were found on all three victims. We can connect her to all three murders."

Detective Stevenson said, "Now we just have to find her. Let's get a photo array over to that clerk. Hopefully she can positively identify Betty as the woman she spoke with in the store. That will give us a time frame so we can narrow our search. Put a twenty-four-hour surveillance detail on her house. Let's get her picture out to the bus and train stations too."

◊◊◊

Shelby opened her eyes to the dark box she'd been imprisoned in for hours. At least the temperature had risen enough in the trailer that she knew it would be safe to remove the plastic from around her body. Her toes and fingers hurt, making it difficult to remove the plastic. She stopped when she thought she heard voices outside the trailer. She tripped and fell to the floor as she tried to get to the trailer wall near the voices. After recovering her stance, she began to pound hard. The pain in her hands made it difficult, but she was determined to get someone's attention. "Please, help me, PLEASE! I'm trapped in this trailer and I can't get out. PLEASE, ANYONE! SOMEONE HELP ME!" She pounded for several minutes, but no one seemed to be able to hear her.

Shelby fell to the floor in frustration and burst into tears. "I'm never going to get out of here." She let herself cry for a while but then wiped the tears away with the back of her hands and got up off the floor. It was still so dark. She reached into her pocket for her cell phone to see what time it was but the battery was dead. She'd left her flashlight near the pallets. She grabbed the edge of a pallet and moved toward her sleeping spot. She bent down on her knees and felt around the floor in the dark until she located her flashlight. She picked it up and shone it on the vent she had punctured. Not sure if the light she saw was from the flashlight's beam, she turned off the torch and felt a sliver of hope as a thin ray of light shown through. "Morning," she whispered.

With the flashlight in one hand and the dead cell phone in the other she circled the trailer pounding on the sides as she shouted, "PLEASE HELP ME! I'M TRAPPED IN HERE! HELP ME PLEASE!" She was exhausted after a few minutes and slumped to the floor. She was too tired to cry and realized she was hungry. She shone her flashlight onto the damaged fruit. She picked up a bruised grapefruit, peeled it and sunk her teeth into it, which calmed her hunger pangs and quenched her thirst. She felt better and told herself that it was possible when she was missing long enough someone from her company or family would come looking for her.

"Jack, where are you?"

◊◊◊

Jack couldn't sleep. He knew in his heart something was wrong—Shelby was in trouble. His pleas for help were unanswered. Both the trucking company and the police would not act until Shelby's load was six hours late and/or she had not called in for six hours.

"Shelby, where are you?"

CHAPTER FIFTEEN

etty burst through the doors of the store. For a moment she thought about taking the dead man's truck again, but knew the cops would be on it in no time. She slithered between the trucks and made her way to the frontage road of the highway. She found a fleabag motel about a quarter mile down the road. She took the last of the cash she had and booked a room under a false name.

Betty remained holed up in the room for a couple of days, trying to figure out what to do next. She thought about calling Joey, but he was too far away and was probably still pissed at her. She was considering calling Tammy to wire her some money when her phone rang.

"Hey, Cheeks. Thought I'd give you a call and see if I could interest you in a sandwich?"

"Hey, hubby. Where are you?" Betty brightened when she heard Fiddler's voice.

"Driving west on Interstate 10. Dropped my load and headed back to New Mexico."

"Hell, yes, I want a sandwich! Come get me."

"Where are you?"

"May I be honest with you?"

"Sure."

"I've had some problems…expensive…I'm so embarrassed…my car was repossessed. I'm stuck here in Eloy, Arizona."

"Look, Cheeks. We've all been there. I'll come get you. Where are you?" When she told him, he said, "I know the place. I'm still in Texas but not too far from the New Mexico/Texas state line. It will take me a few hours to come get you but I'll be there soon."

"Thanks, Fiddler. I really need a fresh start…maybe we can roll together for a while. I mean if you're interested in a traveling companion."

"Let's talk about it when I get there. See ya soon."

Betty took Fiddler's call as a sign. Maybe now that Shelby was out of the way she could settle down. She shoved her things in a backpack and sat on the edge of the bed, watching TV until Fiddler arrived. Her phone rang again and, assuming it was Fiddler, she answered it without checking the caller ID. "Hey, hubby."

"Hubby? Betty, this is Tammy."

"Oh, Tammy. What's going on?"

"Jack filed a restraining order against me. Are you still working on a plan to get even with him for me or not?"

"Well, I'm out of town right now."

"Where?"

"Oklahoma," Betty lied.

"What are you doing in Oklahoma? Is that why you answered the phone the way you did?"

"Yeah. My ex; he wants to see if we can give it another try."

"What about me? You promised."

"I haven't forgotten about you, Tammy. I'll get you back, I mean back to you. See you soon."

Tammy was pissed when the call ended. "Bitch, you'd better come through for me," she said.

◊◊◊

"Hey, Slick. Whatchya doin'?" Mad Dog asked as he approached his fellow driver.

"Well, I'm curious about this truck. It hasn't moved in almost three days," Slick said, standing outside of Shelby's truck. "It stopped running. I'm guessing it's out of fuel. It's strange. I haven't seen a driver near it."

As the two were examining the truck, a third trucker joined them. "What are you up to?" Coyote Killer asked.

"We're checking out this abandoned truck."

Coyote Killer lifted the handle of the driver's side door and noticed it wasn't locked. He stepped up into the cab and looked around. "Something's wrong here, boys. There ain't no woman I know that's going to leave a truck with her purse in it."

The men circled the truck and met up at the back trailer. It was sealed tight with padlocks and even the vents had been sealed off. Mad Dog moved one of the locks. "Looks secure in the back. Maybe we'd better call the cops and let them know."

It was hot and sticky in the trailer when Shelby woke up again in the dark. The freight she was carrying was rotting, and sweat was rolling down her forehead. As she felt around for her flashlight, she'd heard the metal-to-metal sound on the back of the trailer as she moved toward the rear. She slipped on the messy floor as she headed to the doors. "WAIT! DON'T LEAVE!" She screamed as she picked her body up off the floor and scrambled to the trailer doors. Shelby pounded hard on the doors with her fists and flashlight. "PLEASE! DON'T LEAVE! I'M TRAPPED IN HERE!"

Coyote Killer stepped back away from the trailer, sure he had heard something. "Mad Dog, there's someone in this trailer!"

"I heard it too," Mad Dog said.

"How is that possible?" Slick asked. "It's locked up tight."

Mad Dog pointed up to the vent. "Listen."

"PLEASE, OH PLEASE, HELP ME! I'M LOCKED IN HERE!"

Slick jumped back and grabbed his phone. "We've got to get the cops here. Mad Dog, go get the bolt cutters out of my truck's toolbox. Coyote Killer, see if you can get whoever is in that trailer to hear you. Let 'em know we're working to get 'em out!"

Coyote picked up his cell phone and banged a rhythmic response. "Hang in there! We'll get you out," he yelled, not sure he could be heard.

Shelby heard the man's voice. She sunk to the floor of the trailer and cried tears of relief. She had no idea what time it was or what day it was, but she was finally getting out of hell.

It took the drivers only a few minutes to cut the locks on the trailer and pull back the doors. The light from the day showed deep into the trailer as Shelby tried to stand and get outside into the sunshine. The police and ambulance were just arriving as the men climbed into the trailer to help the weak, frazzled-looking woman out. Coyote Killer saw how fragile she was, he picked her frail body up and handed her to Slick who was standing at the bottom of the trailer with open arms. "Come on, little lady. We got you."

"Thank you," she whispered.

The police moved back the crowd that had gathered as the medics took Shelby from Slick and put her on a gurney. A police detective came forward and began to question Shelby. "How did this happen, ma'am?"

Shelby stared blankly at the policeman and then passed out. The officer motioned for the medics to take Shelby to the hospital.

As one officer interviewed the three men about how they found her in the trailer, another police officer secured then searched Shelby's truck for evidence as to how she might have gotten locked in the trailer. It was clear to all by the time the investigation was complete that Shelby had been locked in that trailer on purpose. Having all the information they needed for the time being, the police told the three truckers they were free to go, but took down their phone numbers just in case there were follow-up questions.

Slick, Mad Dog, and Coyote Killer were all waiting in the lobby of the hospital when the nurse came and told them that Shelby was going to be fine. "Can we go in and see her?" asked Mad Dog.

"Sure, but don't stay too long. She needs rest. She was pretty dehydrated and the hypothermia was bad. Besides, she already had a visit from the police."

Two officers had been called to question Shelby while the truckers were being interviewed and her truck had been secured as a possible crime scene.

Shelby smiled as the men approached her bed. "You must be the three guys who saved my life today."

"Yes, ma'am. We're just glad Slick here was smart enough to know that something wasn't right about your truck's being there so long."

The men each walked forward and shook Shelby's hand. Coyote Killer gave Shelby a hug. "Dammit, Killer. Let the woman be. She's in a hospital."

The men and Shelby laughed. "Can't help it, boys, she's pretty. Gotta get a hug from all the pretty ones," Coyote Killer said as he moved back.

"It's fine. Thank you so much you guys for saving me. I thought I was going to die in there."

"How'd you get locked in that trailer anyway?"

"Like I told the cops, I'm not really sure. I was getting ready for bed and I couldn't sleep, so I got out of the truck and walked to the back. I noticed that the doors were swinging. Someone had cut the security seals and opened the trailer. At first, I just thought I had caught someone trying to steal. Then when I got in the trailer the doors closed on me. I guess the wind or something."

"Wasn't no wind, ma'am. Someone shut those doors on you on purpose."

Shelby felt a shiver run up her spine. "Really? The police haven't let me know that yet. In fact, they just let my company know a little while ago that they found the truck. I guess the company finally reported the truck missing."

"Does your family know?"

"Yes, I called my boys as well as my husband."

"I'm sure they're glad you're okay."

"Oh, they're glad I'm okay, but I'll never hear the end of this from Jack."

"The hubby doesn't like you driving, huh?"

"Not one little bit. He'll see this as just one more reason for me to quit."

"Well, don't give up, girl. Shit, I mean stuff, happens out here."

"Forgive Mad Dog, he's not much of a gentleman most of the time."

"Excuse me, ma'am." The men elbowed each other, letting the other one know he was being a jerk. "Don't you never mind about those two bozos over there. Neither of them knows how to treat a lady."

Mad Dog and Slick both gave Coyote Killer a swift jab to the arm and tap to the back of his head as Coyote moved in to kiss Shelby's hand. "Be careful, ma'am. He comes by the name Coyote Killer rightfully so." The room filled with laughter as the new friends continued to talk.

◊◊◊

Jack hung up the phone and slumped down in his desk chair. Shelby was safe, but as he had figured, she'd been in serious trouble. He wasn't going to go to Arizona to get her—not because he didn't want to, but because she didn't

want him to. Jack Jr. and his wife were on their way, which is what she wanted. He knew that he was going to have to work even harder at getting Shelby
back. He loved her no matter what and her not wanting him to be there for
her when things were bad proved just how badly he'd screwed things up this
time. He also couldn't shake the feeling that there was something funny about
what had happened. Betty had to be involved somehow—he just knew it.

CHAPTER SIXTEEN

Betty felt great riding along with Fiddler. They were headed for the East Coast. Fiddler had several loads to deliver and pick up out there. As Betty rode in the passenger seat, she was amazed how much Fiddler reminded her of her father. He was quiet, but would smile at her from time to time. He played old country music on the radio and sipped at his coffee as they put miles under their wheels. Betty leaned back and put her feet in the windshield like she did when she was a kid. She was happy. Shelby was dead. She had wanted to take care of those lawn guys and Tammy, and maybe would someday. Right now she was with Daddy.

After covering several hundred miles, Fiddler pulled into a truck stop so the two could get a bite to eat. They sat in the drivers' section of the restaurant and ordered coffee. "Wow, this is great," she said, with a big smile. "I'm so happy being out on the road again, and it's been nice being with you these last few weeks, Fiddler."

Fiddler didn't say much because the waitress approached and he turned his attention to her. Fiddler was sitting with his back to the TV, so he did not see the news report that came on about the truck stop killings. Betty almost choked on her coffee when her mug shot was shown. "You okay, Cheeks?"

"Yeah, the coffee's just a little hot."

Although Betty liked Fiddler, she had not given him her real name. She figured the cops in Utah were still looking for her. She told him her name was Nancy Mayfield. She also told him that her real husband had been abusive and it was his car she had tried to run away in…the car that had been repossessed. Fiddler was very caring and supportive. He never called her Nancy, only Cheeks.

When she told him she felt ugly and dowdy, he agreed to front her the money for a hair color and cut in an Albuquerque mall hair salon. When she told Fiddler it would take a couple of hours, he pressed $200 into her hand and told her he was going to take a nap and to call him when she was ready. After her hair appointment, Betty went to a one-hour eyeglasses place and purchased contact lenses that did not correct vision, only changed eye color. When Fiddler came to pick her up he was met by a woman with soft auburn curls with streaks of strawberry blond that shimmered in the sun. Her eyes were a hazel green.

"I never knew your eyes were green," Fiddler said.

"What color did you think they were?"

"I'm not sure. Gray, maybe?"

"Oh, they change color, depending on the light. How do I look?"

"Like a beauty pageant contestant."

She was glad Fiddler was distracted from the news. It made her nervous, although she knew she did not look anything like the picture on the TV screen. All she had to do was keep herself focused on her new life and avoid anything that might let Fiddler know about her past.

◊◊◊

Shelby was ecstatic when Jack Jr. and his wife arrived at the hospital and even more thrilled when the doctor said she could go home. The police released her truck back to the trucking company when they were through with it as a crime scene. Insurance would cover the damaged load. She was not held responsible for the unfortunate incident.

Shelby slept during most of the trip back home, and when Jack Jr. finally drove them into her driveway, she let the first tears flow since leaving the hospital. "Mom, what's wrong?" Jack Jr. asked, putting his hand on her arm.

"Nothing, baby. I'm just glad to be home. Maybe your dad has been right all along. Maybe I should just give up driving and stay here once and for all."

"Get some rest, Mom. Things will look different tomorrow. Now is no time to make any big decisions."

Jack Jr. and his wife put Shelby to bed and then Jack Jr. called his dad, who was still staying at Ralph's house. "Dad, you know I don't get involved with yours and Mom's stuff, but you really need to fix things between the two of you. She needs you. I know it's just pride keeping the two of you from getting back together."

"I understand, son, but she doesn't want me there. I would be making more problems trying to butt into her life right now."

"What life, Dad? She's dipping into depression and thinking about giving up driving. I know you don't want her on the road, but she loves it and you need to let her know that it's okay with you...even if it's not. She needs you and wants you to interfere. You hurt her with that stupid affair. Now fix this any way you can."

"Okay, son. I'll do what I can. Is she at home now?"

"Yeah, we just got here with her."

"I'll be over there in a little while."

"We've put her to bed. We need to get back to the kids. Do you still have your house key?"

"Yes, but she's not going to like this, son."

"She needs you...she's just too stubborn to realize it and too proud to admit it. Don't screw this up Dad. Don't talk about the truck—just talk about you guys."

"Okay, Dr. Phil. I'll do my best."

"Thanks, Dad."

Jack was happy about having some alone time with Shelby. He was nervous things might not go as well as Jack Jr. had anticipated. Plus, with Betty still determined to kill her, he wasn't sure how they could avoid talking about her being on the road—he needed to try and keep his mouth shut. Perhaps if the two of them could get away from things for a while and be alone together somewhere without any distractions, they could work on getting things back together. Jack decided that was what he was going to recommend—a vacation.

◊◊◊

After getting a bite to eat, Fiddler and Betty headed east again. Betty sat with her feet on the dash, reading a magazine and feeling like a little girl again with Fiddler. It was amazing—she couldn't have been happier if her daddy was really sitting in that seat next to her, driving the big truck. She had her new life and everything else from the past was gone. Even the breeze blowing through her hair from the open window felt amazing. *Nothing could possibly ruin this day*, she thought.

After being on the road for several hours, Fiddler stretched his arms over his head and looked over at Betty. "Hey, baby. I'm getting a little sleepy. You mind if we pull over and take a little nap?" Betty smiled up at him. "No, not at all. We have plenty of time to make this delivery, right?"

Fiddler pulled the truck over into a picnic area and put on the air brakes. He put the cruise on and ran the RPMs up to about 900, which Betty knew all good drivers did with their trucks when they were idling to save wear and tear on their engines. "I'll just sit here and read," she told him. "How long do you want to rest, or do you want me to drive for a while?"

Fiddler moved to the back of the truck and kissed Betty on her forehead as he went by. "I was thinking maybe you might want to join me for a nap."

Betty liked the soft gentle kiss she received on her forehead but she was slightly taken back by Fiddler's request. She'd been so overwhelmed with the commonalities between Fiddler and her father that she let the sexual part of the relationship slip into the back of her mind. Although sex had never meant anything to her, she wasn't sure she was willing to let it interfere with what she felt she had with Fiddler. "Maybe in a little while," Betty said.

"Okay. I'll be waiting."

The nausea she once remembered feeling in her stomach many years ago as a little girl welled up deep inside her. Tears—a phenomena she hadn't felt in decades—rolled slowly down her face. The memories of years past flashed through her mind and she tried hard to block them out. *How could he even think about having sex with me? I'm his little girl and he's supposed to protect me from the bad people.* Betty stared at her magazine. Maybe she'd misunderstood Fiddler. Maybe he didn't want sex from her. Maybe he really did want her to just rest with him in the sleeper. She figured she'd find out his intentions once she didn't go and lay down next to him.

◊◊◊

Jack didn't know why he felt like a criminal when he entered the front door of the house he and Shelby had built together. The home where they had raised their children. He hoped Jack Jr. was right about Shelby's needing him, but if he wasn't, Jack knew Shelby would be pissed off about him coming into her house uninvited. Jack made his way down the hallway to their bedroom and found Shelby asleep on her side of the bed. She had all the pillows stacked around her, as usual, and Jack laughed quietly at how it was the little things he suddenly remembered about his wife that were so special. He pulled the chair next to their bed and decided to just watch her sleep for a while. He wanted desperately to undress and crawl deep under the covers with Shelby and feel her soft skin next to his while he held her close, letting her know she was safe. But his insecurity about their relationship held him back as he sat and watched her breathe.

He remembered all the wonderful things about Shelby that had made him fall in love with her all those years ago. She'd always been such a sweet and tender woman to everyone. It was like having a light turned on when she walked into a room. Besides being smart and pretty, she just had a way about her that made you feel happy and comfortable when she was around you. She would have done anything for anyone if it were possible. She was a scrapper when she was angry, though, and stubborn when she wanted her way. Jack laughed a little to himself thinking about how Shelby could bring on the fire in the bedroom. Thinking about those things made him angry at himself for the way he'd treated her. She hadn't done anything to deserve his terrible behavior.

Suddenly, Jack got out of the chair and started taking off his clothes. He wasn't going to let her go. She'd been there for him when he almost died and he was going to be here for Shelby no matter what she said or did. Jack slid in under the covers on his side of the bed and moved the pillows out of the way so that he could wrap his arms around her.

Shelby was heavily medicated, but she was well aware of the arms being placed around her waist. She attempted to break loose from the hold on her body, but Jack gently moved in close to her and turned her toward his face so that she could see that it was him. "It's okay, baby. It's just me. Don't be angry. I love you and I'm sorry for everything I have put you through. I'm staying here whether you want me to or not. I'm here because I want to be and I want you to know that you mean everything to me." Jack gently kissed Shelby.

Shelby without words returned the kiss she'd been wanting for so long. Finally, Jack was hers again forever and she was his. Nothing would get in their way ever again.

◊◊◊

Fiddler woke to find himself alone in his sleeper. Betty was still sitting in her seat with her magazine. He moved to the driver's seat and bent over to put on his boots.

"I was just about to wake you up. Did you rest well?" Betty asked, still looking at her magazine.

"Yeah, it was okay. It would have been better if you'd joined me. I know your ex was a jerk, but I thought…"

"I just wasn't tired. You're not mad, are you?"

He wanted to tell her yes but decided to leave it alone—for now. "We better get going we've got some deliveries to make."

Betty felt her heart sink, Fiddler was just like every man she'd ever met. The only difference was he wasn't forceful or mean. Betty was angry that the one man she thought she could replace her father with wasn't interested in being her daddy…no one would ever replace her daddy. Small tears fell to her cheeks as she turned her head slightly toward the window so that Fiddler would not spot her emotions.

Betty would never let anyone see her weaknesses. *Now I'll have to figure out a way to get rid of Fiddler, too.*

CHAPTER SEVENTEEN

Jack got up before Shelby and went to the kitchen, making coffee and a light breakfast for his wife. She was still sleeping when Jack came in with her breakfast, but just as he was about to take the tray back to the kitchen, Shelby moved and spoke. "Hey, you. Where're you going with my breakfast?"

Jack turned and brought the tray to his wife. "I wasn't sure I should wake you. But I'm glad you're awake." Jack kissed Shelby and she gently rubbed the side of his face with her bandaged fingers, which had been bruised by the constant banging on the trailer. Jack softly took her hand and kissed the bandages. "Do they hurt?"

Shelby let him hold her hand. "Not anymore, but they did for a while."

"I'm glad you're okay."

Shelby reached for her coffee but found it difficult to hold. Jack noticed the difficulty and gladly helped Shelby take a sip.

"By the way, how did you get in here last night?"

"Well, if I tell you that, our oldest will kill me."

"Oh, I see." The couple laughed together and Jack moved in for a kiss, which Shelby was more than happy to accept. She was through being angry with Jack and wanted him home, but she was still afraid of his trying to control her, especially when it came to trucking. She had a lot to think about. Maybe it was time to go back to teaching school or something else less dangerous. But anything else wouldn't be the road.

Jack began to feed Shelby her breakfast. "Here, try this. We need to get you well so you can get back to work."

"Do you want me to go back to trucking or do something else?"

"Shelby, I know I've been an ass and not supportive when it came to your driving. I'm really sorry for that. Driving is what you love and what you want to do. So I'm behind you one hundred percent. It also has nothing to do with wanting to come home and being your husband again. Even if we never get back together, I want you to be happy and I want to support your choices."

"So you want to come home?"

Jack sat closer to Shelby on the bed. "Yes, baby. I want to come home and be a family again." Jack kissed Shelby's forehead and gave her another sip of coffee.

Shelby sipped at the coffee and then rested her head on her pillow. "I'm not trying to bring up the past, but I have to know. Did you love her?"

Jack turned away from Shelby. "No, I never loved her. In fact, I can't for the life of me figure out why I ever got involved with her, except that I was angry with you and acting a fool."

"So you're done with her?"

"Yes, but I had to get a restraining order against her…she's been stalking me."

"I didn't know she was that strange." *First Betty, now Tammy. Why do I attract crazy women into my life?* Shelby thought but she said, "I'm sure everything is going to be okay."

Jack turned back to her and continued to feed her. She signaled she was full and said, "I don't know, Jack, maybe it is time for me to stop driving and go back to school. Maybe you've been right all along."

Jack sat up straight and looked Shelby straight in the face. "Enough of this. When you're well, you're going back to driving. You love your job and we'll work together to keep you safe."

Jack's cell phone rang. He looked at the caller ID. It was Tammy. He blocked the call and her number.

◊◊◊

Fiddler had hardly spoken to Betty as they made their way down the highway toward one of his drops. He wondered if he'd made a mistake taking this woman into his truck. Fiddler wasn't upset about her not wanting to be in his bed right away, but now she was acting strange. Something was on her mind. "Hey, what are you thinking about? You seem a million miles away."

Betty didn't expect the calm questions. She thought that Fiddler would lash out at her for not having sex with him. Testing him she replied, "Oh, nothing really, just thinking about my father and how much you remind me of him."

"Your father? I'm not sure how to take that. Tell me about him. Is he a driver?"

"Not anymore. He's dead."

"I'm sorry, Cheeks."

"Yeah, me too. He was all that I had. He promised that we were going to have a little house in the country where we would go when we had down time. But he died before we could make it happen."

"What about your mother?"

"I don't care to talk about her. Let's just say I spent the rest of my childhood in and out of trucks and various government programs until I became old enough to drive and get my CDL. I've been in a truck ever since."

"Well, maybe in a while you can take the wheel and show me just how good a driver you are."

The two laughed. "I'm a terrific driver, and the best female driver in the country."

Betty liked that Fiddler was interested in her, but talking about her past was something she wanted to avoid—especially her recent past. She was surprised that Fiddler hadn't been the asshole she figured he was going to be after she didn't jump into bed with him. That made talking to him easier.

"So I take it things didn't go well for you after your father passed on? Tell me about yourself. I want to know everything. The good, the bad, and everything in between."

Betty hesitated. She sure couldn't tell him about the last two years. She decided to just tell him most of the truth about the past and avoid the present.

"Well, there's not much to tell and most of it isn't pretty. I was a whore for about five or six years after escaping from the foster system. Maybe longer, I don't remember that part of my life…it's easier when I don't try and remember. I did what I had to do to survive while I was trying to get enough money together to get a truck of my own or at least a job driving a truck. I spent the next years of my life driving trucks all over the country. I drove big rigs in the snow, ice, and every natural disaster imaginable. I've been down some of the most treacherous mountains and highways you can think of in this country. Those were the best years of my life, next to the years I spent with my dad. I think he would be proud of me if he knew I kept up his legacy. He was the best in the country, too." Betty looked out her window and thought about her father.

"I have no doubt he's proud of all you had to do to make it," said Fiddler.

"I hope not." Betty mumbled, hoping Fiddler didn't hear her.

Fiddler didn't catch the soft comment. "So what happened? Why aren't you driving now?"

Betty sat up straight in her seat and stared ahead. "Oh, it's a long story, but that problem has been eliminated," she paused. "Let's talk about you."

"Okay, but my life is pretty boring."

◊◊◊

"Well, at least she didn't kill her," Stevenson said, after he read the report the task force had received on Shelby's abduction.

"Maybe we should go speak with her," Petersen said. "Maybe she can shed some light on some things about Betty that weren't in the report."

Shelby had been sedated when she gave her statement to the policemen at the hospital. She did not remember most of what she had said. She'd had a strange feeling ever since Betty was released in Utah and was dismayed the police did not know where the woman was now. The men who had come to her house were sincere about wanting to apprehend Betty before she could kill her or anyone else, she answered their questions as best as she could.

"To be honest with you, Detective Stevenson, I have no idea why she targeted me. Like I told you, I accidentally caught her and her lover in a very compromising situation, but I never told anyone but Jack about it. It wasn't my business, but I guess that's what started it all. And she just never liked my working on her 'turf,' as she called it. She was extremely territorial. Do you guys really believe she's committed all these truck stop murders?"

"She's our prime suspect. But for now, we need to keep most of what we know about Betty to ourselves until we find her."

"Do you have any idea where she might be?" Shelby asked, nervously.

"There is some evidence she has been in Odessa. She's trying to stay under the radar. The truck stop murders have made the national news, her mug shot is everywhere. She knows we're hunting for her."

"Wow—she really has gone off the deep end. So my suspicion about her being the one who locked me in my trailer is valid?"

"Maybe. Can you tell me a little more about what happened, where and when, too, please?" Shelby went into details about what had happened in Arizona.

Jack sat back in his chair and listened to the detailed description of what his wife had been through. He was mortified that she'd endured such horrible things without his being there to protect her. He felt responsible because he had let Tammy distract him.

"Well, this information, in addition to what she did to you in Utah, helps us fill out our profile on her," Stevenson said. "Thank you so much for being willing to talk to us. We are going to do everything we can to track her down and bring her to justice."

Jack walked the investigators to the porch. He stopped and shook hands with them and asked them to keep them informed on the progress of the investigation. As the men made the way to their rental car, Jack looked up and saw a familiar car parked down the street. Tammy's car was parked at the edge of the restraining order limits.

A strange thought crossed his mind, *Is Tammy somehow connected with Betty? Quit it, Jack. You're just being paranoid. How could they possibly know each other?* He went back in the house to take care of his wife. He locked the door and wondered as he moved down the hall if the locks on his house and the security system were enough to keep his family safe.

CHAPTER EIGHTEEN

The road was just what Betty needed to put all of her problems behind her. She and Fiddler had spent days traveling the highways together delivering loads and picking up loads. They followed the main highways that Betty seemed to know by heart as they passed through every town that lined the I-20 and the I-10 to the south, the I-70 and I-80 to the north, and with the I-40 in the middle. She'd traveled them all.

Most of the adventure had been with her father, but she had her own memories as a seasoned driver. Betty put her head against the back of her seat and thought about all the places she'd been. For most drivers, traveling the highways wasn't just movement from one place to another. People and places along those highways made lasting impressions in their minds. It was no different for Betty except for a few places she didn't care to remember. Her whole identity was around being a trucker, which is why she felt so threatened when another woman, especially an attractive one, treaded on her territory.

Traveling the same main roadways could be monotonous. Betty's dad had introduced her to back road hideaways that took away the boredom. One of her favorites was a little station off I-49 near Frierson, Louisiana. The place had changed some from when she and her dad had been there, but it was still the same good ol' southern food and broken-down parking lot. Betty and Fiddler stopped there for a bite to eat and a shower after dropping some of their load and then moved on into Mississippi.

In Jackson, Mississippi, the couple took I-55 north toward Memphis. They didn't stop in Jackson, but Betty remembered a time she'd spent in Booneville at Massey's. It wasn't a big place, but Betty had enjoyed time there with her father. She recalled the details of that day as Fiddler moved the truck down the tree-lined highway toward their next drop and pickup in

Memphis. It had been a beautiful day and her father had bought them ice cream, which they ate while taking a walk around the parking lot. They had talked about the little place they would buy when her father had enough money. It saddened her that her father's dreams never came to light. She shook off the memory.

"After we make this drop and pickup we need to find us somewhere to get us some food. Right, kiddo?"

Betty lifted her head off the back of her seat and sat up. She looked around and stretched as she moved to put her shoes back on. "Sounds good to me. Let's just avoid West Memphis if you don't mind. I'd rather find a little 'hole in the wall' place."

"I think I know just the place."

Fiddler maneuvered the truck in and out of the streets of Memphis until he'd managed to get to his first stop. After backing into the dock and taking his bill of loading into the office, several men on the dock drove forklifts up to remove the pallets off Fiddler's trailer. It took about an hour before they were headed to their next stop in Memphis. The town was beautiful. Betty loved Elvis, which made being in his town more interesting to her. The view of the Mississippi River was spectacular as Betty looked out her window while Fiddler brought them back down to I-40 off of Highway 51 north of Memphis. Her attention to the view was interrupted as she realized Fiddler was steering them toward one of the very truck stops she didn't want to go to.

"I thought I asked you not to stop here," she said, frowning.

Fiddler wasn't shocked at Betty's displeasure. In fact, he was glad she objected to his choice in parking lots. He smiled while bringing the truck to a stop and pulling his air brakes. He picked up his phone and called for a cab. After ordering the cab, he turned to Betty and kissed her on the cheek. "I am taking you to the best burger place in town on Beale Street. But we can't park our truck at Dyer's, and this is the closest place to park. After we eat, we can head west to Murfreesboro and then down to Chattanooga to make these two drops we just picked up from here. You're going to love these burgers, Cheeks. I promise."

Betty was annoyed with Fiddler, not only because where he had chosen to park but the fact he kissed her without asking. She decided to let it slide—this time. "Okay, but you'd better be right about those burgers."

◊◊◊

"What if there is some way we can let it be known through the press that Shelby Mathews is still alive?" Agent Silverman suggested to the rest of the task force. "It's possible that Betty will come out of hiding and finish the job if she hears about Shelby."

"Are you crazy? How are you planning on protecting the Mathews family if you let Betty know Shelby isn't dead?" Stevenson asked.

One of the detectives from the Odessa Police Force spoke up, "I agree. We don't have the resources or manpower to cover twenty-four-hour surveillance on the Mathewses. Is the FBI going to handle that chore?"

Silverman didn't like the fact he'd have to call his commander and find out if he could use agents and funds for this case. But he felt that his intuitions about Betty Burton were on target. If he were right, Betty would head for West Texas in a heartbeat if she found out her number-one target was still breathing. "Okay," he said, nodding. "Let me see if I can get the funds and man hours cleared by headquarters for the surveillance team, but I want her to get that message."

"Only if it gets cleared by your agency and the surveillance is in place first. Plus, the Mathews family will be notified of the plan, and if they have any objections then we will find another way to locate Betty Burton," Stevenson said.

Silverman crossed his arms over his chest. He wasn't used to being told how to do his job. "I'll do the best I can with those requests, but since Ms. Burton is suspected of being a serial killer and crossing state lines to do her dirty work, we'll do things my way."

Detective Stevenson wasn't about to get into a pissing contest with a know-it-all FBI agent. He just hoped the Mathews family didn't end up getting hurt in the process. "Fine, but I will personally notify the Mathews family about the release of that information just so I know they get notified."

Silverman nodded in agreement.

"There is something else to consider," Petersen interjected. "If Burton thinks Shelby Mathews is dead, maybe she'll let her guard down. That could make her easier to locate without putting the Mathews family in danger."

"That's an interesting point," Stevenson said. "There is also the possibility she has someone helping her."

"Could be," Silverman said.

"I'll bet he or she doesn't even realize they are helping her," Petersen responded.

Stevenson pushed his point. "Letting her know that her problem isn't gone will probably send her over the edge. She may kill to get back here, putting whomever she's with in grave danger along with the Mathewses," he said.

"How do you plan to find out who she's with and where she might be hiding?" Silverman asked.

"She's most likely with a truck driver since that is all she knows," Stevenson said. "She knows probably better than most every truck stop and roadway in this country. I believe she's more than likely exposed and right out in the open since she feels that she's covered her tracks."

"Where do you propose we start looking?" Silverman asked.

◊◊◊

Tammy had watched the men leave Jack's porch, get into their car, and leave. When a patrol car drove up she was sure they were going to hassle her about the restraining order. Not wanting to get caught, she left for the bar, knowing Jack was in his house.

Tammy hadn't heard from Betty for a few weeks. Jack had blocked her number, and a patrol car was parked outside his house whenever she passed his street. She was frustrated and angry that everyone had just tossed her aside. She hadn't been to the bar for some time, but decided she might get some information there. She went into the bar and ordered a beer. She was anxious and wanted to talk to Betty. She saw Ralph and Tucker with Jack's other friends sitting at their usual table. She sauntered over to them. "Hey, guys," she said in her friendliest voice. "Have you seen Jack around lately?"

"Nope," Ralph said. "Haven't heard from him since he went home to Shelby. Heard someone tried to kill her. Locked her in her trailer without heat or air."

"That's terrible. Who would do such a thing?" Tammy feigned.

"Don't know," Tucker chimed in. "My wife works at the courthouse. Word is there is some task force in town looking for the Burton woman who tried to kill her a couple years ago."

"That so?" said Tammy.

◊◊◊

Fiddler had found his way back into Betty's good graces by backing away from the affection issue and just spending time with her. He figured Betty was dealing with some deep personal stuff and decided to just let her make the first moves if that's what she wanted. Dyer's burgers were a hit, and after they made their way to Murfreesboro they moved down I-24 to Chattanooga. The city glowed at night and made the green tint of the lake water sparkle from the lights as the big truck rolled over the bridge. Betty had been in Chattanooga many times and she never got tired of the sight, especially at night. Fiddler had told her that he would be dropping a small load in Chattanooga and then picking up another small one for Knoxville. They would, however, be stopping in Charleston for sleep before going on to Knoxville and then back to Nashville.

Fiddler hadn't let Betty drive much, but she didn't mind. It was kind of nice just being a passenger. "Do you want me to drive so we can keep rolling?" she asked, hoping his answer would be no.

"Nah, not tonight," he answered. "You haven't had any sleep either, so maybe tomorrow we can switch out some and keep her running. When we stop up here in Charleston I'll put the other bunk down and we can both get some rest."

Betty was glad Fiddler had said that. She had been wondering how she was going to deal with having to sleep in the same bunk. She liked him, but just wasn't ready for anything physical. She looked through the window and went back to thinking about her father while Fiddler unloaded.

Over the next few weeks Betty and Fiddler ran loads all over the East Coast. After getting some rest, the two left Charleston, Tennessee and traveled I-75 into Knoxville. Fiddler took the time to take Betty to a couple of places while they were there. They went to the Candy Factory and then to Union Avenue to the Market Square. Betty loved the special attention Fiddler was giving her.

From Knoxville, they took I-40 to Nashville, then I-24 towards Evansville, Indiana. They had a load to deliver in Nashville and one to pick up, so they didn't have time to check out any sights. Fiddler promised that the next time they were this way he would make a weekend of it. Maybe even during the Country Music Festival week. In Evansville, the couple ate at the Longhorn Steak House. Betty took over driving for a while, and took them out I-64 to St. Louis. Fiddler slept as she made the drop on her own. After making the drop, she headed out I-55 north towards Springfield, Illinois, where she picked up a load.

Fiddler woke up just as Betty was returning to the truck from picking up their load in Springfield. "You were supposed to wake me up when we got to St. Louis."

"Yeah, I know, but I've done this a million times and I figured if you got some rest we can run further with two of us driving."

"What about your log?"

"Don't worry about it. If I get stopped, we'll worry about it then. I can always just say I forgot it at home or something. They'll give me a ticket and then you'll have to drive us out of there because they won't let me drive without a log."

"Guess you got it all figured out."

"I'm not sure how you're going to explain it to the people you work for, but they keep giving you loads, so I guess they know."

"Well, kind of. Lori is my dispatcher, and she covers my butt a lot when I run over hours on that damn thing."

"Well, good. We need more dispatchers like that. Unless, of course, she's sweet on you, then I might have something to say about that."

Fiddler was a little shocked at the comment but left it alone.

"So where're we at, Super Trucker?"

"Just picked up our load out of Springfield and now we're headed out I-55 to I-39 into Rockford, Illinois where your dispatch wants you to pick up another load and take both to Madison, Wisconsin. We'll drop them, and then head back down I-39 to I-80 and over to Joliet, Illinois to drop the last of the first load. Then we'll have to wait and see what your dispatch wants us to do, but since we are so close to Chicago I bet they send us up there to load."

"Wow. You really do know these roads out here."

"I told you I started on the road with my dad when I was really young and haven't done anything else since."

"I think when we get to Madison we need to find something to do for a while."

"Sounds good."

Betty and Fiddler spent the entire afternoon in Madison checking out the lakes after lunch. Betty felt like she could finally put her past behind her and maybe even build a new life with Fiddler. They moved from Madison to Chicago and then onto I-90 for Toledo, followed by Detroit, Indianapolis, and Akron. Betty was having the time of her life with Fiddler. He'd taken her to places she'd not been before, and to some places that brought back great memories of her times with her father. "Fiddler, I'm not much for words and never been very good at sentiments, but thank you for the past few weeks. I've enjoyed it so much."

"Me too, but we better get some sleep. We need to deliver in the morning." She seemed to be warming to him, but he figured playing a little hard to get might make her a little more interested in him physically. He was willing to wait.

◊◊◊

Shelby was enjoying her time at home with Jack, but as her body healed she found herself getting restless for the road again. She'd been to the yard several times to catch up with the folks there, but she was ready for more. One morning after Jack left for work, she was cleaning the house when she decided it was now or never, especially since the doctor had cleared her to go back to work. She went to her son's room and knocked on the door. "Steven, can you get up and take me to my yard, please?"

"Mom, I worked really late last night and studied for a test 'til four this morning. I have to take that test in two hours. Can't you get Dad to take you?"

"He's at work and I don't want to leave my pickup at the yard. Come on, it will only take a few minutes."

"Okay, Mom." Steven pulled himself out of bed and down the hall to where his mother was waiting at the front door.

"Thanks, baby."

"You're welcome, I guess. If I fail that test because of no sleep, it's on you."

"Got ya covered."

Shelby hadn't told Jack she wanted to go back to work, and for now she wasn't going to say anything. She was going to check in with Jayne and see what was going on. She wanted to check out her truck and bring it back to the house so she could stock the refrigerator and put things back in it. She wasn't even sure that her truck was still in the yard. Jayne might have let someone else use it for all she knew. She didn't care—she was going to get her truck or any truck and get back on the road.

When Detective Stevenson had come by to share that the task force wanted to let the press know Shelby had been abducted but was still alive, Jack pitched a fit, letting him know in no way were they going to use his wife as bait.

Betty Burton had been reported on in the news as a person of interest in the truck stop murders, but as of yet the media hadn't connected her to the most recent events. A police report had been filed on Shelby's abduction, so she figured it was just a matter of time before they put it all together.

Betty hadn't been located, and that still bothered Shelby some, but decided that she'd had enough of being nice. If that bitch Betty was going to come after her again, she wasn't going down without a fight.

◊◊◊

Betty was still asleep and Fiddler was taking a shower when her cell phone rang. The sound startled her because no one had tried to call her since she'd left Arizona. "Hello," she said cautiously into the phone.

"Where are you, Betty?"

"Who is this?"

"It's Tammy. Remember me? Was it you who tried to kill Jack's wife? Thought you might like to know she's still alive and Jack is back with her. Thanks for nothing, bitch!"

"Shelby's alive? How?"

"Don't know. And don't try cashing any checks. I've closed that checking account." Tammy hung up.

"Shit," Betty said. "How many lives does this bitch Shelby Mathews have?" Betty had enjoyed being back on the road. There was no way this was going to be taken away from her again. No one was going to take away her freedom and lock her up. She had done a good job of covering her tracks—the only one who could ruin it for her was Shelby. She needed to get back to West Texas and take care of her once and for all.

She was pacing back and forth outside the truck when Fiddler returned from his shower. Fiddler cleared his throat as he approached the obviously agitated woman. "Cheeks, what's the matter?' he asked.

Betty stopped in her tracks. "Nothing," she said. "I just couldn't sleep so I came out here to walk. You got a cig I can have?"

Fiddler pulled out a pack and handed it to her. Her hands shook as she took it from him.

"Why are you shaking? Did something happen?"

Betty tried to pull herself together. She'd been happy with the way things were going with her "Daddy" and she didn't want anything to mess it up. Betty leaned against the truck. "I don't know. I'm just feeling a little anxious and overwhelmed for some reason."

"We've been going at it pretty hard. We should shut down for a few days and just relax. We can go to a motel and spend some time out of the truck."

"That sounds good. Thanks."

As they went to deliver the last load, Betty thought about her options. She would need to get rid of Fiddler and head back to West Texas. She hesitated at the thought of killing him. But she would need his truck and needed a plan to steal it without his reporting her.

CHAPTER NINETEEN

Jack left work early, wanting to spend more time with Shelby. When he pulled into his driveway he was surprised to see Shelby's big rig parked outside with the doors open and a little pair of flip-flops sticking out, wiggling in the air. He forced himself to tamper down the anger and frustration welling up inside of him. "Well, I see my beautiful little truck driver has decided to go back to work," he said, approaching the truck.

Shelby moved out of the front seat and stood on the steps of her truck. Her hair was a mess; she wiped the sweat on her forehead with her arm. "Hey, baby. Yeah, I went and got her today. I really want to go back to work, honey. You aren't upset, are you? I can't go back for a couple of days because I have to get back on the schedule. Plus, the doctor has to send a formal letter of release before Jayne can let me roll. But I want to get back out there. I promise I won't take a lot of long stuff either, just local loads. Okay?"

Jack grabbed his wife and pulled her into his arms. He kissed her deep and put her back onto her truck. Shelby was shocked at her husband's sudden playful behavior, but was relieved when Jack smiled at her.

"Guess your old man needs to help his sweetheart clean up this dusty thing," Jack said, smiling. He was resolved to support his wife this time, even if his gut still told him to worry about her.

Shelby smiled. "That would be great, Jack. So you're not upset that I want to go back to work?"

Jack grabbed a rag and started cleaning the dust out of the floor on the passenger's side. "No, baby. I am not and I will never be again. I want you to be happy and I think I'm going to take some time off soon so I can ride with you."

Shelby couldn't believe her ears. She just smiled and went back to cleaning the driver's side floor.

After the couple finished on the truck, they went into the house to make some supper. Shelby got into the shower and Jack made them sandwiches. After her shower, Shelby sat at the table in her towel. Jack placed a sandwich and glass of tea in front of her and at his place at the table. Shelby was thrilled with Jack's new behavior and smiled as she watched him eat.

"What?" he asked.

Shelby grinned wider. "Nothing."

Jack reached for the remote and turned on the television in their kitchen. "Let's see what's going on in our world."

"Do we have to?" Shelby complained.

Jack muted the television.

Shelby looked up and noticed Betty's face on the screen. "Turn it up!" she yelled, shaking her finger at the TV.

Jack quickly grabbed the remote and spotted Betty's face as he did.

"This woman is considered armed and dangerous. She's wanted in connection with several murders and an attempted murder of a woman by the name of Shelby Mathews. If you know where this person is or if you see this person, please contact the local police. Do not for any reason make contact with the suspect. She is considered armed and dangerous."

"Jack, how could they do that? How could they release my name publicly? I thought the police were going to tell us before they did this?"

"I don't know, Shelby, but I'm going to find out." He picked up his phone to call Detective Stevenson.

"If she sees this, she'll know that I'm not dead. They just let her know I'm alive. Now I'll have to watch my back when I go back to work!" Shelby cried.

Jack tried his best to comfort Shelby by holding her hand while he waited for the detective to answer his phone. "Yes. Can I speak with Detective Stevenson, please?" After a short pause, Jack responded with displeasure. "When do you expect him to be back in the office?" Another pause, and again Jack spoke with more displeasure. "This is an emergency! I need to speak with him right away. I want you to contact him immediately and have him call me." Jack gave the responding party his is name and phone number.

Jack hung up his phone and placed it on the table. He went around the table took hold of Shelby who was still stunned and staring at the television. "It's going to be okay, baby," he said in his most soothing voice. "The detective is going to call us back in a few minutes and we'll find out what's going on."

Shelby let Jack hold her for a little while and then she broke away from him in anger. She picked up her sandwich and threw it across the kitchen. "Forget it, Jack. You and I both know they did this on purpose! They are using me as bait to bring Betty back here! They couldn't find that slimy bitch, so they're using me to get to her. That's fine! I'll do their job for them, but I promise, I'm done being the nice little schoolgirl! She wants a fight? She's going to get one! I'm done being intimidated and I'm sure as hell not putting my life on hold anymore because of her."

She got up and stomped toward the bedroom. Jack sat in amazement. He drank some of his tea and ate some of his sandwich. Shelby wasn't one to say something she didn't mean, which left him wondering how he was going to protect Shelby now that she was determined to be exposed, no matter what.

Jack was cleaning Shelby's sandwich off the floor when his phone rang. "Yes, Detective Stevenson, this is Jack Mathews," he said. "I was calling about the bulletin we just saw on television, which puts a target on Shelby's back." Jack listened for a moment. "How long has it been on the air? We really need to know how much advance notice Betty may have." Jack was quiet for a moment. "Okay, we appreciate the information. Thank you... No, we understand... Okay, we will let you know... Yes, okay. Thanks again. Talk to you soon."

"Stevenson said that Agent Silverman from the FBI made the call to alert the press. Stevenson said he didn't agree, but the FBI is in charge of the investigation since it involves multiple jurisdictions."

"It doesn't matter, Jack. I'm still not backing down. I'm going to be ready for her this time. Let that bitch bring her best game, because I am not going to alter my life in the least for her."

Jack didn't respond as Shelby got a glass of tea and went back to their bedroom. "Coming to bed, baby?" she called.

◊◊◊

Betty was extremely agitated as Fiddler delivered their last load in Harrisburg. She knew if she was going to get Fiddler's truck and get back to West Texas without Fiddler knowing her secrets, she was going to have to think of a well-devised plan and quickly. "I'm fine, I just really need to get off this truck for a few days."

"Okay…" said Fiddler, baffled. Betty had spent practically her whole life on a truck, so he couldn't understand why she was so anxious to take a break now. "I need to go by our field office here and turn in some paperwork. Our next load isn't due to load until Thursday in Baltimore, Maryland. Do you want to stay here or go on to Baltimore for our break?"

Betty thought for a few moments. "Where are we loading in Baltimore?" "Somewhere down near the harbor in the industrial area. Why?"

Betty again thought for a few moments. She knew Baltimore very well and was familiar with several places in the industrial areas near the ports that would serve her purposes well. "I think I would like to stay in Baltimore," she said. "We could go to D.C. and sightsee. And if we really want some privacy and good seafood we could go to Solomons Island."

"That sounds like a great idea," Fiddler said, relaxing a little. "I didn't realize you were so familiar with the area. Guess I'll have to let you drive." He laughed as he pulled the truck off the dock and forward out into the street.

"Yeah, you should if you don't want to get lost."

Betty wondered how she was going to overpower Fiddler without killing him. She stared out the window and concentrated on her dilemma while Fiddler moved the truck down I-83. As they crossed over the Susquehanna River, it came to her. *Bingo!* she thought. She had a plan.

She pointed out toward Fiddler's driver's side window. "Look over there. That's Metro Bank Park. I haven't been there in a long time. There's a restaurant behind it called The Spot. They have wonderful food and we could get a few drinks there before we head to Maryland."

Fiddler looked in that direction. "Well, we can't get our truck in there, but I know where there's a truck stop off I-81 and I-39. We can get a taxi from there."

"Fiddler, you're the best. I want you to try a drink my father used to drink when he brought me there. They have great seafood, too. Oh, and by the way, you can call me Betty, if you want. My real name is Betty Burton."

Fiddler never understood Betty's change in moods, but hoped this change meant she was going to be more personal. "Okay. Great, Betty."

◊◊◊

Jack was so worried about Shelby that he couldn't sleep. Unfortunately, there was nothing he could do to stop her—not without risking his marriage again, and he wasn't willing to do that. Shelby had gotten up early to finish the cleaning on her truck while waiting for her first load assignment. Jack stood at the front door, sipped his coffee, and watched his beautiful wife. He decided that he would do what he could to protect her without her knowledge.

Shelby climbed out of her truck and came to the door where Jack handed her his coffee cup. "So, lady driver, I see you're getting that big rig ready to roll."

Shelby sipped his coffee and then smiled. "She's going to shine when I get her to a truck wash and get the outside just as clean as the inside." Shelby handed the cup back to Jack and the two of them went into the house.

Jack poured Shelby her own cup of coffee. "So where is Jayne sending you first?"

"I don't know yet. I have to wait for my turn on the dispatch list. Plus, I requested close-to-home deliveries, which takes time to set up. I should be on a job in a couple of days." Shelby sipped at her cup of coffee. "Are you going to be okay with my doing the local stuff?"

Jack sat his coffee on the counter and put his hands on Shelby's shoulders and then around her waist, pulling her to his body. "I'm going to be fine with whatever you want to do. I won't try to tell you I won't worry, especially now that Betty knows you're still alive. But I promise I won't interfere or hold you back. I know you can handle yourself and I believe in you." Jack kissed his wife deeply with every ounce of passion he had in him.

◇◇◇

Betty and Fiddler spent the evening drinking and eating. She kept drinks flowing for Fiddler, but avoided drinking very much herself, knowing that she needed to be sober to implement her plan. When Fiddler became so intoxicated he could barely walk, Betty took money from his wallet and paid the check. "Come on, baby, it's time to get you back to our truck." Betty asked the waiter for a cab and within a few minutes, she and Fiddler were on their way back to the truck stop.

Fiddler was about to pass out when Betty tapped the cabbie on the back and asked him a question. "Do you think you could help me get him inside the truck?"

"Sure." The cabbie helped Betty get Fiddler into the sleeper and then waved them both goodnight.

Fiddler was drunk, and he knew it. "Baby, you are going to have to drive."

"No problem." she pulled out of the parking space and headed down I-83 toward Baltimore. So far, her plan was working.

The trip to the Holabird Industrial area off I-95 didn't take Betty too long since it was late at night. Betty knew of a truck stop nearby where she could execute the rest of her plan. She needed to find a drug dealer and knew there were always guys around the truck stops pushing meth, cocaine, and other substances.

Betty parked near the back of the lot. She backed the truck into the spot and turned to look at Fiddler who was sound a sleep. "I'll be back in a few minutes, Daddy." Betty got out of the truck and walked toward the store. She scanned the parking lot for a lizard who could direct her to a dealer, but didn't spot one. She went into the store and saw one headed to the restroom. Having been a lizard herself at one time, she knew what to look for in a gal. She went to the counter and bought her coffee and then waited outside the store against the wall until her target exited.

When the girl came out, Betty approached her. "Hey, can I talk to you?"

"What do you want? I don't do women but I can put you in touch with a friend who loves women."

"No. I'm not interested in that, but I am interested in some medicinal help if you know where I can get some?"

The hooker sized up the redhead in front of her and concluded she was not a cop. Without saying a word, she pointed toward an SUV parked in a space near the front of the store. "Check with him. He can probably get you anything you want, for a price."

Betty walked out of the store and signaled to the guy in the SUV with the nod of her head. He returned the nod and motioned with his head to the side of the store. She casually lit a cigarette and sauntered to the side of the building. The dealer was behind her in no time—she never heard his footsteps. Betty told him what she wanted. He could tell by looking at her she could afford what she'd requested. He reached into his pocket and withdrew her request. Betty paid him, and he disappeared in as stealthy a manner as he had appeared. She took a couple more drags off her cigarette, dropped it on the pavement and ground it out with the heel of her shoe. Then she made her way back to Fiddler's truck.

She entered the vehicle from the driver's side door. Fiddler was sitting on the edge of the sleeper with his head in his hands. "Man, my head hurts," he said in a groggy voice. "Where are we? Where've you been?"

Betty turned to Fiddler, reached for his left hand and put two of the tabs in his palm. "I figured you would need something for a hangover so I went to the store. Take that aspirin. It will help with your headache."

Fiddler took the tabs she'd given him and washed them down with water. Betty helped him take off his boots and helped him to lie back on the bed. He was asleep in no time. Betty moved into the driver's seat, released the air brakes and started pulling the truck out of the parking space. She knew the particular warehouse in Holabird she wanted to take him to.

When she got to Holabird, she maneuvered the truck down a dark, deserted semi-private road near the harbor. The road was laden with cracks and potholes, which made the truck bounce uncontrollably as Betty guided the truck to a secluded warehouse at the end of the road. Fiddler was in such a deep sleep that he didn't notice the sway and pitch of his truck. She remembered the warehouse from a dispatch she'd been mistakenly sent to years ago. She hoped the building was still standing, and was glad to see it when she turned the corner.

She parked the truck and went back to the sleeper where Fiddler was snoring. It would be so easy to smother him with a pillow as she had her previous victim. "Daddy," she whispered as she shook him by the shoulders. "I need your help with the load."

"Now? I'm so sleepy," he groaned. "We'll do it tomorrow."

"No, they need us to get it now, we're holding up other drivers."

Fiddler had no concept of day or time as Betty put her hands under his armpits and maneuvered him to a sitting position.

"It won't take long, then you can sleep." She put his boots back on him.

"Okay, fine," he groaned.

Betty got out of the truck on the passenger side and went to the driver's side of the truck. She opened the door and Fiddler almost fell out of the truck. Betty helped him try to stand. "Oh, man, Cheeks. I can't stand up. I don't think I've ever been this drunk."

"Come on. We'll go for a little walk to sober you up." Betty walked Fiddler into the abandoned warehouse. He stumbled over the slats of a broken pallet. The further Betty guided him into the building, the dirtier and darker it was, and it smelled like must, urine, and rotting animal flesh. When Betty thought she'd taken Fiddler far enough into the building she guided him to the floor. "Sit here. I'll go and get the paperwork. I'll be right back. I'll bring back some more aspirin too."

Fiddler laid down on the cool cement floor. "Okay," he drooled.

Betty went back to the truck and got some tape, rope, and a water bottle. She hurried back and gave Fiddler the additional tabs. "Here, take some more aspirin."

Fiddler took the tabs and fell over again after taking a couple drinks of the water. Betty quickly tied his legs and arms with the rope. She reached into his pocket and removed his wallet. There was a small amount of cash and a fuel card for the truck. She was going to put tape over his eyes and mouth but decided against it when she looked at Fiddler laying on the floor totally helpless. She left the water next to his head and stood up. "Goodbye, Daddy," she said.

Betty drove Fiddler's truck back to the truck stop. She didn't think anyone noticed it had been gone for a while. She wanted to get a good night's sleep before she headed back to Texas to deal with Shelby.

She slept like a baby for six straight hours. It was still early when she woke up. She grabbed a couple of cups of coffee and donuts from the store. Then she moved over to the fuel island and filled up the rig using the card she had swiped from Fiddler. It was 6:30 a.m. when Betty rolled the eighteen-wheeler onto I-95. She wanted to be well on her way before anyone discovered Fiddler's drugged body in the warehouse.

She turned on the radio to listen to the chatter, but had no intention to speak herself. What she heard infuriated her.

"Hear about that crazy bitch Betty Burton's being on the FBI's most wanted list?"

"Sure did, Tweedy. I hope Barbie stays off the road until they catch that psycho."

Betty's adrenaline was flowing. She had eleven hundred and fifty miles to Odessa. "I'm coming for you, Shelby," she said under her breath, "No matter where you are, I'm going to get you."

CHAPTER TWENTY

Fiddler moved slightly but was still under the influence of the drugs that Betty had given him. He was tired and weak and his wrists and ankles hurt from the ropes that were around them. He wasn't conscious enough to really know what had happened to him or where he was. "Cheeks!" he called out, his voice cracking a little. "Where are you, Cheeks?" There was no response but he was too tired to care. His mouth felt like it had dirt in it and his lips were dry and cracked, but he was too sleepy to realize his situation. He let his mind drift back into unconsciousness.

◊◊◊

Shelby was happily back out on the road, picking up loads out of Dallas and San Antonio and delivering them throughout the great State of Texas. She also picked up and delivered loads in and out of eastern New Mexico. Shelby did not miss the long distances as much as she had expected. She was glad she could be home every other night, which allowed Jack and her to work on their relationship.

She was so familiar with her assigned territory that it made deliveries and pickups easier. She loved traveling Interstates 10 and 20 and she could travel highways 158, 302, 176, 87, 377, 115, and many others in her sleep. She was familiar with a lot of the other drivers who frequented the same highways. All her trucker friends communicated with her on the CB. They were all glad she was on the road again and having heard the bulletin, assured her they had her back.

On an early trip to New Mexico on 176 Shelby heard a familiar voice, "Hey, Barbie. How you doing? Haven't seen you in a while. This is Southpaw."

"Hey, Southpaw. Yeah, took some time off to take care of some personal stuff. How are you? Where are you headed?"

"I'm headed back to OD and then probably up to Brady. Where are you headed?"

"Oh, I'm just headed over here to Hobbs. You look good back to Andrews. Haven't seen a thing. I see you're still hauling sand."

"Yeah, that's where the money is. You're looking good back to Hobbs."

"Thanks, Southpaw. See you again soon. Be safe."

"You, too. We heard the news. We all got your back."

Shelby loved the way she felt when other truckers recognized her and accepted her as one of their own. She felt a little less afraid knowing they were there for her. "Thanks, Southpaw."

Shelby had made her load drop in Hobbs and was dispatched to Dallas to pick up another load headed for El Paso. She decided that she would call Jack and let him know she wouldn't be home until tomorrow.

"What's my trucker baby doing?" he asked as soon as he picked up the phone.

"I'm headed to Dallas," Shelby said. "Going to get there around ten tonight and then head to El Paso for delivery. I'll stop by the house and shower on my way to El Paso. You miss me yet?"

"You know I do. Maybe I can join you for that shower when you come through."

"I like that idea."

"See you when you get in tomorrow. I love you."

Shelby drove down the I-20 in silence. It was a quiet evening on the interstate, and it would take her about five and a half hours to reach her destination in Dallas. She would load out of a warehouse that was open all night and then deliver in El Paso sometime either tomorrow night or the next morning. She would have time on this log day to get back to the house and spend a little time with Jack. Although he was attentive and supportive, she was still having trouble trusting him. Every once in a while the nagging question, "What are you hiding?" popped into her head. She really wanted to forgive him and wondered if she was ever going to be able to let everything go and get them back to where they use to be. *Is it always going to be like this?* she wondered.

In Dallas, Shelby used I-20 to get around the south end of Dallas and Fort Worth instead of I-30 through town. Traffic wasn't heavy and she liked I-20. Besides, her drop off point was at the south end of I-45, so she would be closer hitting I-45 from that end. She decided to stop at the Exit 472 truck stop for coffee. She chose the north side truck stop because it was easier to get into and although it was smaller, it was cleaner.

Shelby remembered that the chatter from the truckers in Dallas particularly around 472 was always intense around the truck stops. Everyone seemed to have strong opinions, whether it was about sports, politics, or whatever was taking over social media. Shelby learned early on that her female voice with these particular drivers brought out men and women looking for an argument. It was her habit when running through Dallas to turn her CB either down or off around the exit.

After getting her coffee, Shelby pulled out of the truck stop and headed over the overpass to the south side of the interstate. There were a few trucks coming off I-20 and Shelby had to brake hard for one particular driver who had pulled out in front of her. She was a little irritated with the trucker, but figured he was probably tired and just wanted to get a space for the night. Shelby didn't let it bother her, though. She only had a couple exits before getting off again, and she was glad that she was so close to her pickup point. She couldn't wait to get loaded and head back to the house. If she got loaded quickly she could be at the house by six in the morning and she could spend some time with Jack before he went to the office. She would get some rest at home and then head to El Paso for delivery.

◊◊◊

Betty was hungry and exhausted and was ready to give in to a little rest when she saw the lights of Dallas glimmering in the distance. She figured if she rested for a few hours she would be more focused on her goal. She ran the I-20 until she got to Exit 472 and then took the under construction exit to the right of the interstate. She decided to go to the truck stop that was positioned to the south of the exit instead of the one to the north. She knew from experience that the north truck stop would be full this late in the night and since the south truck stop was bigger, she'd have a better chance of finding a spot there.

"Get the hell out of my way, dumbass." Betty pulled her truck out in front of another truck that was moving north toward the overpass. She couldn't see the driver and as tired as she was at that moment, she just really didn't care. She wasn't interested in being courteous and didn't worry about who she pissed off.

◊◊◊

Shelby parked her truck in front of her house and quietly unlocked the front door. She hadn't been on the road for several weeks and it was going to take her a few trips out to get used to driving again. She was tired, but she wanted a shower and she wanted her husband. After taking a hot shower, Shelby wrapped her hair in a towel and dried her body. Jack was sound asleep when the naked Shelby climbed into their bed and slid her body next to her unsuspecting husband. It took Jack only a few moments to become aware of the soft, sweet smell of his wife.

Shelby decided that she wanted top. "Not so fast stud."

◊◊◊

Jack sat back in his office chair and smiled, remembering how Shelby had taken control of their lovemaking that morning. She hadn't done that in a long time, but he liked it when she took charge. He believed they were finally getting past some of the bullshit he'd created. He couldn't stop thinking about the soft kiss he left on Shelby's lips before leaving the house that morning. She looked so beautiful naked, her blonde hair spread all over her pillow.

Jack's secretary entered his office and placed some paperwork on his desk. She noticed his mood. "I guess something's good in your life," she said.

"Things are good. And once the FBI catches Betty, things will be even better for both my sweet wife and me."

"I can't believe that woman is running free. Do you really think she killed those men?"

And Tammy, he thought. "Yes, I do. I pray they get her before she comes after Shelby again." Jack's phone rang and he reached for it.

Alice pointed at the paperwork she'd brought in, mouthing, "Sign those please," as she left.

Jack nodded and then answered the phone. It was Agent Silverman. "I want to stress that it's not FBI policy to share procedures with civilians. What I am about to share is strictly on a 'need to know basis.' I convinced the agency to give me permission because of how concerned you are for your wife and to ensure you don't try to take matters into your own hands."

"I'm listening," Jack said, skeptically.

"First, we do have a detail on your wife. We arranged for it when the bulletin went live on national television. It is the agency's priority to protect Shelby, so we'll be tailing her whenever she leaves your home. I know you're both upset and believe our intention was to use her as bait to flush out the Burton woman."

"Wasn't it?"

"Truthfully? Yes. I don't have to tell you that Burton hates your wife. But she's also become an expert at disappearing. She needs a reason to reveal herself and Shelby is that reason."

Jack knew that Silverman was telling him the truth, but he still wasn't happy.

"It's good that Shelby is back at work. We're sure she's feeling anxious, but the more natural things appear, the better the odds that Burton will let down her guard and come out of hiding."

"Just know that I will hold you personally responsible for anything that happens to Shelby. I won't tell her you're watching her so she doesn't accidentally tip Betty off, but you better catch that bitch and fast…and Shelby better not get hurt."

"You have my word that I will personally keep Shelby safe."

"I want a daily update."

"I'll do my best to keep you informed."

◊◊◊

The light of the day shone through the zipper spaces in the sleeper of Fiddler's truck. Betty wiped the sleep from her eyes and opened the curtain. She brushed her red curls in the mirror that hung on the sun visor near the driver's seat. She pulled the truck around to the fuel island and used the last of her cash to get fuel and coffee. She knew it would take her about five hours to get to Odessa. This time she wasn't going to make any mistakes. She would get Shelby no matter how long it took or what she would have to do to make it happen. She would take care of that sniveling Tammy, too. She got her fuel and maneuvered the truck down I-20 toward Odessa. The road was clear and she made good time to Odessa.

Betty parked Fiddler's truck at the back of the parking lot at the War Truck Stop. She knew she would have to maintain a low profile since everyone would be watching for her. She needed a car or truck, but did not see anything in the parking lot that she could steal without drawing attention. Checking to make certain no one was nearby, she released the hood, reached up to open it and then climbed up on the wheel well and took the battery cables off of the terminals. She made sure no other auxiliary power was going to the truck, so it could not be located. She went into the store and called for a cab.

◊◊◊

Tammy was in a Chicago hotel room on a business trip when she saw the news bulletin on TV about Betty. She could not believe what she was seeing and became furious with herself for allowing Betty to convince her to harm Jack and his wife. She was worried that if and when Betty was apprehended, the crazy bitch would try to implicate her in her murderous schemes. Jack had a restraining order against her, which intensified Tammy's worry that she would somehow be associated with Betty. She picked up her cell phone and placed a call. "Hey, Barbara, is that transfer to the New York office still available?" She smiled when she heard the answer. "Hell, yes, I want it. How soon can I start?" More good news. "Great, I'll see you there in a week."

Tammy was grateful she was being offered a fresh start. She would get back to Odessa, put her things in storage and pay any penalty to break her lease. She was anxious to get out of Texas as soon as possible.

◊◊◊

Betty barely had enough cash to cover the cab fare to Tammy's apartment. The driver was pissed with the fifty-nine cent tip. "I'll get you on the way back, I promise," Betty said, but the driver didn't believe her. Betty's dye job had held up and she was still using the tinted contact lenses, she had filled out from being on the road with Fiddler, she was unrecognizable to the driver or anyone else who may have seen her mug shot on TV.

She saw Tammy's car parked in the covered parking space and considered just stealing it, but she was certain Tammy still wanted to hurt Jack so she went and rang her doorbell.

At first, Tammy did not recognize the redheaded woman standing at her door. "May I help you?" she asked.

"Actually, I came back to help you," Betty said. "How's Jack doing?"

"Look, Betty, I'm over Jack. I'm moving to New York to start over. I don't want to be a part of anything you have in mind."

"Too late. You're already involved," Betty said, pushing her way into Tammy's apartment. When she saw the packing boxes and empty walls she knew Tammy had told her the truth, but there was no way she was going to let Tammy go. She knew too much about her.

"Get out!" Tammy yelled at her, "Or I will call the police."

Betty walked toward her, speaking slowly and deliberately. "No, you won't, Tammy. If you call the police, I'll tell them you hired me to kill Jack. I still have the check you made out to me to do the job."

"You stole my checkbook. I…"

Betty stood in front of Tammy and placed her hands on Tammy's shoulders. Helping Fiddler drive and pick up and deliver loads had improved her upper body strength since getting out of jail. Tammy felt that strength as Betty pressed down on her shoulders. "No, Tammy. You and I are the same. We don't like men taking advantage of us and we don't like women moving in on what is ours." She turned Tammy around so her back was to her and pulled the frightened woman close to her body. "You're no different than me," Betty said as her right arm went around Tammy's neck and squeezed, choking off any air Tammy needed to yell. She placed her hand on Tammy's left temple and in one swift move, twisted and broke the woman's neck.

Tammy slumped against her and fell to the ground. Betty grabbed Tammy's purse, linen coat, and car keys and walked out the door. She locked the door and walked over and entered Tammy's car.

◊◊◊

Steven was happy he had had a chance to talk to both his parents at breakfast that morning. He wanted to tell them at the same time that he was planning to move out and get his own apartment. "A buddy of mine said a place is opening up in his complex," he said. "A tenant got a job transfer and needs to leave right away. I'm going to go take a look at it later this afternoon." He kissed his mother on the cheek and left for school.

"Looks like we're going to be empty nesters," Jack said.

"It makes me sad, but I'm proud of him. I'm proud of all three of our sons," Shelby said, choking back the tears.

Steven met up with the landlord later that afternoon between school and work. "The place should be ready within a week. This lady is making a quick exit. Has to be at her new job in a couple of weeks." The landlord knocked on the door and when there was no answer, used his master key to enter the apartment. "Shit," he said when he saw the body.

Steven ran over, bent down and felt for a pulse. "Call 911," he said. "She's dead."

CHAPTER TWENTY-ONE

Fiddler moaned from the pain pounding in his skull. He tried to move his hands but found they were bound. He attempted to free himself, but the pain from trying to do that was too much. His mouth and lips were so dry that the salty taste of the blood from the cracks in his lips burned as it seeped into his mouth. His legs had no strength in them, and they too were bound. The circulation to his extremities had been cut off, making movement virtually impossible. Even if he weren't tied up like a rodeo calf, he would not have been able to move since every bone in his body ached.

Fiddler laid on the dirt-covered floor, trying to figure out where he was and how he got there. He opened his mouth and attempted to call again for Cheeks, but only a slight whisper came from his dry and swollen mouth. *Where is she? Where am I? Were we in an accident? Why can't I move?* he thought. Fiddler was weak, and before he could figure out any answers he passed back into unconsciousness.

"Over here! The body is over here." The EMTs and police moved through the abandoned building toward the ragged-looking man. They pushed past several homeless men who had gathered to watch the drama. The EMTs checked Fiddler's body for life. "He has a slight pulse, but it is faint. We need to get this man out of here."

The police moved the tattered and dirty spectators back to give the EMTs more room to work. The EMTs cut through the ropes that bound Fiddler's wrists and legs and put him flat on his back. "He's extremely dehydrated and unconscious. I would suggest a possible suicide were it not for the bindings on his legs and wrists. Let's stabilize him and get him on the bus. We can try to figure out what happened to him on the way to the hospital."

Fiddler was placed on a stretcher with an IV running through his veins. He was transported to a local hospital in Baltimore but was lost in his unconscious state and was unable to help the EMTs or the police figure out who he was or why he was left for dead in the abandoned building. "He's too clean to be a homeless person, but he's carrying no identification. Whoever did this probably robbed him."

The doctor looked at his unresponsive patient. "Who are you, mister? And what happened to you?" he asked the man. "Keep the IV flowing, watch his vitals, and let me know if there are any changes in his behavior. He has brain activity, but he's not responding to outside stimuli. Let me know if there are any changes." He handed the nurse Fiddler's medical chart.

◊◊◊

Jack felt shame and remorse when he learned about Tammy's death the night before. He felt responsible but could not articulate why. As he left for work, he had a strange feeling that her car was on the street near his house, but knew it was not possible. *It's just guilt,* he concluded. *Besides, her car is a common model and color. Lots of folks have silver Hondas.* Shelby had left before Steven called him with the news. He had a few days to figure out how he was going to tell his wife that his son had found his mistress dead.

He looked up the street one more time and a chill went up his spine when he saw the familiar-looking car. It was too far away to see if anyone was in it. He got in his pickup and left for work.

Betty had spent the night in Tammy's car, watching the Mathews house. The son had come home late and appeared agitated about something. He left just after sunrise. Jack left about an hour later. She had not spotted Shelby and wondered if she was running loads. She decided she'd break into their house to see what she could learn. She started the Honda, turned up the radio, and was moving up the street when she heard the news report about Tammy's body being discovered.

"Shit," she muttered, knowing she would have to dump Tammy's car. Then she had an idea. She pulled the car into Jack's driveway. *What are the cops going to think when they find your lover's car in your driveway? You're going to be the prime suspect, Jack,* she thought. Betty smiled at her own cleverness.

She put on her dark sunglasses, turned up the collar on Tammy's coat and exited the car. She took all the cash out of Tammy's wallet, but left the purse sitting on the passenger's seat. Certain no one was watching, she turned down the sidewalk, put her hands in her coat pockets and casually walked down the street and out of the neighborhood. The cool morning air cleared Betty's head and allowed her to think. Wearing a designer coat and styled hair meant she fit into the upper middle-class neighborhood she strolled through. People leaving their homes to go to work thought nothing of a woman walking down the sidewalk. A few even waved as if they knew her. As she was planning her next move, she walked by a yard where a few newspapers, still in their plastic bags, were scattered on the lawn. This was a signal to her that no one was home. She rolled her shoulders back with an air of authority, went over, and picked up the newspapers as if she were the homeowner. Then she crossed the yard, went over to the gate and into the backyard. It took her less than a minute to recognize it. It was at the edge of the porch next to a flower box planted with herbs; it looked nothing like a rock. Betty wondered if people got stupider the more money they earned. She slipped the key out from the hide-a-key rock, left the newspapers on the porch, and slipped back to the front of the house. As she turned the key to the front door, she hoped the people did not have an alarm. They did not. Her stomach growled and she went to the refrigerator.

Betty made herself a sandwich, found a bag of chips and a package of cookies with double stuffing, and took her brunch into the living room with the pitcher of ice tea that was also in the fridge. She moved around the living room and made sure all of the blinds and drapes were closed. She sat on the sofa, picked up the remote, turned on the TV, and flipped through the channels until she found the twenty-four-hour news station. After three commercials and a story about a corrupt politician, her mug shot came onto the screen. They were interviewing some cop about a trucker bound and drugged in Maryland; he was speculating on whether it was related to the three truck stop murders.

"They found Fiddler," she said, knowing time was running out to get Shelby.

◊◊◊

Jack felt nauseous when he saw the silver Honda in his driveway. Tammy was dead and Steven had been the one to feel for a pulse. His head began to throb. *How did her car get here?* He remained in his truck, took out his cell phone, and called the police. He was told not to touch anything and that a detective would be on the scene soon.

A squad car arrived followed by the forensics unit. The crime scene techs swarmed Tammy's car as a uniformed officer approached Jack's truck. Jack rolled down his window.

"You can wait in your house until the detective arrives," the officer said. As Jack was leaving his truck, one of the techs showed the officer a piece of paper. "Go ahead and call it in," the officer said.

Jack was pacing his living room, trying to decide if he should call Shelby when Detective Stevenson entered his house without knocking. "Did you find Betty?" Jack asked when he saw the man, assuming his presence had something to do with Tammy.

"No, Jack. I've been called in on this recent murder."

"Tammy? Why?"

"You have to admit, Jack, it looks suspicious. First your son finds her body and then her car is found is your driveway. Anything you care to share?"

Jack thought about calling his lawyer, but decided to come clean with Stevenson about his affair with Tammy. Stevenson took notes as Jack spoke. He asked a few questions, but once Jack began talking, he seemed to have a need to confess it all.

"So you spent time with her at your favorite bar and at her apartment. Did you two go anywhere else?"

"She wanted to, but I knew the guys at the bar wouldn't tell Shelby what I was up to. I was afraid if we went any place else, someone would see us."

"Did Tammy know Betty?" Stevenson asked.

"What kind of questions is that? How would she?"

166

"The crime techs found a piece of paper with a phone number scribbled on it. It looks like a number Betty was using. It's one of those disposable phones, but our cyber guys were able to figure out the cell phone towers that picked up or delivered that number. Why do you think Tammy would have Betty's phone number?"

"I have no idea," Jack replied, stunned.

◊◊◊

The sound of a phone ringing woke Betty up. She had fallen asleep on the sofa of the house she had entered. The ringing stopped and the answering machine clicked on, "This is Joni and Todd. We can't come to the phone, please leave a message…*beep*."

"Joni, this is Mom. I couldn't remember if you said you were coming home on Friday or Saturday. I tried your cell phone, but I must have written the number down wrong because a Spanish-speaking man picked up when I called. Your dad is going in for a stent next week. Please call me when you get home." The call ended.

"Looks like I can hang out here for a couple of days," Betty said as she stood up. She went upstairs and found the master bedroom. She opened the folding doors of the large closet and began going through the clothes. She took out a couple pairs of designer jeans, but it was obvious the tops would not fit over her large breasts. She went to the smaller closet where men's suits and shirts hung. She selected a couple of men's dress shirts and then went through the drawers. The oversized sweatshirts would camouflage her body. A knit ski cap would cover her hair and even her face if need be.

She took a hot shower, washed and conditioned her hair, and after drying off and dressing, went back to the kitchen and made herself another sandwich. She opened the door that led into the garage and turned on the light. There sat a chocolate-colored Fiat. She went to the hall and saw several sets of keys hanging from a rack by the front door. The Fiat key was easy to spot.

◊◊◊

Detective Stevenson decided to check out the bar himself. He let his eyes adjust to the dark, before approaching the counter. "Do you know Jack Mathews?" he asked.

"Yeah, he used to be here most evenings."

"Not anymore?"

"Nope, not after he and Tam…"

"The woman who was murdered?"

The bartender nodded and Stevenson took a photo from his jacket pocket. "Did you ever see this woman in here?" he asked, showing the shaken man Betty's mug shot.

The bartender studied it. "I'm not sure. The hair's different, and she's thinner… It could be her. She came in once or twice. She and Tammy seemed friendly."

"Do you know what they talked about?"

"No. Tammy was pretty upset about Jack's breaking things off. I guess it was just girl talk."

"Maybe…Thanks, you've been very helpful." Stevenson got up and left. He got into his car, took out his cell phone and called Jack. "Well, Jack. You're no longer the prime suspect in Tammy's murder. Looks like she and Betty were friendly. And it appears she's back in town."

"I need to get hold of Shelby…"

"Let me know when you do. We'll get a protection detail on her."

◊◊◊

Betty sat for hours watching Shelby and Jack's house. Late at night, when it was obvious no one would be coming, she returned to the neighboring house to eat, shower, and sleep. She found the perfect spot to park the Fiat, not too close to Shelby's house. With the help of opera glasses of all things, which she found in the top drawer of Joni's desk, she was able to keep the front door under surveillance.

"Where are you, little Miss Barbie?" The longer she sat in the tiny car, the angrier she became. "I gave up everything to come back here and take care of this bitch, and she's not here," she said, banging her fist against the dashboard of the Fiat. She had one more day until Joni and her husband returned. She determined that she would have to return to the house, park the Fiat back in the garage, get her things and head back to the truck stop, and try again tomorrow. She started the car and was heading down the street when she saw the headlights of a big cab coming in the opposite direction. They could only belong to one person: Shelby. "There you are, Shelby. I've got you now."

Just as she was about to go back to the spot she'd been occupying in order to keep an eye on the Mathews residence, Betty slammed on the brakes. A vehicle with two men in it crossed in front of her and she could tell from their clothing that they were law enforcement of some kind. She turned the Fiat around and returned it to its garage. She left the house with the ski cap pulled down below her ears, and walked to the alley behind Shelby's house. She saw another vehicle of the same color parked at the opposite end of the alley. It had one man and one woman in it; no doubt they were also cops. None of the people in either vehicle made contact with Shelby and Betty surmised they were a protection detail. She would have to be careful.

She went back to the house to figure out how to get to Shelby and avoid the cops. Betty was not deterred. She would take down anyone who got in her way. "You have to be smarter than your target, ladies and gentleman. You're not, but I am," she murmured.

Normally, her neighborhood association would object to Shelby's parking her truck on the residential street. Without giving a reason, Jack had called and gotten permission for her to park there for a few days.

Shelby went into the house, put her things down on the couch, and kissed her husband. Jack grabbed his wife and put her on his lap and kissed her back. "I'm glad you're home, baby."

Shelby wrapped her arms around Jack's neck. "Sorry I've been gone so much this week. The loads just turned so quickly and it just turned out that way. I promise it won't be like that all the time."

"Don't worry about it. You have to do what you have to do. I'm just glad you're protected and safe."

"Protected? What do you mean protected?"

Jack tried hard to backtrack. "Oh you know what I mean, protecting yourself, being cautious and safe about stuff."

"I'm trying." She wrapped her arms around him. "It was a good trip, Jack. I got to hear and see several of my friends out there. It is so amazing to know that so many people recognize me when I'm on the highways."

Jack hugged Shelby. He was appreciative she had friends on the highways especially with Betty still out there. "Who did you run into this time? Anyone we met up with in Utah?"

"No, just some guys I've made friends with over the last couple years."

Shelby got off her husband's lap and took her things to their room. Jack followed her, teasing her with touches to her butt. "Jack, stop it. Or you can carry my stuff."

"What? You don't like my hands on your ass? That isn't what you said the other morning in bed."

Shelby dropped her things on the floor. She and Jack rolled around on top of each other in their bed laughing and kissing. "Of course I like your hands."

"I know you do." Jack kissed his wife and they played for a while until Shelby was suddenly scared by a noise near the window. "What was that?"

Jack stopped. "What?"

Shelby and Jack listened and then the noise came again. "That!"

Jack went to the window. "It's just the shutter I forgot to fix. I'll get on that tomorrow. Do you have to go out tomorrow?"

Shelby got off the bed and walked toward the restroom. "No. Dispatch didn't have a load for me right away. Plus, there's a noise in the engine that I want to have checked out so I'm going to the yard in the morning."

"Do you think we could have lunch together tomorrow?"

"I think that would be wonderful."

◊◊◊

Betty checked the news again before leaving Joni's home. On the local news the police were still looking for leads on Tammy's murders, the national news had no new information on the truck stop attacks, and nothing more was said about Fiddler. The nation's attention had turned to some celebrity scandal, which was of greater interest than some dead or injured truckers. Betty did not know if they had IDed Fiddler or if anyone was looking for his truck. She needed to get out of Joni's house, so she called a cab and went back to the truck stop.

Fiddler's truck was where she had parked it. She spent the night in it and thought about how she was going to get to Shelby. She had no information on the detail. *Is it only when she's not on the road? Are they at her house 24/7? Who's paying for that?* She hadn't noticed anyone watching the house when Shelby wasn't home, which meant they might possibly be following her on her routes, but not here in Odessa, Betty suspected.

Betty decided she'd try to keep as close to Shelby as she could without being discovered. "I will just take my time and get that bitch at the first opportunity that presents itself," she thought. She turned over in the sleeper and put her face in Fiddler's pillow and inhaled his scent. She grabbed the pillow and threw it against the sleeper wall, refusing to miss him.

Betty woke up before the sun came up. She was determined to find a way to get to Shelby, and she decided that she needed to use a big truck, but she didn't want it to be Fiddler's. She looked around the parking lot but did not see anything she could steal without drawing attention. She knew of only one yard where she could get a truck this early in the morning—her old yard. It was doubtful anyone would notice if one of the older trucks was gone for days. Betty went into the store and hitched a ride from a driver to her old yard.

With the ski mask covering her face, she broke into the office and once inside went to the key box. She wasn't that surprised to discover it hadn't been moved. She grabbed the keys to a truck that had been a dinosaur back when she worked for ESCC. Like the key box, it was in the same parking spot as always. She climbed in, revved the engine, and headed to Shelby's house.

She knew it would look suspicious to have two rigs on the residential street, then she had an idea. She remembered during her initial walk in the neighborhood that there was a house undergoing serious renovation. She drove around until she found it and then parked along the curb, letting people think it was owned by the construction company.

"Shit. How am I going to get to that bitch?" Betty swore when she saw the unmarked police car in front of the house. She pondered going back to Joni's house to lay low but didn't know if the woman had returned from her trip. She went back and climbed into the old truck to figure out her next move.

◊◊◊

Shelby got up when Jack's alarm went off. She went to the kitchen to make coffee but he'd already made it and he was in the shower now. She took off her t-shirt and panties and opened the shower door. Jack openly welcomed his wife as she helped herself to his naked body. "You're going to be late."

"I like it when I'm late."

She and Jack made love in the shower and then on their bed. Then they had breakfast together. Jack left for work late with a smile on his face. The agents saw him leave and took note of the time.

Agent Silverman checked in with the watch detail but they had nothing new to report. Jack had left for work and Shelby was still in the house. They asked what the response should be if Shelby left.

"You stay in the house even if she leaves. I have a feeling our suspect will be casing the house if she isn't already. I got the report about the dead mistress and her car being parked in their driveway. I think I know who left it there. Keep a watch out for suspicious vehicles. I don't believe she'll show up in an eighteen-wheeler, so concentrate on pickups and cars."

"Looks like she's leaving now. You still want us to stay in the house?"

"Yeah. I'll check with her husband to see if he knows her plans for today."

It was close to 10:00 a.m. when Shelby reached the truck yard. She took her truck to the mechanic. "There's a ticking sound. It happens when I turn on the heater or air conditioner."

"I know exactly what it is, Ms. Shelby. Give me about an hour and I'll have it ready for you."

Shelby was greeted by a familiar voice when she entered the office. "Hey, Shelby. How are you doing?"

Shelby turned and gave her boss and friend Jayne a hug. "I'm good, but how are you? You haven't been in the office for weeks."

"Opening the new yard in Colorado."

"I heard about it. You're expanding. That's great!"

"It will be good to have another yard available further west."

Shelby told Jayne about getting her truck fixed and thanked her for the modified assignments. Jayne had been her mentor from the start, but as much as she appreciated her friend, she wasn't ready to reveal her concerns about Betty or her situation with Jack.

"It was good seeing you, Shelby. I need to go see my banker. Make yourself comfortable until your truck is ready. You take care and be sure to check with dispatch this afternoon. I think they have a load for you."

"Okay, I will."

◊◊◊

Betty woke up to the sound of a guy knocking on her window. "We've got work to do here," he said.

"I know. I was told to bring a load of sand over."

"Don't know nothing about that. You'll have to move the truck out of our way until the contractor gets here."

"When's that?"

"Not sure. He's at another job. Maybe an hour."

Betty moved the truck down a couple of blocks and then got out. "I'm gonna get some coffee," she yelled, but the guy just waved her off.

She walked around the neighborhood and saw Shelby lock her front door and head to her truck. Betty expected the unit to follow Shelby but it remained in front of the house.

Betty moved quickly back to where she'd parked and in no time had Shelby in her sights, turning onto loop 338. She kept a safe distance, anticipating where Shelby was going and let out a sigh of relief when she saw her pull into her company yard off the I-20. Several yards down the road was a towing company and salvage yard. Betty pulled into the tow yard and found a place to park. She looked around, but no one came out of the steel building, so she got out and walked up the road to where she could watch Shelby and still not be noticed.

◊◊◊

Jack called Shelby and invited her out to lunch while she was waiting for her truck.

She was about to leave when the mechanic caught her at the door. "Hey, Mrs. Mathews. I was wondering if it would be okay to keep your truck here for another few hours? There are a few things I want to double check before you take it back out. Plus, Ms. Jayne asked me to download the onboard computer."

"No problem. My husband's picking me up for lunch."

Jack pulled up and Shelby got into his pickup. Before he pulled out onto the road, his cell phone vibrated. It was Agent Silverman. "Okay. Yes, sir," Jack said into the phone. "Uh huh, right here…okay…will do…call you soon."

"Who was that?" Shelby asked, suspiciously.

"The office, wanting to know when I'd be back."

Shelby doubted he was telling her the truth, but let it slide.

Silverman had intended to report in to Jack as promised, but could tell by Jack's evasiveness that it wasn't a good time to talk. He did glean from the short conversation that Shelby was with her husband.

Jack knew that Shelby suspected something and was uncomfortable about what it might be. Still, he couldn't let her know that the FBI had a detail on her. He could tell Silverman wanted to tell him something, but it would have to wait until he got back to his office. Jack grabbed Shelby's hand. "So, where am I taking my beautiful wife for lunch?"

Shelby squeezed Jack's hand and tried to shake off her suspicions about the phone call. *Will I ever totally trust him again?* she wondered. "I think I want Mexican food. Let's go to Las Margaritas."

◊◊◊

From her observation point, Betty saw Shelby get in Jack's car, which meant her truck was still at the yard. She had to make a quick decision: follow the two or stay put. She decided to hang around. She walked over to Jayne's yard. No one was around. She glanced around and saw Shelby's truck in the mechanic bay. She walked back to the tow yard and got into the truck. She drove around for about an hour and then turned back onto the road to see if Shelby had returned. She brightened when she saw Jack's pickup coming down the road toward Jayne's yard. She pulled to the side of the road and ducked down.

Shelby recognized the truck. "Look, Jack! That's old 171. That truck was a relic when I drove her at ESCC. I wonder why she's parked over there near the entrance to the tow yard? Guess she must have finally given up." Shelby looked the truck over as they went past it. "That's odd. No driver and it's not on a tow truck."

"Maybe something happened to the tow truck," Jack said.

"Maybe…"

Jack dropped Shelby off and headed back to his office. He called Silverman back on the way. "Sorry I couldn't talk earlier. I had Shelby with me."

"I thought that was the case. Where is she now?"

"At her yard, getting her truck fixed."

"Is she headed out on the road?"

"I'm not sure. Why?"

"I just received two calls from the Odessa PD regarding your neighborhood. A woman by the name of Joni Goodall called and said someone had broken into her house while she was out of town. Looks like whoever it was stayed a couple of days. Ate some of her food, took clothes from both her husband's and her closet and may have even driven her Fiat."

"Do you think it was Betty?"

"Don't know. A forensic team is headed over there now to dust for prints."

"What was the other call?"

"A contractor from a house under construction said that a woman in a sand-hauling truck was parked outside the site when his crew arrived. She told the foreman she was sent to deliver a load of sand, but no request was ever made for sand. Then the driver said she was going to get coffee, and then she drove off and never came back."

Jack's heart raced with fear. "Shelby and Betty used to drive sand-hauling trucks for ESCC. She noticed one of their old trucks on the side of the road near her new yard. Shit…," he said and ended the call before Silverman could respond.

◊◊◊

Shelby was in her truck about to cross the railroad tracks when the lights came on and she had to wait. She heard the whistle but could not see the train. Many of the tracks in this part of town had warning lights but no arm to deter motorists. As she sat waiting for the train she received a call on her cell phone from Jack. "Hey, baby. What's up?" she chirped.

"Shelby, I have to tell you something…," he started and then he heard a blood-curdling scream. "SHELBY!" he shouted. All he heard was Shelby screaming as she tried to shift gears.

Betty, driving the large 171, had rammed Shelby from behind, pushing her onto the tracks. Although Shelby's truck was newer and stronger, Betty had built up speed and had momentum as she rammed into Shelby's idling vehicle.

The jolt caused Shelby to drop her phone. Shelby looked out her mirrors but all she saw was the red color of a truck hood. She tried to put the truck in reverse but was so panicked by the sight of the oncoming train she screamed, "OH MY GOD! I'VE GOT TO GET OUT OF HERE!" She knew it was too late to try to get her truck off the tracks. She needed to bail.

Betty was still pushing as hard as she could against the back of Shelby's trailer as Shelby pushed open her driver's side door and quickly jumped out of the cab. She fell by the side of the road and rolled into the ditch. The train sounded its horn in an attempt to warn the driver of the truck. Shelby covered her face and waited for the impact to be over.

Betty continued ramming Shelby's truck and was in such a frenzy she did not realize that Shelby had ejected herself from the truck. "DIE, BITCH! DIE!" she screamed.

The freight train hit the nose of Shelby's truck, causing it to spin 360 degrees and then hit the side of several speeding boxcars where it folded like a discarded soda can. Shelby remained curled up in a ball with her hands covering her head trying to shield herself from the devastation. Then every-thing went quiet. Like a gopher on the prairie, Shelby lifted her head up and surveyed the site around her. Mangled pieces of metal that had once been her truck were strewn up and down the track. And then she saw it: truck 171 was at the base of the road that led to the track crossing. The truck's cab was pushed in, but it was the profile of the driver that caught Shelby's attention. "BETTY!" she shouted.

Without thinking, Shelby leapt to her feet and with adrenaline pump-ing ran toward the 171. "BETTY, YOU FUCKING BITCH! COME OUT OF THAT TRUCK AND LET'S FINISH THIS RIGHT HERE! I'M NOT AFRAID OF YOU! COME ON, LET'S DO THIS THING!"

Betty could not believe what she was seeing. Shelby was supposed to be in that mangled mess of metal. "Fuck! How did you manage to get out of this one?" Betty screamed. She was about to get out of the truck and take Shelby out when she heard the sirens in the distance. As she pulled out onto the road she stuck her head out the open window and yelled: "THIS ISN'T OVER, BITCH! WATCH YOUR BACK! I'M GOING TO GET YOU. I PROMISE."

Shelby ran as fast as she could but could not catch up to her. "YOU COWARD! COME BACK HERE AND DO IT NOW IF YOU THINK YOU CAN!" she shouted.

Betty peeled out and drove as fast as she could down the road, she took a quick right turn onto an old Farm to Market road and parked the truck in a vacant lot not far from the train wreck. She had been wearing gloves and assumed her fingerprints would not be found on the truck. She took off on foot, wanting to put as much distance as she could between her and the cops. She knew she needed to move parallel to the highway and after getting lost on a couple of private roads, she finally made it to Exit 115. She knew she would need to find a place to stay and some transportation. For now, she needed to stay clear of the cops, who no doubt would be combing every truck stop within a fifty-mile radius.

◊◊◊

Dirt covered Shelby's face and body, her elbows were scratched and bleeding, and she was shaking uncontrollably. Even though she hadn't been hurt, she was having a hard time focusing when she saw thought about what had just happened. She surveyed the devastation. *Why is Betty so evil? Why is she so determined to kill me? If someone doesn't stop her soon, she's going to kill more people,* she thought. She wished she had her phone.

When the police came onto the scene, they saw a shocked and disoriented woman staring at the debris on the tracks.

CHAPTER TWENTY-TWO

J ack became frantic when he was unable to get Shelby back on the phone. He placed a call to her yard. "This is Jack Mathews, Shelby's husband. Is Shelby still there?"

"Hold on just a minute, Mr. Mathews."

Jack did not have time to wait. He put the phone on Bluetooth and sped as fast as he could back to the yard. Jayne finally came on the line. "Jack, this is Jayne. I don't want to alarm you, but Shelby has been involved in an accident."

"What? Where?"

"Jack, calm down. Shelby isn't hurt. Come to the yard and I will go with you to the site of the accident. I just got off the phone with the police and was heading that way."

"Okay. I'm almost there. You sure she's okay?"

"Yes, Jack. The police said she was fine, just shaken up."

Shelby was sitting sideways in the backseat of a patrol car when Jack pulled up to the scene. The door to the car was open and she sat with her feet firmly on the ground. An ambulance was also on site, but she told the EMT that she did not want to go to the hospital. A uniformed police officer was interviewing her.

"I was waiting for the train when Betty Burton pushed me onto the tracks. I got out just as the train was about to hit me. Then, when all the noise stopped I looked around and saw an ESCC truck, truck 171 to be exact, behind my truck…'til it got scattered from here to hell."

"How did you know it was truck 171? Did you see the truck number?"

"No, I didn't see the truck number. I used to work for ESCC and I drove that truck for a long time. Betty Burton was behind the wheel. She was trying to kill me again. I went for her but she took off before I could pull the bitch out of that truck by her hair."

"The Odessa PD has been briefed about Ms. Burton. You know how dangerous she is. You should not have tried to apprehend her. Did you see where she went?"

"No. She peeled out very fast and caused a big dust cloud."

Sergeant Petersen arrived with a local unit in an unmarked car. He and an Odessa detective stopped and spoke to two other patrolmen who were canvassing drivers who had arrived within moments of Betty's pushing Shelby onto the track. He nodded and walked over to Shelby and the policeman questioning her. "Officer Hernandez, there are a couple of truck drivers over there who spotted Ms. Burton out on FM 1788. You and your partner head out there. I'll take over here with Mrs. Mathews."

"Yes, sir."

"Who are you?" Shelby asked.

"Arnold Petersen. We met briefly in Utah. I am very familiar with the Burton case and have been tasked with bringing her back to Utah. The task force has been wondering when she was going to surface."

"A task force? Because of me?"

"Not exactly. Betty Burton has been on a cross-country killing spree from California to Maryland. Only the guy in Maryland is still alive. We've got state, federal, and local law enforcement on the case."

"I thought her vendetta was towards me."

"It started out that way, but she's developed quite a taste for killing. She's a textbook serial killer."

Shelby was stunned. *Did other people die because of me?* she wondered. "I need to find my purse and my phone," she said to Petersen. He walked with Shelby to the wreckage, flashed his badge to the crime scene unit and helped her into what was left of the front cab. Shelby looked and found most of the contents of her purse. The sight of her mangled phone made her grateful that she'd jumped out of the truck when she did.

Jack was standing there when they returned to the patrol car. He opened his arms and brought Shelby in tight against his chest.

Jayne had arrived on the scene and went over to where Jack and Shelby stood.

"I'm sorry about the truck, Jayne."

"Shelby, you have nothing to be sorry about. I'm just glad you weren't hurt. I'll see what I can do about getting you another truck."

"Hold off on that for a bit. I think I'm going to have Jack take me out of town for a while…at least until they find Betty. She did all this and I'm not going to put anyone else in danger. She wants me and she's not going to stop until she kills me or they capture her. Jack has convinced me it would be best for us to find someplace quiet to go and let the police find her."

"Maybe you're right, Shelby. At least you'll be safe until they find her." It was also a prudent business decision for Jayne, but all she said was, "Keep me informed and let me know when you want to come back to work."

"Okay, I will."

Jayne turned to leave but stopped in mid-step. "Shelby, I just had an idea. Can I talk to you a minute before you leave?"

The two women walked several yards away from the scene. Jack watched, but the two had their backs to him and all he could see was Shelby nodding a couple of times. When they turned around and headed back in his direction, Jack was pleased to see a smile on her face and she strolled toward him with her hands in her coat pockets.

The police did not have any more questions for them, so Jack and Shelby walked to his pickup. As he pulled the truck out on the road, he grabbed Shelby's hand and asked. "Are you sure taking a vacation is what you want to do?"

"Yes, Jack. Betty's a monster. Innocent people are getting hurt and killed because she's insane. You didn't see her eyes like I did today when I went after her. She has to be stopped."

◊◊◊

Betty was breathing hard when she finally made it to Exit 115. She had to make it back to Fiddler's truck while remaining out of sight. She thought about hitch-hiking. She hoped that if her coat collar was pulled up over her ears and her hat was pulled down low enough, she would not be recognizable to drivers speeding past. She got on the feeder and stuck out her thumb. A young man in a 1999 green Honda Civic with a donut wheel for one of his towers passed her, then pulled over to the shoulder and waited for her a few yards away. Betty put her hands in her pockets and walked to the car. The young man took her to the northeast side of the 126 and let her out on the roadside. She waited for traffic to clear and then walked across the street to the War Truck stop.

To stay concealed, Betty moved along the rear of the trucks until she got close to the back of the truck stop store. She went into the store by the back door and then went out through the front, walking toward the street. Fiddler's truck was parked in the back of the parking lot and Betty moved quickly to her safe haven. She knew she couldn't stay there since Shelby had identified her in the ESCC truck. Every truck stop in the area would be crawling with cops before too long. She unlocked the door, climbed in, popped the hood and went back out to reconnect the battery cables. She hoped the truck would start without needing to be jumped. She got back into the driver's seat and breathed a sigh of relief when the engine roared to life.

Betty pulled the truck out and just as she was pulling out onto the feeder road her suspicions were confirmed. Two DOT units came over the overpass with lights on. One went to the truck stop to the east and one went to the truck stop to the west. Betty knew immediately which direction to take. She made a sharp right and moved the truck down I-20 to the west and figured she would find a place down the road and lay low until things cooled off.

◊◊◊

Fiddler moved slightly in the bed he'd been confined to for the last few days. He'd been having a hard time focusing, and his head still hurt. He tried to move, but the tubes connecting his body to the array of machines next to him were restrictive. A nurse who had been monitoring him came into the room to check on her patient. "Well, Mr. John Doe. I see you have decided to open your eyes."

Fiddler let the nurse remove some of the tubes. He rubbed his hands and arms as she removed several of the unnecessary wires and needles. "We didn't know if you would come back to us."

"Where am I?"

"You're in one of the best hospitals in the Baltimore area."

"How did I get here?"

"Well, they found you in an abandoned warehouse near the harbor. You were almost dead when they brought you in. You don't know how you got there? You don't remember anything?"

"No. The last thing I remember was having dinner with someone but I can't really remember much of anything, really."

"Do you know who you are?"

"Yeah, you just told me. John Doe."

The nurse chuckled. "Sorry, John, but that's what we always call patients who come in without identification. You really don't remember who you are?"

"No. Everything seems fuzzy."

The nurse finished with Fiddler's IVs and went to the door. "You sit tight and I'm going to call your doctor."

Fiddler looked around the room and tried hard to remember something about who he was but all he could remember was his recent conversation with the nurse. It wasn't long before a man in a white coat came into Fiddler's room. "How are you today? I'm Dr. Denton and I've been taking care of you since you came in here. The nurse tells me you're having some trouble remembering things."

"I can remember the stuff that's happening now and a few stupid things from before, I guess. But that's it."

The doctor looked into his patient's ears and looked into his eyes. "What things do you remember?"

"Stupid little things, like eating in a restaurant and a truck, a big truck. I remember a person but I can't see the face."

The doctor stopped looking in Fiddler's eyes. "It's normal for the body to protect itself after something like this."

"Like what, Doctor? I don't even know why I'm here."

"Well, you were found half-dead in an abandoned building. You had high levels of painkillers and alcohol in your blood. You were dehydrated, and the EMTs found you bound at your hands and feet. You don't remember anything about how you ended up that way?"

"No. I wish I did."

"Well, you rest up. I'm pretty sure in a few days, things will start coming back to you." The doctor said, and then left the room.

Fiddler put his head down on his pillow and tried to remember anything. Nothing came to him. It was all a big blank.

◊◊◊

Shelby curled up against Jack in their bed. "Jack, I still want to get out of town until they find Betty. When Jayne and I were talking earlier, she told me about the new yard she just opened in Colorado. She also bought a little cabin near Gunnison. She asked if I might want to go up there and work in the office until they capture Betty. I think I want to take her up on her offer. That way you can save your vacation."

Jack thought about it for a minute. He had hoped to take Shelby some place more exotic, but knew she wanted her life to be as normal as possible. "I think that sounds good, Shelby, but I have plenty of vacation time, so I'm going to take you up there."

Shelby turned to face Jack. "I'm thinking if you want to come with me, then we need to go up there separately. We don't know where Betty is, but I'm sure she's laying low for a little while to avoid the cops. If I leave first thing in the morning, we ask for the detail to make sure I'm not followed. She'll think I'm still here if you are still following your normal routine for a while."

"Yeah, maybe, Shelby. But Betty is evil and she's smart. I'm not sure what you're planning will work. I think she might figure it out and come after you."

"I don't think so, and I want to try this," she said, getting off the bed. "Besides, I'm tired of my life being interrupted because of that bitch. If she comes after me, I'm going to use this."

Jack jumped back when he saw Shelby pull the gun from her dresser drawer. "Shelby, where the hell did you get that gun?"

Shelby handled the gun with caution but Jack could tell she wasn't afraid of the barreled metal piece in her hand. "Jayne gave it to me. I'm not backing down from that bitch ever again."

"But a gun, Shelby? That's not you. You hate guns."

"No, Jack. I don't hate guns. I hate what people do that makes guns necessary. If I had this gun with me today, that evil witch would be in hell right now."

Jack walked over to Shelby and tried to gently take the gun out of her hand. "Put the gun away, Shelby. Have you lost your mind?"

Shelby took the gun out of Jack's hand and put it back in her drawer. "No, I haven't lost my mind. I will defend myself against that woman. You can count on it."

Shelby and Jack got back into bed. Jack wasn't sure he liked this new side of his wife. "Okay," he said. "So you're heading to Colorado tomorrow and I'll come up later."

"I think that is going to be the best way to deal with Betty for now. If they still don't catch her, then we will have to resort to other measures."

"Wonderful. My wife—the gun-slinging trucker," he said.

The couple laughed, but both knew the situation was serious.

◊◊◊

Betty found herself in a small truck stop on the south end of Monahans, a little town in West Texas. The truck stop was more like a convenience store. It wasn't secluded by any means, but it was close to the interstate and provided Betty with some place to lay low until the heat was off of her. She wasn't going to wait long. In fact, she planned to go by Shelby and Jack's either tomorrow or the next day.

Betty started to get out of the truck to get something to drink but suddenly turned and went back into the truck when she spotted a police unit rolling slowly through the parking lot. She wasn't thrilled with the place where she was parked, but after realizing that the cops might still be looking for her she decided she didn't want to leave just yet. She crawled into the sleeper and made sure the curtain was closed.

"Wonderful. Pigs. This is entirely your fault, Shelby Mathews. I can't even walk across the parking lot," she said to herself.

◊◊◊

Fiddler woke up in his hospital bed the next morning surprised he was beginning to remember more and more. Today he remembered his name and where he went to high school and little bits of other things about his life. He let the nurse know what he thought his name was and the other things he remembered. She documented everything for the doctor and then went to her computer to see what she could find out about the John Doe who was finally remembering things about his past.

CHAPTER TWENTY-THREE

Jack was leaving for work when Agent Silverman called with his daily update and surveillance schedule.

"I don't think you're going to be needed here much longer. Shelby is taking a job in Colorado and she's leaving this morning. I would appreciate it if you could at least watch out for her and make sure Betty isn't following her when she leaves."

"We'll do that. Do you think it's wise for her to leave town until we capture Betty?"

"Shelby wants out of here until Betty is apprehended. I agree with her that leaving now is best since Betty may be laying low for a bit, after the train stunt."

"Okay, I'll bring in some extra units for surveillance and make sure that the area is completely secure."

"Good. Maybe you could leave a unit on the house for a couple of days, so if Betty is in the area, she'll think Shelby is still at home."

"I'll see what I can do."

Shelby was packing while Jack was on the phone with Silverman. Her cell phone rang and she saw it was Jayne. "Hey. I'm packing now."

"Good. I was wondering if you might want to drive one of my new trucks to the Colorado yard. I mean, if you think it will be safe?"

Shelby hesitated but then said, "Sure. After I get my stuff together, I'll call you and you can come get me."

"Okay, see you in a little bit."

Shelby hung up the phone and wondered if she was doing the right thing. She hadn't told anyone—not even Jack—that she was having nightmares about Betty. But after Jayne's call she decided that maybe getting back into a truck was just what she needed to help her deal with everything.

She went into the kitchen just as Jack was rinsing out his coffee cup. "Jack, Jayne is coming by the house to pick me up. I'm going to take one of her new trucks to the new yard in Colorado."

"Are you sure that's a good idea?"

"I'm thinking trucking there by myself is what I need right now."

Jack wasn't thrilled with the idea that Shelby was going to be driving a big truck to Colorado, but he wasn't going to try to talk her out of it—not after everything they'd been through the past few months. "I'll come by the yard and see you before you leave."

Jack got into his truck and took out his cell phone. "Agent Silverman, this is Jack Mathews. There's been a change in plans. Shelby isn't flying out to Colorado, she's going to be taking one of Jayne's new trucks out there."

"Are you sure that's a good idea?"

"Nope, but Shelby wants to do it. I really need you guys to do your job and make sure Betty isn't anywhere around. I want Shelby out of town with an escort and I want you to make sure she doesn't have anyone following her."

"Okay, we can do that. I wish we could escort her all the way, but the director won't approve any long trips."

"Just make sure Betty isn't around."

"Trust me. This time if she shows up we will arrest her."

"Yeah, we'll see."

As Jack was pulling into the parking lot of his company, his cell phone rang. It was Detective Stevenson. "You talk to Silverman?" Jack asked.

"Yeah, he told me Shelby is heading up to Colorado."

"Did he tell you about the detail?"

"Yep, that's why I'm calling."

◊◊◊

Jayne picked Shelby up and carried her and her bags to the yard, unaware she was being followed by a police detail. Several units stayed by the house and patrolled the perimeter to make sure Betty wasn't anywhere around.

Shelby was loading the new truck when Jack arrived at the yard. "Hey, lady driver. You ready to go?"

Shelby put down what she was doing in the truck and welcomed Jack into the truck. "Come in here, baby."

Jack got into the truck with Shelby and sat on the sleeper bed. "This is a nice truck. Are all of her new trucks this nice?"

"They all look like this one and even have plenty of room for all my shit."

"I doubt that."

They both laughed.

Shelby finished loading her truck. "Well, that should do it."

"I think I saw the truck take a deep breath."

Shelby slapped at Jack's belly. "Asshole."

Jack laughed and grabbed at his belly. "Damn, you got some swing."

"Be careful. I'm working out, big boy."

"Yeah, I know you worked out with me quite a bit lately." Jack wrapped his arms around his wife.

"I'm going to miss you, baby."

"You know I'll be just a phone call away and I'll be up there soon."

"Yeah, I know."

They climbed out of the truck. As they were kissing goodbye, an agent drove up. "Sorry to interrupt," he called out through his rolled-down window, "but we gotta go. The Director is pulling some of our agents off this detail and putting us on another one."

Jack was pissed at how unconcerned they seemed to be with Shelby's safety and knew he knew he had to get her on the road. He was going to get the protection he wanted for her before she left the area. "Okay," he said, sighing. "She's coming. Shelby, you are to call me every hour until you get to Jayne's cabin. Detective Stevenson has a friend in that area and he's going to have him check things out before you get there. He's also going to check on you from time to time while you're there."

"Okay. Well, I have to go by the yard first and drop off this truck and get the company pickup."

"Just let me know where you are and what you're doing so I won't worry."

Shelby kissed Jack as she climbed into her truck. "I promise."

The agents from the FBI had made sure Shelby was secure before letting her go down the highway on her own. The agents that had been watching the Mathews home cleared the area and reported in. "We patrolled the entire area for a five-block radius and found no one suspicious or even remotely close to the description of our suspect. We are stationed out of sight but near the house, waiting to see if the suspect arrives. At least on our end, we believe Mrs. Mathews was not followed."

"Sounds good, gentlemen. We are currently coming back into town from escorting Mrs. Mathews out of town. We, too, were successful in making sure Mrs. Mathews made it out without a tail. Mr. Mathews should be on his way home so secure the area one more time and then you're released from duty."

◊◊◊

Shelby was on her way to Colorado; a cool breeze blew in through her slightly open window. It was beginning to get chilly outside in Texas and she knew the further north she went, the cooler it would become. It felt good to be on a long run again, although she wasn't loaded with anything and she didn't have a delivery or pickup time to make. Highway 385 through Texas wasn't a very exciting highway. It was mostly small towns and farming communities, but Shelby didn't mind. She loved the feelings of peace and safety she felt driving on small highways like this one.

Shelby had never been to Gunnison, Colorado but Jayne made the town sound so beautiful. Shelby would travel west on Highway 50 out of Lamar, Colorado to Gunnison and then she would travel another sixty-five miles on into Montrose to deliver the truck to Jayne's new yard. Jayne had chosen to put the truck yard in Montrose because it was a larger town between Grand Junction and Durango and it was nestled in a beautiful part of Colorado. She'd chosen Gunnison for her private cabin because Gunnison was smaller, providing her with not only a variety of outdoor activities, but also the quiet serenity a small town savors. Shelby knew without ever having been in Gunnison that she was going to like it.

Shelby kept her word and called Jack every hour. "Hey, baby. Just checking in."

"Where are you at?"

"Between Seminole and Brownfield."

"Any sign of the witch?"

"Nope. My stalker seems to still be in hiding." Shelby changed the subject. "I can't wait for you to come to Colorado. I haven't seen it yet, but Jayne was telling me a little about the place and I think we'll enjoy spending time there together. Maybe a second honeymoon."

"That sounds terrific. You just be careful getting there and let me know all about it when you check things out up there."

"Okay, talk to you in another hour."

Shelby called Jack again when she got to Littlefield, Texas and again when she reached Hereford. She had traveled 385 many times during her time as a sand-hauler and she decided that she would stop in Vega, Texas for coffee. She would also call Jack again so he wouldn't worry. When Shelby pulled into the truck stop south of I-40 she parked in the fuel island. Strictly speaking it wasn't allowed, but since the place wasn't very busy, she figured it would be fine.

Inside the store, Shelby used the restroom, bought a sandwich and a cup of coffee. She walked around the store for a few minutes and looked at the trinkets that were always available in truck stops. She didn't buy anything else and was about to go to the truck when someone touched her shoulder. "Barbie?"

Shelby pulled away from the touch with a jerk. Very few people knew her CB handle unless they knew her from her sand-hauling days and since she wasn't on her home turf and on edge with Betty running loose, she was particularly jumpy.

"Oh, I'm sorry, Shelby. I didn't mean to frighten you."

Shelby looked at her old friend and smiled as she gave him a friendly hug. "Praise Warrior, how are you? I haven't seen you in forever."

Praise Warrior hugged her back. "I'm good, Shelby. How have you been?"

"Okay. What are you doing out this way?"

"Just coming back from Colorado and Wyoming. Been doing some jobs up there. What are you doing out here?"

"Oh, I'm taking that new truck to a new yard in Colorado. Then I'm going to stay and do some work in the office for my boss."

"Well, that sounds like a good thing. Where in Colorado?"

"Near Gunnison."

"Oh, that's a beautiful area."

"Yeah, that's what my boss says. I can't wait to see it. My husband Jack is coming up soon so I think we will have fun checking out the area."

"Well, that will be fun, I promise. It's getting cold so you won't be able to do some of the water stuff, but the skiing is terrific up there. If he comes up soon you guys can probably still do some fishing and rafting."

"Awesome."

Shelby talked with Praise Warrior for a while and they walked out to the parking lot and to their trucks. Shelby gave Praise Warrior a hug goodbye and got into her truck. Warrior got on the CB as he left the parking lot. "See you next time, Barbie."

"Okay, Praise Warrior. You be careful out there."

"I will."

"You were looking good all the way down 385 to Odessa. I didn't see anything all the way up here."

"Okay there, driver. You looked good to Lamar."

"Thanks, Praise Warrior. I'll see you later."

"10-4."

It took Shelby less than an hour to get to get to Dalhart, where she called Jack and then headed to the Oklahoma state line, crossed it and then went on another twenty-two miles to the Colorado state line. She then drove another forty-nine miles into Springfield, Colorado. Shelby again called Jack. "Hi, baby. Just checking in again. I'm going through Springfield, Colorado right now. I got another fifty miles to Lamar."

"How are you holding up, babe?"

"I'm doing okay, but it's getting late so I'll probably shut down at the truck stop near the weight station in Lamar. I would rather find Jayne's yard in the daylight. I'll only have three hundred and eighty-eight miles to Gunnison and then a few more to Montrose."

"Okay, sweetheart. But be careful and park in a safe place, please. Any sign of anyone following you?"

"Nope, haven't seen anything suspicious."

"Call me in the morning, Shelby. I love you."

"I love you, too, baby."

◊◊◊

Betty wanted to check out Shelby's neighborhood, but was worried about bringing another big truck into the area. She knew she wouldn't be able to go to the construction area. She decided to park Fiddler's truck behind a small strip center about two and a half miles from the neighborhood. She pretended she was a jogger and when she ran past the Mathews house saw the cops were not there. "That's good, it will give me a chance to check things out and find a place to keep a closer watch on Shelby."

Betty speed-walked around to the back of Shelby and Jack's house. She noticed that Shelby's car was there and that Jack's truck was gone. She found a little spot she thought would work as a nice place to watch the house. She was going to stay right in the open and hoped that the law wouldn't notice her.

Betty liked the fact she was possibly alone with Shelby, but she didn't know who else might be in the house. It was also possible that cops were hiding somewhere near the front of the house that she couldn't see. Betty watched the house for a little while, hoping to see Shelby come outside in the backyard or walk through the house. After sitting there for quite a while Betty became bored. She began to walk back to the truck through the alley when she noticed an unmarked unit with a well-dressed man pass the entrance to the alley. The unmarked unit went around the block and several other blocks before leaving the area. Betty decided that the cop car was too close of a call when she finally made it back to her truck. She went to the truck stop for a little while to figure out what to do next.

◊◊◊

After getting up with the sun, Shelby went into the truck stop and took a shower. She got breakfast and then walked back to her truck with her shower bag and coffee. She looked at the sky as it started getting light out and noticed that the sun was behind clouds. "It looks like rain," she thought. Shelby got into her truck and put her things away. She was five and a half hours from Gunnison and another hour from Montrose. It would be sometime early afternoon when she would arrive at Jayne's yard. Before she left the parking lot, she called Jack. "Good morning, my love."

"Good morning, baby. How did you sleep?"

"Really well. How about you?"

"Without you it was terrible."

"Well, you'll be up here soon. I'm on my way to Montrose."

"Any sign of Betty?"

"Nope. I'm sure if Betty were following me she would have let me know while I was asleep."

"Okay, but you continue to call me every hour and let me know when you get to your drop off point."

"Yes, sir. I love you."

"Love you, too."

When Shelby finally reached Gunnison, she called Jack, but this time it wasn't just to check in. Shelby was so excited about the area that she was seeing. "Jack, you aren't going to believe this place. It's beautiful. I went past Jayne's cabin coming into town. It's so big and gorgeous. Oh my goodness, Jack. The town is so cute! It has all these little businesses together, making the downtown look like an old Western village."

"Calm down, sweetheart. I gather from your excitement that you're glad you went to Gunnison."

"Oh yes, Jack. You are going to love it."

"I know I will, honey. Where are you right now?"

"I'm on my way to Montrose to check out the yard and drop the truck off."

"Okay. Well, you be careful and call me when you're done and headed to Gunnison again."

"Okay, baby."

Shelby loved the mountains and the trees and how green everything was. She had a hard time watching the road on the way to Montrose because she was so distracted by the scenery. There were signs for recreational areas, mountain trails, lakes, rivers, an old mill, and lots of other towns. *This place is going to be awesome to explore,* she thought.

The weather was cooling fast, so Shelby figured a lot of the activities she and Jack would get to do would eventually be in the snow. She was thrilled (especially coming from the desert in West Texas) that she was going to get to spend some time in the snow: skiing, snowmobiles, ice fishing, and ice-skating. Shelby figured she and Jack would have time before it got too cold to go to the lakes and rivers and spend time hiking.

It didn't take Shelby long to find Jayne's yard. It was fenced with a security gate so Shelby had to put in the code Jayne had given her before she could enter the property. Shelby was impressed when she rolled the new truck into a parking spot behind the new building next to the well-manicured yard. There were already some of Jayne's new trucks and trailers parked behind the building. It was obvious that Jayne had spent a great deal of money to make this yard very appealing—it definitely had a woman's touch.

Shelby gathered her things together from the truck and put them in the front passenger seat. She took the keys out of her purse that Jayne had given her for the building. The company pickup was parked in front of the building. Jayne had not hired anyone for the office yet because she wasn't going to open the yard until all of her trucks arrived. Shelby was going to be taking care of the new place for a while and was anxious to check it out.

She unlocked the door to the shiny building, stepped into the lobby, and turned on the lights. Once again, she was amazed at the expense Jayne had gone to in order to make the lobby and offices state of the art. Shelby went to the receptionist's office and made a call. "Hey, Jayne. Just wanted to let you know that I made it to the yard with the truck. You told me this place was nice, but wow!"

"I'm glad you made it safely, Shelby. Thank you and I'm glad you like the new yard and office. I tried hard to make sure it was nice."

"It is beautiful and the area up here is super. I went by the cabin, but I didn't stop. I wanted to get to the yard before it got too late. The cabin looks like it's huge."

"It's pretty big. I just had it remodeled on the inside so I hope it turned out well. If you don't mind, would you send me some pictures of the interior? I haven't seen it since the decorator was in it last week."

"I'll be happy to. I'm just checking things out today, but I will be here in the morning and I'll call you so you can let me know what you want done."

"Sounds good. You be careful and enjoy yourself."

Shelby finished her phone call and then called Jack, letting him know that she'd made it to the yard and that she was headed to the cabin. Shelby turned off the lights and locked the building up. She got in the pickup and drove it to the truck she'd just brought to the yard. She gathered her things out of the passenger side of the truck, loaded them into the pickup, and left the yard through the security gate.

It took her about an hour to drive back to Gunnison. She was anxious to get to the cabin. Shelby drove into the driveway and opened the garage with the garage door opener Jayne had given to her. She parked the truck in the garage, but didn't close the garage door. She wanted to look around the outside of the cabin before she went inside.

The cabin had triple-level architecture with a two-car garage on the bottom level, partially embedded in a hill of earth. The second level had steps to a balcony where the front door was located. The front surrounding the entrance was totally glass. The separated pane, odd-shaped glass windows gave the front of the cabin a look of splendor in the midst of the woods. The second floor also had steps to a covered patio to the back of the house where the back door was located. The third level had a smaller balcony also to the back of the house with steps from the ground to that balcony.

Each balcony and patio were nicely furnished with wood and wicker outdoor furniture. A round outdoor wood-burning pit was the center of attention on the patio located a few feet away from the built-in hot tub and outdoor built-in grilling kitchen. Shelby knew Jack was going to like the grilling area and she was definitely going to enjoy the hot tub.

The property was heavily covered in trees of all kinds but mostly pine. Because the snow was not due to fall for a few more weeks, the grass, bushes, and a few flowers were still visible, making up the beautiful landscape of the property. There were several rock boulders that partitioned sections of the yard in several places. A small gravel driveway that went from the front yard to the back of the property led to a small corral and barn. There were several paths leading from the well-manicured backyard into the wooded areas that surrounded the entire white picket fence. Shelby loved the outside of the house and knew she was going to love the inside.

Shelby went back to the pickup and got some of her things. She hit the garage door opener on the wall next to the door, which turned on the lights in the garage automatically. The door was locked so Shelby had to put her bags down and locate the keys she'd placed in her pocket.

She opened the door, gathered her bags and entered the cabin at an entryway with an open staircase. She could tell that a hallway just to the right of the stairs contained several half opened doors, and she figured they were probably extra bedrooms and baths. The stairs going up led to a beautifully designed and decorated living room. The living room was open, spacious, and well lit from the windows that covered the front wall. The only thing separating the modern stainless steel appliance kitchen from the living room and dining room area was a granite counter top bar with stools. The furnishings were warm and luxurious with stunning electronics fashioned tastefully into the décor.

Shelby put her bags down near the glass top dining table that was nestled with its six chairs close to the rear entrance door. Close to the open staircase Shelby found a small wet bar that was well-stocked with liquor and beer. Shelby took one of the beers out of the refrigerator, walked down the hall past the kitchen and located an office and half bath. She then climbed the stairs to an open sitting room and double doors that opened up to the biggest master suite she'd ever seen.

Still sipping on her beer, she went through another smaller set of double doors that opened up to a huge bathroom. It contained a counter with double sinks, a double tiled shower, and a whirlpool tub. It had soft bath towels and candles placed around the whirlpool that Shelby knew she would enjoy lighting while taking a long leisurely bath later on in the evening. She flipped on the light to the walk-in closet and saw it was huge.

She walked out onto the balcony feeling totally awed as she took in a deep breath of the pine smell that lingered in the evening air. "This is going to be the most wonderful place to spend time getting my life back on track with Jack."

CHAPTER TWENTY-FOUR

Shelby had been in Gunnison less than a week when Jack decided he missed his wife and didn't want to be away from her for much longer. He'd been in contact with her every day, several times a day, and she kept him informed of everything that she was doing. She'd enthusiastically told him how much she loved the area, describing every activity to him in detail—ones she hoped they could enjoy together, including walks in the woods and wine dinners on the patio. Her job at the yard didn't take up much of her day since it was mostly answering the phone and waiting for things to be delivered. She knew they would have plenty of time to enjoy each other when he was able to come to Gunnison.

Jack was excited about spending time with Shelby. He couldn't wait to get there and see everything she'd been talking about over the phone. "I'll be there in a few days," he told her on their last call.

"Any word on whether they have located Betty?" she asked.

"Nope. Haven't heard a thing from Silverman, Stevenson, or Petersen, but that really isn't surprising."

"Yeah, well, it's obvious they haven't a clue about how to catch her."

"Since they haven't seen her around here they think maybe she's gone underground again until she thinks the heat is off."

Shelby was frustrated. "I guess, but I sure wish they would find her."

"Yeah. Me too, honey. They will. It just might take some time."

"I guess it won't matter when you get up here and we can spend time together."

"That's just what I was thinking. I think I will be able to leave on Saturday and be there with you on Sunday."

◊◊◊

Fiddler was making great improvements. A week after he had been brought to the hospital, his nurse entered his room with the information she had discovered about him on the computer. She'd been making notes every day of the things that Fiddler was remembering and just as the doctor had predicted, his memory was slowly coming back.

The nurse opened his curtains and then began taking his vitals. "So, how are we today, Kenny?"

"Good, Nurse Roxanne. How are you today?"

"Having a great day. Doing what I do best—taking care of my patients."

"Well, you've taken good care of me."

The nurse finished with the vitals and was writing in his chart. "Thank you. How's the memory today?"

Fiddler began to run down some of the things he was remembering but most of it was information from when he was a youngster. The nurse recorded the information in his chart and then closed it. "Well, sounds like it's coming back, but the doctor wants to see what the brain looks like, big guy. I have you scheduled for an MRI today. Betty the orderly will be here in a little while to take you downstairs for that."

Fiddler gasped.

The nurse looked at her patient and frowned. "Kenny, what's wrong?"

Fiddler stared at the wall as if his eyes were going to burn a hole in it.

"Kenny?" The nurse rubbed the top of her patient's hand. "Are you okay?"

Fiddler was angry as he pulled his hand away and got out of bed. "That bitch! She drugged me at dinner on the river and then left me to die in that building. Where the hell is my truck?"

The nurse quickly pushed the emergency call button and several other nurses and male attendants came to Fiddler's room. Nurse Roxanne tried to calm Fiddler as the other nurses and attendants entered the room. "Kenny, who are you talking about? Come sit back down and let's talk about it. I'll call the doctor and you can tell him everything."

Fiddler was agitated as he looked out the window. "That bitch Betty told me she loved me. I reminded her of her father. How could she do this to me? Where is my truck?"

Fiddler was emotional now as the memories began to flood back. He turned toward the nurse and was shocked to see the barrage of nursing staff in his room. He backed away slightly, showing Nurse Roxanne that perhaps she'd overreacted to his anger outburst.

"It's okay, Kenny. They just came to see if you're okay." The nurse motioned for the nursing staff to step back out of the room. All but the male attendants complied. "Come on, Kenny. Lay back down and let's talk about what you are remembering."

Fiddler slowly moved toward his bed and put his head on the pillow. The male attendants left after Nurse Roxanne assured them that she was fine.

"Okay, Kenny. Tell me everything you remember. Tell me what I said that brought all those memories flowing back."

Fiddler began from the beginning and told the nurse everything that he remembered before he lost complete consciousness. "Betty Burton. That was her name. She took my truck and almost killed me. I can't believe I trusted her."

Nurse Roxanne was shocked when Fiddler finally told her the name of the "bitch" he'd referred to earlier. "Did you say Betty Burton?"

Fiddler nodded. "Yes, Betty Burton. Why?"

The nurse didn't want to upset her patient any further until she could confirm her recollection from the news she remembered hearing yesterday. "Nothing, Kenny. Just wanted to make sure I had the name correct."

"Please, call me Fiddler." Fiddler then continued with details as the nurse scribbled down notes.

◊◊◊

Spending her time going from exit to exit and truck stop to truck stop in and around Odessa was frustrating. Betty had tried a couple of times to get back to the Mathews house to check if Shelby was still around, but the incident at the construction site and not knowing if there was a detail still on Shelby made her cautious. She was also down to just a couple of dollars in cash and would soon need to put fuel in Fiddler's truck. Although she hated the thought of it, she knew she was probably going to need to hook up with some johns to get the money she needed to pursue Shelby.

The color and cut she had received thanks to Fiddler's generosity had held up well and she still had Tammy's stylish cashmere coat. She had lifted some frilly black panties, a matching bra, and two crotch-less teddies from Joni, hoping she would not need to use them, but was glad she had thought to nab them. She pulled into a truck stop around Midland and parked in the back. Truck stop culture was consistent no matter the state or town. Truckers knew exactly what areas to go to score drugs or a hooker. Betty looked so much better than the average lizard that she not only would get more money, she was going to get fed too, maybe even get set up in a motel room for a few nights. The other advantage was that the cops were looking for a female trucker and not a hooker.

Her first John was a young trucker from Tulsa named Evan. The young man was no more than twenty-five years old and still had the acned complexion of a sixteen-year-old. He was scrawny and definitely inexperienced. The only good thing is that he didn't argue about her price. She did the deed in his truck and the anxious young man was finished in no time. Just being with the Okie infuriated Betty and she felt a burning desire to strangle him. The urge to kill was so much a part of Betty's nature that she had to remind herself of her objective: killing Shelby. She was out of the guy's truck before his pants were pulled up.

Although she made good money in a matter of hours with each successive trick, her urge to kill the men she was with became stronger and stronger. By the third day, she was itching to track Shelby down before she took her rage out on some unsuspecting horny trucker.

She changed back into blue jeans, a sweatshirt, and boots and put her hair up under a ball cap. She fueled up Fiddler's truck and headed back to Odessa. Hopefully, she would get a chance to see what was going on at Shelby's house. She pulled into the truck stop near Exit 115 and parked around the back. As she went through the parking lot to the store, she surveyed the parking lot, hoping to see a pickup truck or van she could "borrow" for a few hours to drive over to Shelby's neighborhood.

She went into the store to get coffee and some breakfast. As she approached the counter to pay, she saw her mug shot from Utah on the front page of the *Odessa American*. The headline read, "Feds Launch Nationwide Search for Truck Stop Killer." She pulled the bill of her cap lower and tried to remain discrete. Betty did not realize anyone was behind her in line until she heard the voices.

"So this new gig sounds pretty sweet."

"Yeah, Jayne Edwards says everything is going to be state of the art. You should contact her. She's offering drivers a nice signing bonus. Barbie is already up there setting things up for Jayne."

"I don't know. Colorado? I'm not sure my wife would ever leave Texas."

"Montrose is a pretty nice area, and it pays well. Everyone has their price."

Betty took her change from the cashier, slipped it into her coat pocket and slipped out the door of the store without a word. *I'll be damned. Shelby is in Colorado*, she thought.

◊◊◊

Jack hated how quiet his house had become. Although Steven had been shaken up from discovering Tammy's body, he was still determined to move out. He had moved in with his girlfriend until he could find his own apartment. He wanted to give his parents privacy. Jack desperately missed Shelby. He considered going to the bar to play some pool with his buddies, but if Shelby got word he was over there, he could lose any modicum of trust he had gained back from her. He didn't want to go to the bar. He wanted to go Colorado.

He decided he would go into work, give his secretary a detailed to-do list and let Shelby know he was headed her way. He poured himself a cup of coffee and went to the front porch to fetch the newspaper. He was furious when he saw the front page with Betty's picture and the headline about the manhunt. He picked up the phone and dialed a now-familiar number. "Agent Silverman, this is Jack Mathews," he said. "Who the hell thought it was a good idea to put Betty's picture on the front page of the paper? Whatever happened to the element of surprise?"

"It wasn't us, Jack. Your paper must have picked it up from the wire service. A trucker in Maryland was left for dead in a warehouse. He's named Betty Burton as the perpetrator. The press out there must have gotten wind of it."

"Well, we know she isn't in Maryland. Have your guys learned anything?"

"We figured that close call at the tracks probably sent her underground. Betty is gutsy though. She has been profiled as a serial killer. She'll be more careful and less exposed but not completely withdrawn. She's has an appetite for killing."

"You don't have to tell me. You do realize she is fixated on Shelby."

"We know. Have you had any sense she's been watching your house?"

"Well, it's hard to say if she's been around. That's supposed to be your job. What if she finds out that Shelby isn't here or figures out where she is?"

Silverman could tell Jack was anxious. "I'm sure she doesn't know where Shelby is, Jack. But you and Shelby need to continue to be diligent in watching out for her."

"I'm leaving in the morning to go to Colorado and spend a couple weeks with Shelby. How long do you think it will take the FBI to find Betty? I don't want Shelby to have to stay in hiding forever."

"We don't either. I think it's a good idea that you're going to be with her. Continue to stay in touch with me. If something doesn't look right, don't hesitate to call the police. We'll make sure the Colorado State Troopers are briefed."

◊◊◊

Fiddler had spent a good portion of the day talking with his Roxanne. Getting his memory back was helping the healing process, but he still felt like a fool for having allowed himself to be taken in by Betty. She'd taken his truck, his money, his pride, and his trust. Fiddler couldn't believe he'd been fooled so easily. He was coming to terms with his physical trauma, but mentally, he was just pissed off. He wanted his truck back and he wanted to hurt Betty like she'd hurt him.

Roxanne walked into Fiddler's room just as he was about to fall asleep. "Hey, Kenny. I'm sorry to bother you and I won't stay long, but I thought maybe you would like to know what I've learned about your friend Betty."

Fiddler sat up on his bed as she sat down in the chair next to it. "What did you find out?" Fiddler was impressed by her personal interest in his case. He knew she was doing more investigation than the police were.

"Well, I knew that I had heard that name somewhere before and then it came to me. I had heard her name on the news. So I looked it up and it seems that your little girlfriend is wanted in connection with several murders and an attempted murder of some lady from Texas."

Fiddler's eyes widened. "Oh, wonderful. I was falling in love with a killer."

Roxanne rested her hand gently on his arm. "I'm sorry that she hurt you so badly, Kenny. But you can take comfort in the fact that apparently she loved you in some sick way, too. She didn't kill you like she did the other people who came into contact with her."

"Yeah, I guess, but what caused her to turn on me?"

"Maybe she saw the news reports somewhere and she was afraid you would see them and figure out who she was?"

"Yeah, maybe. Or maybe she's just a total wacko and I was too stupid to realize it."

"I don't believe that, Kenny. You're just a nice guy who lost his heart to someone he just didn't know very well."

"Thanks. But what now?"

"Well, I've been thinking I know you have talked some to the police. But I think you should follow up with them. Tell them everything you've been remembering. They might be able to find your truck and maybe your information will help them find Betty. You know, the other thing you can do is talk to the press."

"I don't want the media showing me as an idiot."

"Don't feel that way, Fiddler. She's the one who was the fool." Roxanne got up and went toward the door.

Fiddler put his head on his pillow.

"I'll see you tomorrow, Fiddler. You get some rest."

"She called me Fiddler," he grinned, before he drifted off to sleep.

◊◊◊

Jack's cell phone rang as he was packing to go to Colorado. "Hello, this is Jack Mathews." Jack listened to what the caller wanted. "There isn't someone else who can handle this? I'm supposed to start vacation in the morning." Jack wasn't happy. He threw the shirt in his hand into his suitcase. "Fine," he spit out. "I'll go to the location, but I'm only staying there until you can find someone to relieve me." Jack was pissed. "Shit, now I have to tell Shelby I won't be there for a few days."

Jack called Shelby. "Hey, sugar. I got some bad news. They just called me and there's a mess on one of my wells that I have to make sure gets fixed before I leave. It's going to be a few days before I get there."

"Oh, well, I guess I'll have to just keep this bed nice and warm for you then." Shelby giggled. "It's okay, sweetheart."

"You're not upset?"

"Well, it's not the news I wanted to hear, but I know you have a company to run. I accept that things are going to happen with that kind of responsibility."

"Thank you for being so understanding. I'll call you tomorrow and let you know how things are going."

"Okay, talk to you tomorrow."

Jack hung the phone up and immediately called Silverman. "I just wanted to let you know that there has been a change of plans. I have to go take care of a well in the Gulf, so I won't be leaving for Colorado for a few more days."

"Call Stevenson. Ask him if his buddy will go check on Shelby on a regular basis," Silverman suggested.

"I will, but he's just one guy."

"I'll see if there is any way we can arrange for a detail."

"Thanks."

"How's Shelby doing?"

"She's doing well, and she is in good spirits. She feels safe because Betty doesn't know where she is…and I'm going to do everything in my power to keep it that way."

"Hopefully, we can keep her protected, too."

"Okay. Let me know if you find Betty."

"You know we will."

◊◊◊

After Jack finished with the emergency in the Gulf, he flew back to Odessa. He stopped by his office to drop off some paperwork on the well and then went by his house to get the bags he'd packed for Colorado. He was on the road before noon. He called Shelby to let her know he was on his way.

CHAPTER TWENTY-FIVE

Betty got in Fiddler's truck, pulled out of the truck stop, and headed north. She turned on the CB to listen for any chatter. What she heard disturbed her.

"River Rat here. Ya'll hear about that trucker they found in Maryland? Think he may be a victim of the Truck Stop Murderer?"

"Is it true they think the killer is a gal?" Bat Boy asked.

"That's what they're saying. Gotta be one cold-hearted bitch."

Pacman joined in the conversation, "Rumor is it's that gal they let out of prison in Utah."

"That was the bitch who tried to kill Barbie," Slick Stick said. "I was there and helped save her."

Why is everyone on that bitch Shelby's side? That woman has ruined my life and she has to pay for it. Betty turned off the radio and continued north on the highway. She plotted how she was going to kill Shelby, and if she got the opportunity, Jack as well. She moved down the road, lost in her thoughts.

"Shit," she said when she heard the siren and looked in the rearview mirror and saw the flashing lights. Betty pulled over and waited for the officer to come to her door.

"May I see your CDL and registration please?"

"Sure," Betty said, flashing the cop a friendly smile. She turned in her seat and made a show of looking for her purse. "Oh, no," she squealed. "Oh, no!"

"Is there a problem, ma'am?"

"Yes, Officer…" she looked at his badge. "…Officer Carlisle. My purse isn't here. I must have left it in my storage unit. I had no business stopping there…I'm on the clock and scheduled to make a delivery…I'm already running late…my sister needed a car seat for her baby and…now…stopped for speeding…I'm going to get fired," she moaned.

"Look, ma'am. I'd let you off with a warning, but I can't let you drive without a license. Where is this storage unit?"

"Two miles back." Betty had remembered seeing the sign for climate-controlled units just after she turned off the radio.

"Tell you what," Carlisle said. "I'll follow you back over there. You get your purse, show me the documents, and I'll send you on your way."

"You would do that for me? Oh, Officer Carlisle, thank you so much."

Betty watched in her rearview mirror as Carlisle returned to his patrol car, got in, and flashed his lights that he was ready to go. At first, she thought about just taking off, but knew he would get pissed and pursue her. She had another idea, and it was just what she needed.

Betty made a U-turn and headed back to the storage units. The cop was not far behind her rear bumper. She pulled into the facility and was relieved that the gate was open, but it was clear that her rig would not make it down the narrow passages between the units. She pulled up in front of the office, parked, reached into the glove compartment for something, which she slipped into her pocket, and got out of her truck.

She began to walk toward the patrol car when the storage facility's manager came out of the office.

"What's happening here?" he asked.

"Oh, I'm sorry," Betty said. "That policeman is my husband. I need to get him some things for our kids. I have a long distance haul."

"Okay," the manager said, relieved, and returned to his office.

Betty moved over to the cop who was talking into the radio on his shoulder. He lowered the window as she approached. She leaned in the window and said, "Officer Carlisle, my unit is two aisles down, all the way in the back."

"Get in," he said, cocking his head toward the passenger door.

Betty got in the car and they moved to the end of the units and turned down the rows. "All the way to the end," she said. He parked in front of the unit.

"Let me get my key," Betty said, reaching into her pocket with her gloved hand. She grabbed the screwdriver and in one swift move, plunged it into his neck, puncturing the carotid artery. Blood gurgled from his lips, as bodily fluids released themselves. His head flopped forward onto the steering wheel.

All the tension that had been pent up inside of her was released with the man's death and she felt a sense of euphoria. She put the screwdriver back into her pocket. She got out of the car, opened the back door, and pulled out the officer's jacket. She used the fabric to wipe down the passenger seat and anything else she might have touched. She heard the radio on his shoulder crackle and a voice began to speak. Using the jacket, she pushed the body back against the seat, grabbed the radio microphone off the officer's shoulder and ripped out the wires. Then she grabbed the cop's gun from its holster. "This will come in handy," she said and shoved it into the left side pocket of her coat. She rolled up the officer's jacket and stuffed it under her arm. Then she walked back to her truck.

As she walked back to Fiddler's truck, she walked passed the office door and waved at the manager who, she could see through the window, was talking on the phone.

◊◊◊

The call came into the Odessa Police Department an hour later. When the actual renter of the unit, a forty-something tractor mechanic, went to retrieve some parts, he saw the stalled patrol car blocking access to the door. He cautiously approached the vehicle and immediately threw up when he saw the dead, blood-soaked police officer, his eyes still open.

Detective Stevenson rolled up to the crime scene accompanied by three patrol cars, the crime scene unit, and an ambulance. While Carlisle's body was loaded into the ambulance, Stevenson interviewed the distraught office manager. "She told me the policeman was her husband."

"She?"

"Yes, the lady who was driving the big truck."

"She was in a big truck? Can you describe her?"

Some of the description didn't match what Stevenson knew about Betty and he was having trouble understanding the Indian man's thick accent. He

210

took out his cell phone and called the station, "Get a sketch artist over here immediately." He then joined the crime scene techs to get briefed on the gruesome scene in and around the patrol car.

It took another hour for the crime scene to be photographed and processed and the artist renderings to be completed. Stevenson did not even need the face recognition software to know the pencil sketch of the woman was Betty Burton. He sent out the updated picture of the woman for the BOLO alert and then placed a call to Agent Silverman.

"I sure hope she isn't headed to Colorado," Silverman said.

"Who would have tipped her off as to where Shelby is now?"

"I don't know. Jack's on his way there now. He's not going to be happy about this latest development. How could Betty be in Odessa and no one knew?"

"What are you suggesting?"

"I'm not suggesting anything. I just know if you want to find someone you have to look. I've been down here in Odessa from my department in L.A. for several weeks now. I might as well transfer to this department. All I see is that we aren't any closer to finding Betty now than we were when I was first assigned to this task force."

"Agent Silverman, this is a relatively small police force with limited resources. Besides, it's the FBI who is supposed to thwart terrorists."

"Terrorism. That's quite a leap."

"You can't deny that Betty is terrorizing not only Shelby and Jack Mathews, but she is a threat to anyone who crosses her."

"I know. That's why I spend every free moment I have working on this case. We need to get the task force together again and decide what to do next."

"We don't have time for all that, especially if Betty has found out where Shelby might be hiding."

"You saw the updated BOLO, right?"

"Yeah."

"Well, here's something else I'll get out on the wire. Remember that trucker they found in Maryland?"

"Yeah."

"Looks like she's driving his truck."

◊◊◊

Jack was exhausted when he finally drove into Gunnison. He called Shelby to find out how to get to the cabin. "Hey, sweetie. I'm in downtown Gunnison. Come get me."

"I'll be right there, darling. Where are you?"

"Right in the middle of all these little stores."

Shelby laughed. "Cute, huh?"

CHAPTER TWENTY-SIX

Unbeknownst to Jack or Shelby, Betty was not far behind him. When she crossed into Colorado, she made a brief stop at a truck stop to use the last of her cash for fuel and something to eat. She approached the counter with her coffee and sandwich.

"Anything else?" the cashier asked.

"Yeah. This newspaper."

Betty took her food and paper back to the truck. She fueled up and found a spot as far to the back of the truck stop as possible. She turned to the classified section of the paper as she ate her sandwich. As she'd expected, there was a help wanted ad for truckers. The address for Jayne's new yard was listed. She read the listing carefully and learned not only the premium Jayne was paying for drivers, but how to access temporary housing in Gunnison.

She patted her hand against the hard steel of the gun in her pocket and then went into the sleeper for a good night's rest before getting to Shelby.

◊◊◊

"So, Fiddler. How are you feeling today?" Nurse Roxanne asked as she stepped into the room. The patient had been moved from ICU to a regular room. The administration had originally assigned him to a semi-private room, but Roxanne had been able to arrange a private room for him.

Fiddler smiled at her. "Better, but I think I need to get out of here."

"Well, the doctor thinks you still have some healing to do. I'm glad to hear you talked with the police yesterday."

"Yeah. They're going to put an APB out on my truck. I talked to my company and they said I can drive again as soon as I get a medical release.

They're going to want their own doctors to examine me. But I can't do any-thing until they find my truck."

"I'm sure they will. You'll be a hero when they find that woman."

"I hope they put a needle in her arm."

"You're not the only one. Now let's check your vitals."

◊◊◊

Betty entered Gunnison and was nauseated by the cuteness. "Oh my God, what a sweet little town. I think I'll vomit now." She searched the side streets but she found nothing that appeared to be sufficient for what she needed. She left the town limits and started looking in the wooded areas for something more suitable.

Frustration was beginning to overtake Betty as she worked her way up and down the little country roads. "This is ridiculous!" she said as she peered out the window, looking for a good spot to hide the truck. "Who in their right mind would live in a stupid, dumpy, little piece-of-crap town like this?"

She was beginning to think she was going to have to find another town for a hideout, when she saw it—a little run-down shack in the trees off the main road about three-tenths of a mile. She stopped and pulled the truck off the side of the main road. There was a two-wheel path that led to the shack, but a cattle guard gate blocked it. The road was overgrown with weeds and grass. Trees were thick with broken branches laying everywhere.

Betty got out of her truck and walked to the cattle guard gate. She looked over the cattle guard and tried to move the bar that blocked the entrance off to the side. Rust had accumulated over years of non-use and the bar would not budge. Betty struggled with it until her anger kicked in. She took the gun out of her pocket and slammed the butt of it against the rust, cursing with each blow. Exhausted, she shoved the gun back into her pocket and then shoved the bar with all her might. The bar broke at the turn end and landed within half an inch of Betty's foot. "Dammit!" she shouted. She did her best to muscle the bar out of the way of the road.

Betty dusted off her jeans and walked down the two-wheel path to the shack that was hidden in the trees. The road seemed strong enough to handle her big truck, but she wasn't sure where she was going to park it once she got it on the road. There was a lot of tree cover but not until she got closer to the shack. Once she reached the shack, Betty was surprised to find a rather large clearing to the north of it. It appeared that at one time there might have been a barn or another large building next to the shack, but it had either been burned down or torn down. There was junk everywhere and the shack had more holes in it than a spaghetti strainer. At least it was secluded. She decided she'd stay in the truck and use the nearby trees for cover.

Betty removed several pieces of junk from the spot she'd decided to park her truck. Then she walked back down the path toward the main road. She backed her truck up and then positioned it for a really wide turn since the cattle guard was narrow. She wasn't concerned with destroying the cattle guard, but knew that any sharp metal would damage her tires. It took several back and forth tries to get the rig and trailer through the gate.

Once she'd got the truck through the cattle guard, she moved it without stopping up on the overgrown two-wheel road. She was afraid if she moved too slowly or stopped she might get the truck stuck. As soon as she reached the shack, she turned the truck and trailer around in the open area. She parked the truck behind the shack in an attempt to conceal it from view of the main road as much as possible. Betty backed the truck into position before blowing the air brakes. She got out of the truck and dollied the trailer down after removing the airlines. She pulled the truck away from the trailer before turning the truck off. It wasn't late, but she was tired and she wanted time early in the morning before it got light to find a smaller vehicle and some money.

◊◊◊

Jack was exhausted when he made it to the cabin. Shelby let him sleep in and went to the office for a couple of hours. She returned around one o'clock and pulled her company vehicle into the garage next to Jack's truck. She walked quietly into the cabin and gently opened the master bedroom door to check on Jack. He was no longer in bed. He was in the shower. She decided that this would be a wonderful time to make her husband feel welcome and left a trail of her clothes on the way to the shower. "Hey, big guy. Got room for me?"

Jack quickly took his naked wife in his arms under the water and kissed her. "Always!"

Shelby and Jack spent the rest of the day in the cabin. Shelby cooked and they had dinner on the patio. After they ate, Jack poured her some more wine and stoked the fire pit he'd started earlier. They sat in the moonlight under the stars, taking in the deep smell of pine in the air. The crackle of the fire was the only sound that seemed to break through the quiet serenity of the night. "This is a beautiful place, Shelby. I could get used to being up here with you."

"Yes, I like it, too," she said. She rested her head on his shoulder. "But don't forget, it is going to start getting pretty cold in the next couple of weeks. I hope they find Betty soon. I really don't think I'm going to like having to fight the snow and ice on that highway to work."

"Come on, baby. You're a truck driver. You know you can handle weathered roads."

"Handle them, maybe. But like them? No way."

◊◊◊

Betty woke up at 5:00 a.m. having to pee. She got out of the truck and looked for a place among the trees to relieve herself. As she was pulling up her jeans and zipping them up her eyes squinted to a sight in the distance—smoke. It was thin and curled before evaporating in the darkness. Betty went back to the truck and pulled out a flashlight. She walked back to the two-wheel road and pointed the beam in the direction she thought she saw the smoke. She looked up; there it was again. She inhaled and mixed with the scent of pine was the undeniable aroma of a fireplace.

She walked for almost a half-mile when she noticed a little white house nestled all by itself among some trees. As quiet as possible, Betty snuck close to the house and looked through the windows. She caught a glimpse of someone sleeping in a bed, but there didn't appear to be anyone else around. She moved around to the back of the house, hoping the snapping of the twigs and leaves beneath her feet would not wake the sleeper. When she reached the left side of the cottage, she made her way through a carport, which led her to the back door. In the carport was an old dusty four-door Ford Fairlane. Next to the old Ford was a smaller Toyota pickup. The pickup appeared a few years newer and Betty hoped it was usable. Next to the carport was a rickety storage shed.

She tried the back door to the little house and the knob turned in her fingers. She tiptoed through the kitchen, watching each step as she tried not to alert the sleeper from a loose or squeaky floorboard. Betty moved methodically through the house, making sure there was indeed only one person inside. She stepped momentarily into the living room and snatched a decorative pillow off of the sofa.

After confirming that the person sleeping was the lone inhabitant, Betty slithered along the wall in the hallway to the room with the unsuspecting victim. She moved to the subject on the bed. Betty took the sofa pillow and placed it over the head of the elderly woman in the bed.

The gray-headed woman was startled awake and she jerked and clawed in vain against her attacker's force. Betty held the pillow in place until the woman stopped moving. She then dropped the pillow and wrapped her hands around the old woman's neck saying as she squeezed, "Sorry about that, Grandma, but I need to borrow your ride and some cash."

Betty left the woman on the bed and pulled the covers up around her, up to her neck. The corpse looked like a sleeping woman. She then went to the kitchen. She was exhilarated, but starving. She went into the kitchen, opened the refrigerator and took out some bacon and eggs. She made herself breakfast and coffee and sat at the table, planning her next move. She looked around the kitchen and saw the woman's purse sitting on the counter next to the back door. She snatched it up and emptied the contents onto the table. The wallet contained seventy-five dollars in cash, two dollars and fifty cents in change, her driver's license and a bank debit card. She looked at the driver's license. The late Gladys Walker was eighty-five years old. She memorized the date of birth, fairly confident she knew what the woman had chosen for her pin number.

With money in her pocket and food in her stomach, Betty knew what she was going to do next—she was going to move into this house.

Betty decided to take the woman out of the house and put her body in the storage building. She went back to the bedroom and snatched the covers off the still-warm body. The lady probably didn't even weigh ninety pounds. Betty bent over, reached under Gladys's body, and tossed her over her shoulder. When she stepped outside a pink glow appeared on the horizon. She wanted to get her truck to her new hiding place before the sun was completely up.

Betty concocted a scenario in case anyone came by after she moved in. She would tell them that she was Gladys's niece. Gladys was not feeling well and she had come to Colorado to take care of her.

Betty walked back to the shack to get Fiddler's truck. She brought it back to the house and parked it in plain sight. She'd left the trailer back at the shack, since it was too difficult to get down the two-wheel road.

She was content. She had a television, food, and a bathroom. As long as no one got too nosy or someone showed up that knew too much about the woman, Betty would be able to utilize this place until she could get to Shelby.

◊◊◊

While Shelby spent the morning again in the office in Montrose, Jack spent his time checking out the woods and a small stream that ran behind the cabin. They had made plans to meet in Gunnison for lunch and do a little shopping before heading out on a bike ride through the country. Then they were going to go back to town and enjoy an evening at the local pub.

Jack took the bicycles that were hanging in the garage down and dusted them off. He oiled the chains and checked the tires to make sure they were aired up, and then put them in the back of his pickup. He went up the stairs to the bathroom to take a shower and wait for Shelby to call.

He thought about checking in with Agent Silverman, but decided to put it off. He and Shelby were enjoying their time together and he did not want to do anything to spoil the mood. He showered and dressed and met Shelby in town for lunch.

"How was your morning?" Shelby asked.

"It was okay. But it would have been better with you. Hey, maybe I can go with you to your office tomorrow. I'd like to see Jayne's yard."

"That's a great idea. I don't plan on being there very long tomorrow. Then maybe we can go to Tin Cup Lake and go fishing or rent a boat and catch some sun."

"That sounds like a wonderful idea."

◊◊◊

Betty drove through Gunnison in Gladys's Toyota pickup. She had the window rolled down and her elbow rested on the door as she smoked a cigarette. *Oh my God! Little House on the Prairie reincarnated into the modern era—yuck!* she thought.

Betty looked at all the vehicles parked along the street and finally found a parking spot near a café. She went in, found a seat near the window, and ordered a cup of coffee. As Betty sat there, she sipped coffee and peered out the window, watching people stroll up and down the main street. Betty knew that Shelby and Jack would eventually find their way into town for shopping or food. She just had to wait.

Meanwhile, Jack and Shelby ate their lunch and then walked hand in hand out the door and down the street. "Come on, Jack. I want to show you this little town. It is so cute. It takes you back in time to when people owned their own businesses instead of big corporate chain stores."

"I want to see it all, but don't forget I brought the bikes with me if you still want to go for a ride on the trails."

"First let's shop."

Shelby began at the first store on the main street and took Jack through every store that faced the street. They spent most of the afternoon shopping and talking to the local people. Jack was becoming tired with the shopping. As they approached where his pickup was parked, he said, "Come on, baby. Let's go for a bike ride."

Shelby heard the plea for relief in her husband's voice. "All right, sugar. Let's go biking." Jack unlocked his pickup and put Shelby's packages in the back seat.

Betty couldn't believe her luck as she watched a man unlock the passenger door of his pickup and help a lady climb in. He then went to the driver's side of the truck. "Got you, Shelby!" Betty threw three dollars on the table and left the café in a hurry. She almost knocked over a woman and her child coming into the café in her hasty retreat.

"Watch out!" the woman said, pulling the little girl close. "You're rude."

Betty ignored the comment as she darted toward the Toyota while at the same time keeping tabs on the direction Shelby and Jack were traveling.

"So where we going?" Jack asked.

Shelby pointed to the west. "Just stay on Highway 50. I saw a couple of places that I think we will be able to ride a few miles up into the mountains toward Montrose from some spots there."

Shelby and Jack stopped several miles from Gunnison where there was a dirt cutout for parking and a path that led toward the mountains. Jack took the bikes out of the back of his truck while Shelby tied her hair back. "Okay, babe. Here's your helmet." Shelby took her bike off the kickstand.

"I'm not wearing that silly thing. I want to feel the wind in my hair." Jack laughed as he tossed the helmets into the back of the pickup. Then he mounted his bike and the couple started following the path.

"If you wanted to feel the wind in your hair you should have brought the Harley," Shelby said, giggling.

"Oh, wow. I didn't even think about bringing the motorcycle," said Jack. "Man, that would have been a blast up here."

Betty was able to keep up her tail on Jack and Shelby. She drove past the cutoff to avoid any suspicion. After going down the road a few miles, Betty turned the pickup around and headed back to where the couple had unloaded their bikes. Betty parked her truck at a scenic overlook and got out. She walked across the highway and came in behind the couple through the trees. She tried to keep up with them, but as they pedaled, they were too fast for her to stay close. Betty bent over and grabbed her knees while she tried to catch her breath. "I need to quit smoking," she panted.

Betty wandered through the woods for a couple of hours. "God, I know I came this way." She was beginning to think she was lost. "Where the hell am I?" Betty continued to move in the direction she thought she'd come from, but everything looked the same. In every direction she turned, all she saw was more and more trees. Then she heard voices coming toward her. "Come on, slow poke! I'll beat you back to the truck."

Shelby grinned as she and Jack raced back to the truck. Jack was in front of Shelby, but Shelby was closing in fast. "Cheater! You had a head start."

Jack pedaled and laughed as he maneuvered his bike toward the main road through the trees. "Slow poke! We got about three more miles and then we'll be back to the truck. You're going to lose."

Shelby did her best to keep up, but Jack not only had a head start, his legs were stronger. He teased his wife and rode in circles on the forest path, totally unaware of the predator who was watching them.

"You don't play fair," Shelby yelled.

Betty got her bearings and began walking back toward the highway. She knew she wasn't going to get there before they would. She began to run. If she could get there in a hurry she might have an even better chance at getting to Jack and Shelby while they were putting their bikes in the back of the truck.

Breathing hard, she made it back to the main road and found a spot near where the Mathewses had parked. Betty forced herself to slow her breathing and watched as the Shelby and Jack loaded their bikes into the back of the pickup. Seeing her opening, she felt around in the pocket of her jacket for the pistol she'd taken off the cop.

She anxiously patted at all her pockets. "SHIT, SHIT, SHIT!" she whispered. "It's got to be in the truck." Unable to locate the gun she assumed she'd been carrying, she quietly watched as the Mathewses got into their pickup, backed out of the parking spot and headed back to the road. They were gone. "Dammit! Right there!" she said. Betty moved from her hiding spot and placed herself in the exact spot Shelby had been. "You bitch, you were right here!"

Betty stomped her feet on the ground like a child having a tantrum.

◊◊◊

Shelby and Jack laughed with each other as they drove back to Gunnison. They had decided that they were going to have dinner and drinks at a local pub before they returned to the cabin. Jack pulled the pickup into a parking space. He reached over and kissed Shelby. "Can I buy you dinner and drinks, my lady?"

"Yes, of course, sir. But please take advantage of me if I drink too much."

Jack and Shelby kissed again before getting out of the pickup. "You can count on it." The two got out of the pickup and walked to the pub.

Betty pulled into Gunnison. She drove down the main street still pissed that she'd missed her opportunity. She turned her head to the right and there it was: Jack's pickup. Betty laughed to herself as she made the block. "I won't lose you again, little Miss Barbie."

CHAPTER TWENTY-SEVEN

Jack and Shelby woke to the sun pouring through the windows of the master bedroom. Shelby was still struggling with not wanting to get up when Jack rolled her over on her back and kissed her naked body from head to toe. She giggled and squirmed as Jack tickled and kissed his way to her toes. "Jack, you're so bad," she said. Jack continued with his seduction until Shelby willingly gave in to her husband. "You took advantage of me last night while I was under the influence and now you want to take me again. You're good."

Jack tickled his wife as he came out from under the covers. "I thought you just said I was bad?"

Shelby's laughter faded away under the passionate kisses and touches from her husband as he moved his naked body between her naked legs.

After showering together and then having breakfast, Shelby took Jack to Montrose. She drove in through the security gate and parked outside the office building. "Come on in, baby. Let me show you where I work now."

Jack got out of Shelby's company truck and followed her to the door. While Shelby was trying to unlock the door, Jack played with Shelby's butt and nibbled on her neck from behind. Shelby giggled. "Jack, didn't you get enough this morning?"

Jack turned Shelby around and kissed her neck and then her lips. As the door swung open Shelby dropped her keys and purse. Jack pinned Shelby to the door. "Never enough, baby. Never enough."

"Don't you think I should do what I came to do this morning so you can take me back to the cabin?"

Jack continued to kiss and tease his wife while she giggled.

"Stop it, Jack. Not here. There's a delivery due any moment."

"Okay, I'll let you go for now but you're mine tonight."

Shelby laughed. "You're an animal. Grrrr…"

◊◊◊

Betty had followed the Mathewses back to their cabin and then drove to Gladys's house. She knew that she had Shelby and Jack where she wanted them—all she had to do was come up with a foolproof plan to get rid of them. She wanted something that would ensure that Shelby would be gone forever. Betty sat at the little round table in the kitchen, eating the old lady's cereal as she devised her plan.

After she finished eating, Betty decided to go through the old woman's house one more time. As she was going through the cabinets and drawers, there was a knock at the door. Betty backed up against the wall in the kitchen near the back door. She'd grabbed her gun off the table and moved to the wall. She put the gun to her side and slightly moved the curtain that covered the back door glass window. There was another knock at the door. "Gladys, it's Rosie. Gladys? Are you home?"

Betty put the gun in the back of her pants, deciding that the only way to get rid of the old bag was to deal with her. Betty gently opened the door.

The old woman looked at Betty with surprise and suspicion.

"Can I help you?"

The woman tried to force her way into the house passed Betty. Betty blocked her. "I'm Rosie, Gladys's friend. Who are you?" she asked, still trying to get passed Betty. The woman tried to see inside the house over Betty.

"I'm Angie, Gladys's niece. I'm just here for a couple days. Visiting."

The woman narrowed her eyes in suspicion. "I don't remember her ever telling me about a niece named Angie. Where is Gladys?"

Betty pointed toward the bedroom. "Aunt Gladys is still resting. She wasn't feeling too well this morning. In fact, I was just about to go into town for some medication to help her feel better. I guess I kept her out too late last night when I took her to dinner."

Rosie's shoulders relaxed slightly. "Well, tell her I'm sorry she's feeling bad. And tell her I missed her at our card night over at Sid's."

"Sure, I'll let her know when she gets up."

The woman turned around to go and noticed Betty's big truck parked on the other side of the carport. "Is that your big truck?"

"Yes," Betty said with pride. "It's a new profession for me. I had a delivery in Aurora and thought I'd stop by and visit with Aunt Gladys."

"Doesn't seem right, a woman driving one of those big things."

Betty took offense but withheld her anger for the moment.

"Tell Gladys I'll come back later and check on her."

Betty didn't want to raise the woman's suspicion any further, but didn't want the woman coming around again either. "Aunt Gladys and I are going to Montrose to visit with my family tonight. Maybe you can check on her in a couple of days after I head back on the road. It would make me feel better knowing someone is checking in on her."

"Fine." Rosie left the house and drove down the street.

Betty shut and locked the door. She was extremely anxious about the way that the woman, Rosie, had behaved. *That woman is going to be trouble. I need to get to Shelby soon.* Enraged, Betty began throwing dishes against the wall. "Bitch! I should have just brought you in here and eliminated you, too." Betty tore through the house for anything she thought she would need… clothes, toiletries, canned goods, bottled water, blankets, kitchen knives. She loaded everything into her rig. Hoping she'd diverted the nosy old lady's attention for at least a couple of days, she would use the time to set up the plan she'd concocted to take out Jack and Shelby. She'd wanted more time, but the nosy old bitch had put a kink in her plans.

Once Fiddler's truck was loaded with Gladys's things, she went over and got into the Toyota. She was going to track down Shelby and Jack. Once she had them pegged down, she was going to take them out in just the same fashion she'd planned the first time. Only this time she wasn't going to let anyone stop her.

◊◊◊

Shelby and Jack were on their way back to Gunnison. "So, my love, what would you like to do today?" Jack winked at his wife.

Shelby laughed. "You mean besides keeping me wrapped up in the sheets?"

Jack smiled. "How about checking out that lake you were telling me about? We could rent a boat and go fishing."

Shelby was thrilled. "I think that would be awesome, but we need to go back to Montrose."

"Why do we need to go back to Montrose?"

Shelby turned the truck around and pointed it toward town. "We don't need to rent a boat. Jayne gave me the keys to her boat. We just have to go back to the yard and get it."

Jack smiled. "Terrific. Why is it at the yard?"

"She keeps it in a garage and out of the weather."

"Wow. She's set up isn't she?"

"Yeah, she plans to retire up here."

"Well, I don't blame her for that. This place is beautiful."

◊◊◊

Betty had posted herself outside the cabin several feet away from the driveway. She was hidden by a slight curve in the road. After sitting in that position for a couple hours, Betty was becoming frustrated. She had not observed anyone coming or going from the cabin nor had she seen any movement on the property. She anxiously got out of the pickup and walked to the wooded area east of the cabin. She made her way through the trees and checked to make sure she had a clear path across the yard to the cabin. Everything looked good as she made her move quickly across the yard and took cover against the wall to the garage.

Betty made her way to the back and looked into some of the lower windows. She didn't see anyone. Then she climbed the stairs quietly to the second-floor landing on the patio. She looked through the French doors and windows, but the cabin was completely empty. She figured that if anyone was around this time of the day they would be using the kitchen and living areas.

She was suddenly surprised by noise coming from the front of the house. Betty quickly ran down the steps and slid along the wall of the garage.

She heard the garage door continue to move upward and talking coming from the driveway. Jack and Shelby were back. Betty wasn't ready to take the Mathewses for their final ride yet. As she watched from her cover spot, Betty saw Jack and Shelby head into the house through the garage.

Betty took the opportunity to sprint to the trees. She squatted close to the road near her pickup to see what the Mathewses might be planning. It didn't take long for them to emerge from the garage with some things in bags. Shelby closed the garage door and then backed the company truck with the boat hitched to the back out of the driveway. Betty immediately went to her pickup and followed the Mathewses down the picturesque road to Tin Cup Lake. She did her best to stay out of sight.

Shelby backed the boat and trailer down the boat dock while Jack guided her. Once the boat was in the water, Shelby got out of the pickup and helped Jack get the boat off the trailer. Once the boat was in the water, Jack mounted the boat and Shelby pushed it further into the water before starting the engine. "This water is cold, Jack. I'll go and park the truck and trailer and meet you over near the loading dock."

Jack waved at Shelby, letting her know that he understood as she waded out of the water.

Back at the pickup, Shelby lifted up her pant legs and wiped off her legs with the towel from the backseat. She got into the truck, put it in gear, and pulled it and the boat trailer around to the loading dock. It was a beautiful day for boating, but Shelby was shaking because the water had soaked her jeans. Once she had the truck and trailer parked, she got out and pulled the bags out of the backseat. She reached into her bag and pulled out another pair of jeans. "I knew I was going to need these." She set the bags outside the pickup door and then took off her shoes. She gathered up another pair of socks and quickly took her pants and socks off.

Jack was waiting for Shelby at the dock and started to whistle. "Show me more, baby."

Shelby laughed. "Shut up, you pervert."

Jack whistled again as he made a few spins with the boat in the water. "Only a pervert for you, baby."

Shelby laughed again as she wiggled into her dry jeans and replaced her socks and shoes. "Be there in a minute." Shelby grabbed the bags, locked the pickup, and headed to the dock.

Betty watched as Shelby got on board the boat and the two headed out into the lake. She sat there for a few moments and thought about how she could use this area to her advantage. She decided she was going to take advantage of this place, but in order to do that, she was going to need Fiddler's truck.

◊◊◊

Rosie called her bridge partner. "Helen, does Gladys have a niece named Angie?"

"No, she only has nephews. Why?"

"You know how worried we were when Gladys didn't come to our game? I went by her house to check on her. There was a big truck parked outside her house and a woman named Angie opened the door. Said she was Gladys's niece and that Angie wasn't feeling well. She also said they were going to visit family in Montrose for a couple of days."

"Gladys doesn't have family in Montrose."

"I'm going to call the police."

As soon as Rosie finished her call with Helen, she phoned the Gunnison Police Department. It was a small department, consisting of a dispatcher, two uniformed officers, and the chief of police, Alfred Overhill. Overhill listened to everything Rosie told him. "I am glad you called, Mrs. Foster. But Gladys's place is outside the Gunnison city limits. You're going to need to call the county sheriff."

Annoyed, she took down the number Overhill gave her and made the other call.

Sheriff Ulsterman was much more receptive to what Rosie had to tell him. He had recently seen the updated BOLO from Odessa and had received an APB from the Colorado Highway Patrol based on information from the FBI. When she mentioned the truck, he knew she was credible. "Can you describe the truck, Mrs. Foster?"

Rosie told him everything she remembered.

"This information is very helpful, Mrs. Foster. Would you give me your address? I'd like to send an officer over with some pictures."

◊◊◊

Agent Silverman's secretary walked into his office and handed him a print-out. "This just came in on the wire."

Silverman took the document; it was a dispatch from Gunnison County. "Holy shit!" He grabbed his jacket and bolted straight toward his secretary's desk, yelling, "Contact everyone on the task force. Betty Burton's been seen in Colorado."

As Silverman left the building, he realized that he hadn't heard from Jack in a couple of days, which was unlike the persistent Jack. He glanced at the dispatch and took down Ulsterman's number.

"Already tried the Mathewses—they aren't answering their phones. I had my receptionist contact the locals," Ulsterman said.

"Can you arrange for surveillance on the cabin where they are staying and the truck yard where Mrs. Mathews works?"

"I'll see what I can coordinate with the state troopers."

"Just make sure that they don't spook Betty. She's crazy enough to kill that whole town. Call me as soon as your make contact with Jack and Shelby. I'm flying there now."

CHAPTER TWENTY-EIGHT

Betty made it back to Gladys's house before Rosie had made contact with the sheriff's office. She left the pickup in the driveway and went to Fiddler's truck. She started the truck and aired up the brakes. Once the truck was aired up, she headed to where she'd left the trailer.

Betty pulled her bobtail into the drive where she'd left the trailer. To her horror, the cattle guard gate had been replaced and padlocked. She put the truck in park and walked to the shack. The trailer was gone. "Shit!" Betty walked back to her tractor, furious and confused. *Who could have taken it?* She combed over everything in her mind, but didn't have the faintest clue.

Betty got into her truck and decided she could take care of what she needed to do without the trailer. It wasn't ideal, but it would work. She also decided she was going to have to take the Mathewses from the cabin as she'd planned from the beginning instead of the lake. Betty turned her truck around and headed toward the cabin, determined to make her plan work.

◊◊◊

Shelby and Jack made their way back to the loading dock after spending the day fishing. Shelby got out of the boat and took the bags with her back to the pickup. It took them about an hour to get the boat loaded and head toward the cabin. It was beginning to get dark as they drove toward Gunnison. Jack had taken over the driving.

Shelby sat next to Jack with her head on his shoulder, almost asleep. "I had a wonderful day today, Jack."

"Me too, baby."

Shelby was almost asleep when her phone rang. She dug for her phone in the bag but missed the call. She let out a gasp when she realized all the calls she'd missed—nearly twenty, including Silverman, Stevenson, and Jayne. "Jack, something's wrong. I've missed a bunch of calls from the police and from Jayne. That call I just missed was from Detective Stevenson."

"What? Call him back, quick. Maybe they caught Betty."

Shelby pushed redial and dug through the bags, looking for Jack's phone. She found it and handed it to him.

Detective Stevenson answered his call. "This is Shelby," she said breathlessly. "I'm sorry I missed your calls. Is something wrong?"

"Shelby, I'm so glad we got ahold of you. Are you and Jack okay?"

"Yes, we're fine. We've been out fishing. Why?"

"Well, we have reason to believe that Betty is up there near you."

"Oh God, no. Detective, are you sure?"

"Yes, Shelby. She's somewhere up there."

"We haven't seen her."

"Hopefully she hasn't found you, but be very careful. We have contacted the locals and they are keeping you guys under surveillance until we get there."

"You guys are coming here?"

"Yes. Agent Silverman and I are on our way right now. We should be in Montrose sometime in the morning."

"Okay, well Jack and I are on our way to the cabin. We will stay there until we hear from you."

"Good. You guys be careful and call the local police if you see her."

"We will. Thank you, Detective."

Shelby ended the call and looked at Jack. "She's up here somewhere, Jack."

"Shit. How did she find us?"

"I don't know, but Silverman and Stevenson are on their way here. They contacted the locals and we are to keep an eye out."

"Dammit!"

"Let's get back to the cabin, Jack." Shelby looked out the truck window and then back at Jack. "Do you think she knows where we are right now?"

"I hope not." Jack drove as fast as he could to the cabin.

◊◊◊

Betty parked her bobtail off the main road and walked to the cabin. She had no trouble getting into the cabin because the patio door was unlocked. She'd brought her gun, rope, and duct tape. She was determined to deliver Shelby and Jack to their destiny on the side of a canyon cliff. Now all she had to do was wait patiently in the dark for the couple to arrive.

Jack pulled Shelby's company truck into the driveway of the cabin. He parked it outside the garage and opened the garage door. "You stay here and let me check things out before you come in." Shelby reached for her door handle and grabbed the bags off the floor. "Like hell. I'm coming with you. I left my gun in the side table drawer next to our bed. Wish I had it with me right now."

"Come on then. I think everything is fine, but just be careful."

"I'll hit the garage door once we get into the house. We have to leave the truck out because of the boat. We can take it to the yard in the morning."

"Okay."

Jack entered the cabin in front of Shelby and looked through every room on the bottom floor. Shelby looked in the closet and utility room. Then they moved up the stairs to the second floor. Shelby turned on the lights. The area was open so it wasn't hard to tell that the space did not contain an unwanted visitor. Jack checked the rooms on that level before heading up the stairs to the master suite. Shelby took the bags she was carrying and put them on the table. Jack came down the stairs from the master room. "All clear."

Jack stopped in his tracks when he saw his wife with a gun at her head. Shelby was scared as she looked at her husband for reassurance that everything was going to be okay.

Betty spoke up now. "Well, well, well! I guess it wasn't 'all clear' after all, was it, Jack? Aren't you going to say 'Hi,' Shelby? Been a while since we've had a heart to heart talk. I mean I saw you the other day at the railroad tracks, but we didn't get to talk really. We just haven't really had any time to catch up, have we?"

Shelby felt all the blood draining out of her face.

Betty pushed Shelby toward Jack as Jack hit the bottom step into the living room. "We really don't have time to chitchat now." Betty threw the rope and tape onto the floor. "Tie your husband up with the rope, Shelby. Hands behind his back and legs together. You'd better do it tight because I'm going to check it when you're finished and if you didn't make it tight I'm going to kill him here instead of letting him take a little ride with us."

"Okay."

Shelby began to tie Jack's hands behind his back when her cell phone went off on the table. Betty picked the phone up and looked at it. "Oh, it looks like an Agent Silverman is calling you. Shall we answer it or just let him wonder? I think we will just let him wonder."

Jack's phone vibrated in his jean's pocket, but Betty couldn't hear it so she didn't know he had it. Shelby felt the vibration and they both looked at each other, knowing that they could maybe use it later if she didn't find it. Shelby then helped Jack to the floor and began to tie his legs. "Remember, make sure it's tight, Shelby, or I'll kill him now instead of later."

After Shelby had tied up Jack, Betty checked him and then made Shelby turn around. She wrapped the first piece of rope around Shelby's hands and then set her gun on the table. She quickly tied Shelby up and then pushed her to the floor. She took the duct tape and wrapped it around Jack's legs and hands. Then she wrapped it around his mouth. Betty didn't put rope on Shelby's legs, but she did duct tape them together. She pulled Shelby by the legs and dragged her into the hallway. She used rope to tie her to the banister. Then she pulled Jack to the steps and tied him to the banister too. Betty put tape on Shelby's mouth before heading down the steps to the garage. "I'll be back in a few minutes. Don't go anywhere."

Betty left the house through the garage. Jack tried to talk to Shelby and find out if she was okay, but it was no use with the tape on their mouths. Jack could tell from Shelby's eyes that she was scared but okay.

Shelby heard the garage door open and then heard it close again. Betty suddenly came back into the house and pulled the tape without mercy off of Shelby's mouth. "Where is the trucking company you work for, Shelby?" Betty had seen the logo on the side of her company truck.

"It's in Montrose, off Bay Street. Why?"

"You got trucks and trailers there?"

"Yes, but I don't know where the keys are. I don't run a truck, I'm just taking care of the office stuff for a while. The company is new. They aren't even in operation yet."

"Where are the keys to that pickup with the boat on it?"

"On the table."

Betty went to the table and got the keys. She cut the tape off Shelby's legs and untied her hands. She aimed her gun at Jack's head. "Untie his legs and take him downstairs to the garage. If you run or he gets loose I will shoot him in the head and then shoot you. I could kill you right here and be done with you, but I want to finish what I had planned for you from the beginning. Now move him down the stairs."

Shelby helped Jack down the stairs as Betty held her gun close to his head. Once they were in the garage, Betty took hold of Jack and threw the keys to the pickup on the garage floor. Betty warned Shelby, "Pick up those keys and when I open this garage door I want you to go to that pickup and back that boat right into this garage."

Shelby did exactly as she was told. Once the boat was backed into the garage, Betty motioned for Shelby to come to the rear of the boat. "Now pull that cover back and help him into the boat. Put him on the floor and tie and duct tape his legs together. If they aren't tight when I check, I promise I will shoot him on the floor of that boat."

Shelby did as Betty demanded. Betty climbed into the boat and checked the tie. She was satisfied when she climbed from the boat. Shelby wanted to run but she knew Jack would be a dead man if she did.

"Now put the cover over the boat and get into the driver's seat. You're taking me to that new yard of yours. If you try anything stupid, I will shoot you and then I will shoot him."

"Okay."

Betty watched as Shelby covered the boat and then got into the pickup.

"Do you have keys to the yard with you?"

"Yes." She wondered whether it would be better to lie or tell the truth.

"Okay. Let's get going. Close that garage when you pull that boat out."

Shelby pushed the garage door opener, closing the garage behind her.

"Now take us to your yard. No funny stuff or else."

Immediately after pulling onto the highway, a patrol unit passed Betty and Shelby pulling the boat. The officer was looking at the cabin and didn't notice that the pickup had just come from that drive.

Betty didn't care. She was on a mission and nothing was going to stop her this time. "Drive, bitch. Drive."

Shelby was scared, but she wasn't going to lose her head. She would wait for an opening and get her and Jack out of this somehow.

◊◊◊

Agent Silverman had received permission to take an agency jet to Colorado. The pilot met him at the airport, but did not have good news. "Sorry, sir. Thunderstorms. We don't have clearance to leave."

Silverman and the pilot went into the lounge to wait for clearance to take off. The agent took out his phone and called Stevenson.

"Where are you?"

"On my way to Gunnison, I left as soon as I couldn't get in touch with Shelby or Jack."

"Weather has me grounded. I can't get them to answer my calls either."

"I'll call the locals and have them make contact with the house."

"My officer just made a drive by there and everything appears to be fine," the sheriff told Silverman.

"Look, I need for you to send that officer back to that house and contact the Mathewses."

"Okay. I'll send him out again."

"Okay, thank you. Let me know when they've made contact."

◊◊◊

Shelby drove Betty to the Montrose yard. She punched in the security code.

"Pull around to the back," Betty demanded. Betty looked over the yard and spotted the new trucks parked on the line. "Wow, those are some sweet-looking rides. Let's go have a look." Betty reached over, turned the pickup off, and took the keys.

Shelby got out of the pickup. "I want to check on Jack."

Betty pointed the gun at Shelby and motioned for her to come around to her side of the pickup. "I don't care what you want, Princess. Your Jack is fine for now."

Shelby and Betty walked to the line of new trucks. Betty checked each of the tractors out as Shelby led the way with a gun at her back. Shelby shook from fright in the frigid air. Betty instantly knew which one she wanted for the trip. "I want this one. Now let's go into that office of yours and find some keys."

Shelby tried to stall, hoping a cop or someone would come by and see Betty with a gun on her. "I'm not sure we have any keys in the office here for these trucks. They might be in the shop over there."

Shelby pointed to the mechanic building, knowing there were no keys in there, but trying hard to waste as much time as possible. If she could delay Betty, maybe the cops would figure out where she'd taken her and help. Betty, however, wasn't in the mood for a treasure hunt. "No, I think we need to check the office area. I've never seen a company leave keys to trucks in the mechanic building unless they are in repair."

Betty pointed Shelby toward the main offices and handed Shelby the keys to the door when they reached it. "Open the door, Shelby." Shelby did as she was instructed and let Betty into the new building. Betty turned on the lights. "Oh, now isn't this nice, and it smells all new, too. Show me where the keys to those trucks are."

Shelby did everything she could to delay. "I really don't know, Betty. We'll have to look around. I only work in that office there and I don't know what's in the other ones."

Betty pushed Shelby further into the offices. "Look through those drawers while I look over here. I want those keys or I promise you I will blow the head off the shoulders of that hubby of yours."

Shelby knew she wouldn't have much time to stall, so she pretended to look through a drawer while she scratched a small note of only a few words.

"Taken to Grand." Shelby watched to see if Betty was looking and quickly slipped the note on top of the desk before Betty noticed anything. "I can't find anything in here. Maybe they are in one of the other offices."

Betty was annoyed. "This is bullshit. Find me some keys now, Shelby."

Shelby knew Betty's patience was wearing thin so she moved into the office she knew held the keys.

Shelby began with the drawers again so she could leave another note—this time she only had time to write the word "Canyon." She slipped the note on top of the desk just as Betty joyfully found the keys. "Here they are. What number was that truck?"

"586."

Betty grabbed the keys and pushed Shelby out of the office area into the lobby. "Now let's go get me a new truck." As they passed by the office that Shelby used, Betty stopped. Shelby hoped that she hadn't decided to check the desktop for anything, otherwise she'd find the note. "We are going to need a fuel card. You got any of those here?"

Shelby hesitated, but not wanting Betty to find the note, she gave in. "Yes, we have fuel cards, but they are not activated and I can't activate them without Jayne's authority."

"Fine, I've got some cash," she said, thinking of the $400 she'd pulsed from Gladys's bank account from an ATM in town.

Betty pushed Shelby toward the door and left it open and unlocked as they made their way to the pickup and boat. Betty had Shelby get into the driver's seat again and she got into the passenger's side. "Drive over to the truck and back that boat up next to the back of the truck." Shelby did as Betty wanted.

Betty then made her get out of the pickup. "Now open those trailer doors." Shelby opened one door and then Betty stopped her. "That's enough. Now take off the cover to that boat and climb in. Tear the tape only from Jack's feet and the two of you get into the back of that trailer."

Shelby didn't like what Betty was doing, but at least she was going to see Jack and find out if he was alright. She quickly took off the cover and found Jack to be bumped a little, but okay. Shelby took the tape from his feet and helped him climb into the back of the trailer. Then she climbed into the trailer herself. Betty threw a roll of duct tape at Shelby and demanded that she wrap Jack's legs up again. While Shelby was wrapping up Jack's legs, Betty had an idea. "Give me Jack's wallet," she demanded. Betty climbed into the trailer as Jack moved over so that Shelby could get to his wallet. Once Shelby had the wallet in her hand, Betty hit Shelby in the back of the head and knocked her out. Betty grabbed the wallet as Jack tried to move toward Shelby. Betty backed him off with the gun. "Don't worry, Prince Charming, she's not dead…yet."

Betty rolled Shelby over and tied her hands together with tape. She didn't bother with her feet because time was becoming precious. "There now, you and your pretty little princess can be together forever." She closed the trailer door and secured it from the outside. She went to the tractor and started the truck to air it up.

Jack moved close to Shelby in the dark, but because he was bound with tape he couldn't even speak to her. He cuddled with her on the floor and for once in his life prayed that someone would help them. Jack hoped that Shelby was going to be okay, but she just lie on the floor not moving. *Please, Shelby, wake up. Please, Shelby, be okay. I love you,* he thought.

After starting the truck, Betty went to the mechanic shop and located some chain and an old lock that was lying on the bench. She took the chain and padlock and dragged them back to the trailer. She wrapped the chain around the bars on the trailer to further reinforce the security of the trailer doors. She then took the lock and attempted to secure the chain ends together. The lock, however, wouldn't stay hooked. "Shit."

Betty went back to the shop and gathered some duct tape she saw on the bench. She took the tape to the truck and forced the lock together in a secure fashion with the tape. Then she wrapped the tape around the lock until it formed a bundle the size of a volleyball. She took the remainder of the tape and wrapped it up and down the chains. "There now, let's see you get out of that." She got into the driver's seat, took off the air brakes and moved the tractor-trailer around to the security gate. "Dammit, what else can go wrong?" She'd forgotten to get the code from Shelby. "Fuck it." Betty ran the truck through the gate.

◊◊◊

Betty was tired as her adrenaline rush bottomed out. She was away from Gunnison and Montrose and almost to Grand Junction near I-70. She had followed Highway 50 up to Grand Junction and planned to take I-70 westbound towards the Grand Canyon cliffs in Utah to complete her mission. She had wanted Shelby to die in the Utah mountains a couple of years ago, but that vision never came to pass. This time, Betty was going to see that vision through no matter what it took. She spotted a truck stop. Feeling sure that she had gotten safely away without detection, she pulled in and parked for some rest.

CHAPTER TWENTY-NINE

gent Silverman slept in the lounge sitting up. They still had not been cleared to fly. He'd received word at around 3:00 a.m. from the sheriff's office that they were unable to make contact with anyone at the cabin. After further investigation, they had found that the patio door on the second floor was not secure and that the cabin was in disarray. There didn't appear to be any signs of a struggle or blood anywhere, but Shelby's company truck was missing.

Silverman's worst fears were realized. Betty had Shelby and Jack in her possession. She was going to be difficult to stop. *I wonder how she took them down and how she got them away from the cabin? She must have a weapon.* Then he remembered from the report that the dead police officer's gun had been taken. He called Stevenson with an update. "How far are you from Gunnison or Montrose?"

"I'm in Gunnison now. I'm going to check in with the sheriff's office."

"We need to get to their cabin and see if there are any clues that will tell us where they might be," Silverman ordered.

"Wait a minute, Silverman. Shelby works in Montrose at a trucking company that her boss just built, right? Maybe we should check the yard there first. We know she took that truck from that Kenny guy. She's not going to stay in that and she's going to need a getaway vehicle. I think she'll head for the main freeways if she thinks she isn't going to be followed. Food and fuel are more readily available on the main interstates. So I think she took the Mathewses and went to the yard in Shelby's company pickup. She probably took one of those trucks from that yard and headed towards I-70 near Grand Junction, Colorado. That is, if she's headed back to the Utah Mountains to finish what she started with Shelby."

"That's quite a theory. Did they find any big rigs parked anywhere they shouldn't be?"

"I don't know, but I'm going to check with the locals."

"Where are you going with this, Stevenson?"

"I don't know, but I'm trying to think like Betty and I just don't think she'll kidnap the Mathewses and take them on a road trip in a four wheeler. She's a trucker and she feels comfortable in and around trucks. She would be able to conceal her kidnapped victims easily in a box trailer. That's why I want to check out the yard first. I'll bet you twenty bucks Betty forced Shelby to take a truck from that new yard in Montrose."

"Check it out, but how would Betty have known about the new yard?"

"Either she found out from following Shelby, or maybe Shelby's company truck has a logo."

The pilot came in and told Silverman that they could finally leave. Silverman told him to file the flight plan for a different location. "I'll be in Montrose in a few hours, Stevenson. Meet me at the airfield there."

"Hey, I just got a text. The sheriff received a report about a truck abandoned in Gunnison near the cabin where Shelby's been staying. They had it impounded. I'm going into the sheriff's office now."

"I guess I owe you twenty bucks. Think she's headed back to Utah?"

"Maybe."

◊◊◊

Jack felt Shelby move and moan. He moved close to her as she moved some more and then felt her turn over.

"Oh, my head." Shelby opened her eyes and couldn't see anything in the dark. She suddenly remembered where she was and what had happened to them when she couldn't use her hands. "Jack! Jack! Where are you, Jack?"

Jack moved around on the floor but couldn't say anything because of the tape over his mouth. He murmured and made a little sound through the tape.

Shelby felt him move and heard his attempt to speak. She slid close to where the sound came from until she was again next to Jack. "Jack, are you okay? Move against me if you're okay." Jack moved against her. Shelby was able to move her legs, but her hands were tied. She thought about how she was going to get them out of the trailer. First, she'd need to get them out of the tape and rope. She then realized something. "We're not moving, Jack. I need to find some way to get us out of here."

Getting to her feet was difficult because of the pain and dizziness in her head. But she knew she had to get up if she was going to find something to cut the tape on her hands. Shelby couldn't see in the darkness, but she could feel along the walls and floor. She knew from her past experience of being locked in a trailer that the insides of trailers were never perfect. She was going to find a sharp edge somewhere in this trailer. She'd have to be careful not to fall or make too much noise in case Betty was sleeping or near the trailer.

She whispered to Jack, "I'm going to move around the walls so I can find something sharp to cut the tape on my hands. When I get back around to where you are you need to move or make a sound so that I won't fall on you. I hope I can find something sharp before I get back around to you, but we don't want to give Betty any reason to open this trailer up."

Shelby knew that Jack understood. It took her what she figured was about halfway back to Jack when she found a screw about waist-high sticking slightly out from the metal framing. She got on her tiptoes and put the bottom part of the tape between her hands on the screw head. She pulled down and was successful in causing the tape to rip but not enough for her the pull her hands apart and get free. She repeated the technique several times until she was able to make a tear in the tape big enough that she could pull her hands apart and free.

"Baby, I got my hands free. I'm on my way back over to you so I can get you free too," she whispered. Shelby walked gently with her hands on the walls toward Jack. She'd only made a few steps when the truck began to move, causing Shelby to fall to her knees. "Ouch! Dammit, she's moving the truck."

Shelby waited for a few moments before getting back to her feet so that she could figure out what Betty might be doing. She figured if she kept gearing up that she was leaving the place where she had stopped. If she didn't gear up and made swing maneuvers, she was either getting fuel, food, or both.

Shelby waited for the sounds and movements. Betty made swing maneuvers, so Shelby knew what she was planning.

Shelby waited until Betty finished with her maneuvers and brought the truck to a stop before she again moved along the walls. She knew that Betty wouldn't open the trailer for fear that someone would notice that her cargo was human beings. Shelby found her way to Jack and felt for the tape on his face. "Baby, I'm going to take the tape off your mouth now." She removed the tape from Jack's mouth as gently as she could. "Is that better?"

Jack swallowed the urge to yelp and moved his jawbone around. "Yes, sweetheart, it is much better."

Shelby worked her way to Jack's hands, tearing at the tape and then working the knots loose on the rope. It was difficult doing what she had to do in the dark, and when Betty started moving the truck it was even harder. But with persistence and patience, she succeeded.

Jack stretched his arms forward, trying to work the feeling back into his extremities. With his help, Shelby ripped at the tape and rope knots from around his feet. When Jack was free, he hugged and kissed his wife. "Thanks, sweetheart."

"You're welcome, babe. Now let's find a way out of here."

◊◊◊

Silverman and Stevenson made it to Jayne's Montrose yard. Stevenson brought him up to speed. Sheriff Ulsterman, Office Frank Dodges, and other members of the Colorado Highway Patrol, the Utah State Police, and Detective Peterson were there when they arrived. Peterson had come from Utah when the task force was informed about Betty's activities. It was easy to see the place where Betty had crashed through the gate.

"We've been combing through the place," Ulsterman told Silverman. "Let me show you guys something." He took them to the desk where the note with the word "Canyon" was scrawled on it. "Don't know if it means anything."

"Looks like I owe Stevenson another twenty bucks. Anything else?"

"Shelby's company pickup truck is in the parking lot with a boat behind it. They were here. There's no doubt."

Stevenson entered the office where Silverman and Ulsterman were talking. "I found the key box. Looks like truck 586's keys are missing."

"I'll get word out to all the local agencies," Ulsterman said.

"I'll have the FBI get the word out interstate-wide."

"Get this information out as quick as you can to all agencies."

Stevenson continued to look through Shelby's desk drawers and papers and found nothing. Just as he was about to leave her office he noticed a single piece of paper that apparently had been blown to the floor. He picked up the paper and looked at it. He took the piece of paper over to a crime scene tech who was bagging evidence. "Let me see that paper you had with the word written on it." Stevenson took the papers and put them together. He turned the papers over and then held them up for Silverman to see what it said. "Way to go, Shelby."

"Yep, we've got to get out of here. They have several hours on us."

"Go," Ulsterman said. "We'll secure the yard."

"We'll get you an escort," one of the highway patrol officers said.

"Which way do you think she'll go, Stevenson?"

"I'm not sure, but I have a feeling she's headed to the I-70."

"We'll get units out on both routes," the patrolman confirmed.

Silverman and Stevenson got into the unit. Stevenson was driving and they headed north on Highway 50 toward Grand Junction. "I hope you're right about this woman, Stevenson."

"I believe I am. My gut tells me that I am."

"Good, because we need a break here if we are going to get to Betty before she kills again."

The Colorado Highway Patrol was covering all possible routes out of the state. Petersen contacted his department and had the Utah Highway Patrol out in force.

"Five states surround Colorado. What if you're wrong about Utah?"

"Well, the Grand Canyon is only in three and Utah is the closest."

"Still."

"I've got an idea. He picked up the mic for the police radio mounted on the dashboard. Hey, Chips, can you get us patched into a CB radio?"

"10-4," came the reply.

"CB?"

"I think I know how we can find out for sure where Betty might be. We'll have to wait until we get up on I-70, but let's pull in some of the truck drivers out here for help. Let's just hope she isn't monitoring channel 19."

"Cool. I've always wanted to talk on one of these. Breaker, breaker 1-9."

Stevenson rolled his eyes. "How old are you?"

"You're patched in, Detective," the patrolman said over the radio." Then they heard, "Go ahead, break."

"Wow. Someone responded. What do I do?"

"They usually respond if you ask them something. Just talk to him."

"What do I say?"

Stevenson took over the conversation. "Yeah, thank you, break, we're looking for a truck headed down I-70. A brand new Peterbilt with a white box trailer. The tractor is brown with gold and black markings, possibly has some front end damage."

"Well, I don't know if this will help, but I just came from Grand Junction and I did see a truck fitting that description in the parking lot at the Acorn."

"Did you notice if the driver was a woman?"

"Nope. The truck was parked. Guess they were sleeping."

"But it was still there when you left?"

"Yep, at least a half hour ago anyway."

"Thanks, driver. That information is really helpful."

"Wow, that was awesome. Did you used to be a trucker?"

"No. You just talk to them like we talk to each other on the radio. Truckers, believe it or not, are really good people. They get a raw deal if you ask me." He punched the accelerator and sped toward Grand Junction with Peterson in tow.

Stevenson contacted the highway patrol escorting them. "Did you get that?" he asked.

"Yeah, we'll contact the authorities in Grand Junction."

Peterson interjected. "I'll let my men know in Utah. I'll have them have a roadblock ready to go at the state line."

"That sounds good, Peterson, but as determined and crazy as Betty is—I doubt a roadblock will stop her."

"I agree, but it will at least slow her down."

"CHP, have your men and the locals check the truck stop for that truck, but tell them not to approach the subject. We just want them to keep the truck under watch 'til we get there. Get a bird in the air over that town too if you can."

"Bird has already been dispatched, it should be in the air by the time we get there. CHP and the locals are descending in full force on Grand Junction as we speak."

"10-4."

"We're about forty minutes out, right?"

The patrolman put on his lights. "Follow us. We'll get you there on time."

◊◊◊

Betty had slept longer than she had wanted, but figured she had plenty of time while she fueled her truck, waiting in line to pay for it and her coffee. She hadn't checked on her load because she just didn't care. They were going to be dead soon anyway so if they died in the back of the trailer, that was fine with her.

◊◊◊

Shelby and Jack had held each other for a while after the truck had stopped, wondering what was going to happen to them. They both waited for the trailer doors to open, but for several hours they never did. Then Jack suddenly remembered his phone in his pocket. He reached into his pocket and looked to see if he had a signal—he did not.

Shelby took the phone from Jack. "I could have told you that, but we can use it to see around in this trailer." Shelby looked up and down the trailer with the phone before handing it back to Jack. Then she had an idea. She remembered the vents in the doors. This trailer was new, so the rubber seals would be tight and she wouldn't be able to see any light shine through a leak.

Shelby got up and walked to the trailer doors. She bent down and used the phone light to find one of the vents. "Look, baby. See a vent? Maybe we can get a signal if we can get the vent open."

Jack liked the idea. He moved to where Shelby was and together they worked to see if they could get it loose.

Shelby and Jack felt the truck moving, they continued to work on the vent until a very short time later the truck stopped again. They stopped messing with the vent. "Baby, I'll bet she's getting fuel, we better wait 'til we start moving again or she's going to hear us."

Jack was frustrated and started working on it again. "I know, but I think I almost have the vent loose. We need to at least try and send a signal to Detective Stevenson so he knows where to look for us. Shelby, no one knows where we are."

"I know, but she might try to shoot us."

"Yes, she might, but we're dead anyway if we don't do something."

"Okay, so what should we do?"

Jack got up and kicked at the vent. "I don't know. I just don't know."

Shelby thought about it and then she started jumping and running into the walls. She started to scream and yell while she continued to run into the walls. Jack did the same thing. They both hoped that someone would notice.

Betty came out from the store in a hurry. She became extremely angry and nervous when she realized what the Mathewses were doing. She wondered how they were able to move the trailer since they were tied up, but it was too late for that now. Betty wanted to open the trailer and shoot the both of them but knew that she couldn't open the trailer in a truck stop. She dropped her cup of coffee on the ground, mounted the truck, released the air brakes, and got the hell out of there.

"Shit." The morning traffic in the truck stop and on the streets was maddening. There were cops everywhere. She pulled out into traffic and positioned herself to take the westbound on-ramp towards Utah.

"Dammit." Betty quickly changed lanes in the heavy traffic for the east-bound side going towards Rifle after observing several patrol units gathered along the westbound entrance.

Betty fumed, hitting the steering wheel hard with her fist. "Fuck those cops, and fuck you too, Barbie. I may not be able to get rid of you like I planned, but I will see you dead."

◊◊◊

"Detective Stevenson, this is CHP Officer Dodges. My officers in Grand Junction just informed me that our suspect just left the truck stop and she's attempting to enter I-70 eastbound."

Silverman looked at his map, pointing out to Stevenson the next town eastbound from Grand Junction. "She's heading in the opposite direction, Stevenson. Why would she head into such heavy traffic?"

Stevenson shook his head. "I have no idea, but we are almost to that interchange."

Dodges came back over the radio before Silverman could respond. "The local officers positioned a couple of units near the westbound entrance for surveillance. That may have deterred our suspect from the westbound lanes. Our bird has the truck in site and it is jammed up in eastbound traffic."

"Thanks, CHP. When we get to that on-ramp lead us up onto that eastbound side." Stevenson responded, not sure how he was going to get Betty to stop without endangering the public.

"She's just made this pursuit a whole lot more dangerous and deadly." Silverman reached for his cell phone. "I need to call this in. We are going to need some reinforcements before we get a bunch of civilians killed."

"Wait. Before you make that call think about it. It will take your agency several hours to organize anything to get her stopped. Right now, we have a little help because of the slow traffic. I think if we reach out to a few truckers we might be able to stop her."

"Truckers? Just what the hell do you think a bunch of truckers can do?" Silverman looked at all the trucks that surrounded the patrol units.

"Detective Stevenson, the bird just informed me that it's an accident on the eastbound side of the I-70 that's got traffic backed up for about ten miles between Junction and Palisade," Dodges relayed.

"How far is it to Rifle from Palisade, Dodges? Does the bird still have Betty's truck in sight?"

"It's about sixty miles from where you are getting onto I-70 to Rifle. The bird has her situated about three miles ahead of you. Traffic is at a standstill, so I don't think she's going to get very far. The bird also wanted you to know that there's a line of ten frack crew trucks near Parachute. Looks like they are off the side of the road. That would be about thirty miles in front the accident. If you have ideas of going around her in that area, use caution."

"Thanks, Dodges." Before signing off, Stevenson added, "Hey, Dodges, are there any smaller highways off I-70 that she might use?"

"Yeah, but it's near Rifle. The 13 goes north to Meeker. It's a two-lane."

"Okay, Dodges. Have the bird stick with her. I'm devising a plan now. Just flow with the traffic. I need some time to put things together."

"10-4, just give us the word."

"So what we going to do, genius? You're right. I can't have an extraction unit set up in less than a few hours. By that time Betty will have either taken some side road north deep into the cliffs of the Rockies or into the congestion of the Denver Metroplex. She's got us in quite a dilemma."

◊◊◊

"Come on people, I have a hot load to deliver and I don't need all this traffic to keep me hemmed up." Betty moved her truck in and out of lanes when she saw an opening, but it was fruitless. Traffic was at a crawl and the truck was so new that it didn't have a CB installed yet, so she had no way of finding out what was happening in front of her.

Jack looked at Shelby, who had been thrown across the trailer from him when Betty realized that her cargo was loose. She took off out of the truck stop with such vigor that the centrifugal force sent both passengers flying around in the trailer. "Shit, that wasn't very nice of her. Are you okay, baby?"

"Yeah, I think so." Shelby attempted to find something to hold so that she could stand. "That crazy bitch is mine if we get out of this alive." Then she realized she could see the wall of the trailer. "Jack, look. The vent is open."

Jack and Shelby steadily moved towards the vent. "Can you tell that the truck isn't moving very fast? In fact, she's barely moving at all."

Shelby poked at the vent with her fingers, putting Jack's phone as close to the opening as possible. "Yeah, she's probably got herself stuck in traffic somewhere. But unless it's something major, like an accident, we won't be at this standstill for too long. Let's see if we can't get a brief text message out to Stevenson. There, I got a small signal, but your phone is telling me you have a low battery. Better make this quick. 'BETTY HAS US IN TRAILER, HEADED TO GRAND CANYON, UTAH, SEND HELP.'" Shelby pushed send.

Jack leaned up against the wall of the trailer. "God, I hope they find us."

Standing up, Shelby put her arms around her husband. "They will."

CHAPTER THIRTY

"**B**reaker 1-9 for the cops I hear tracking the brown Pete with front end damage."

"Go ahead, break, you got Detective Stevenson."

"Yeah, this is Proud American and I got the back door of that truck you've been spying out. Looks like they got that trailer locked up pretty tight. There's a whole lot of duct tape wrapped around some chain, and there's something the size of a soccer ball secured to the lock area with duct tape as well."

Silverman rolled his eyes and wiped his hand across his forehead. "Dammit, a bomb!"

"Proud American, can you tell me does it look like there are any wires coming from it?"

"You mean like a bomb or something? I'm ex-army, there ain't no wires and it sure don't look like no bomb I ever seen before. No, it's just a bunch of duct tape, what it looks like to me."

"How does he know that for sure, Stevenson? He sounds like a real yokel to me." Silverman said, frustrated with the delay in reaching his perp because of the traffic.

Tired of Silverman's disrespect, Stevenson responded, "Look, Silverman. We can't use the highly paid, slow response team you want, so we are going to do things my way. You just sit back and watch just how intelligent most of these truckers really are, then you can eat those words."

"Thanks, Proud American. Can you do me a favor and keep her in your front door? Let me know what she does. We are moving through this traffic as fast as possible. What type of truck are you hauling in? That way I can spot you better."

"I got me a 379, racing red Pete, can't miss it. I'm carrying a fifty-three-foot, half-loaded flat bed of wood, headed for Nebraska. I'll keep my eyes peeled, and the grill in the back door."

"Thanks, Proud American. You got any buddies out there that might want to help me slow that female driver down when we break out of this traffic jam?"

Before Proud American could answer, several truckers responded.

"You got Lady Outlaw and the Gambler team running our Tweety Bird yellow KW right up next to that wanted Brown Pete. We're ready to help out, just give us a shout."

"This is Steel Jumper from up New York way and I'm swinging into that Brown Pete's front door right now."

A female voice came over the radio. "This here is the Charmed One and I got your front door, Mr. CHP Officer, sir. I can see that Proud American's red tractor is not too far up in front of us in the fast lane. Let me know what you need and I will be happy to help."

"I'm Iceberg and I got the cops' back door in the granny lane."

"Snake and Joe Dirt rolling the fast lane next to Iceberg. Ready and willing."

"Lone Wolf here, I'm in the granny lane, not sure where all this is going down, but I'm game."

"Me, too. The Rubber Ducky is always in the mood for a cradle robbery. I'm almost to the site of the accident, so I must be in front of ya in the fast lane."

Stevenson had Silverman pull out a pocket notebook and pen as the drivers gave their locations. He pointed to boxes that Silverman had drawn on the two east bound lanes on his paper. "Thanks for the help, drivers. That female trucker has two hostages in that trailer and plans to kill them. I need to stop that truck before that happens."

Stevenson's phone buzzed. He handed it to Silverman. "What, I'm your secretary now?" Silverman looked at the text. "It's from Jack, he is letting us know he and Shelby are in the trailer. But they think they are headed towards Utah. His battery is low."

"Send them a message back. Let them know we are in pursuit of the truck. We will be attempting to stop Betty soon. Tell them to brace themselves."

The drivers had been talking over plans among themselves. Proud American had a solid idea and shared it with Stevenson.

Stevenson responded, "I like it, Proud American, but we need to get past this accident and away from Palisade before we do anything. She's going to try to break away from the slow traffic as soon as she can. We have to confine her in one of those cradle things you've been talking about. Then we need to stop the traffic behind us."

"UHP Petersen, Iceberg, Snake, and Joe Dirt, I need you and some of the local cops behind you to block traffic in these two eastbound lanes as soon as you make it to the accident area. CHP Dodges, get on the horn and make sure your officers stop all traffic from entering this side of the highway from De Beque to Parachute. That will keep as many civilians from our flanks as safe as possible. Once she tries to make a break for it, I need Lady Outlaw and Charmed One to move in beside her, putting her in that cradle thing from the granny lane. Steel Jumper and Proud American will hold her tight in the fast lane. Then CHP Dodges and I will come in from the median and try and get her to pull over. Lone Wolf and Rubber Ducky, you maintain the lanes from the front. Let the four wheelers pass and get out of the way. Then slow these lanes down as much as you can."

Every driver responded to their respective assignment. Silverman shook his head. "What are you going to do if she breaks away?"

Stevenson rolled his eyes. "Then we box her up in the right lane. Lone Wolf and Rubber Ducky have the front door and they will block her from getting away."

"Rubber Ducky, Lone Wolf, what the hell kind of people are we dealing with here? I'll tell you what kind, the kind that sues the shit out of us when one of them gets hurt. This is crazy and insane. What are you going to do if this doesn't go according to plan, which most of the time, plans never do, especially in our business? Stevenson?"

"Let's give it a shot and see what happens. If it doesn't work, then we continue our pursuit and figure out something else."

◊◊◊

Jack's phone buzzed. Shelby looked at the screen near the vent. "Oh Jack, they know we're in here and they are pursuing her. We are going to get out of here, sweetheart. But they want us to brace ourselves. I don't know what that means, or even how we'd do that in here."

Jack held his wife. "I don't know either, baby." Jack couldn't help thinking to himself. *I hope we get out of here too, Shelby. I just hope we don't leave this tin can in a body bag.*

◊◊◊

"Okay, folks. You got the Rubber Ducky here, I'm just entering the accident scene and they are moving right lane traffic into the left lane. We might have a problem keeping her hemmed up when the right lane opens back up."

"Lone Wolf here. I got the Rubber Ducky next to me. Steel Jumper, you hold back traffic and let me get a squeeze in behind the Ducky. I'll follow him out to the breakout point and we'll do our best to keep her in check until the others get free of the accident."

"Sounds good, Lone Wolf. Watch them four wheelers. They are hot to trot being stuck in this stuff so long. Must be late for work or something," Steel Jumper responded.

Stevenson confirmed. "Don't put yourselves or any of these four wheel drivers in any danger, truckers. If this doesn't work, we will come up with another plan down the road."

Charmed One chimed in on the conversation. "If this doesn't work, why don't we find a safe spot, use a fifth wheel pull bar, and unlatch her truck from the trailer? If we can keep her speed down, that trailer will drop to the ground. It might slide a bit, and may even turn on its side, but at least the people in that trailer won't be rollin' down the highway with that crazy bitch-ass driver anymore. Plus, she'll be losing air so fast from the broken airlines, the warning sound on her air pressure gauges will take that loony into another realm."

Stevenson and even Silverman liked the idea. "I think we need to try that anyway, Charmed One. Even if she doesn't get around our cradle blockade, we can still unlatch the trailer. Who's got one of those fifth wheel pull bars?"

"I do," Charmed One reiterated. "But it's in my tool compartment. I'd have to stop and get it."

"I got one right here." Lady Outlaw confirmed over the CB. "Gambler's driving and I just lifted up our bed and pulled it out of the storage compartment. Get me up next to her and I'll separate that truck and trailer faster than you can spit."

Stevenson thought for a few moments then pushed the mic button on the radio. "Okay, revisions to the plan." Silverman pointed out what he thought should happen from his sketchy drawing. Stevenson nodded his head in agreement. "Lone Wolf and Rubber Ducky, you maintain front line hold, just as before. Steel Jumper, you hold back traffic and let Lady Outlaw and Gambler in front of you when traffic goes to one lane. Once we get to the breakout point, Lady Outlaw, you stay in the fast lane and let Steel Jumper get around you. The brown Pete will follow him if you keep your speed down, Gambler. Proud American and Charmed One, do the best you can to block her in behind Steel Jumper and Gambler. Once you got her in the cradle, Proud American you back down and let Gambler and Lady Outlaw in beside the brown Pete. Lady Outlaw, you do your thing and release that fifth wheel."

"You got it, lawman," Lady Outlaw responded.

Before any of the other drivers could respond, Rubber Ducky and Lone Wolf were out of the accident area, letting all the four wheelers go around them.

"What the fuck is going on?" Betty flipped Gambler off as he passed her truck and moved in front of Steel Jumper. "Asshole, wait your turn."

"She knows I'm the number one driver on the road. She just gave me the sign. Lady Outlaw and the Gambler are in front of Steel Jumper, but that female driver isn't happy about it."

Charmed One moved in front of Proud American. CHP Dodges, Stevenson, and UHP Petersen put on their lights, forcing the few straggler four wheelers to fall back away from their vehicles and Snake, Joe Dirt and Iceberg's trucks. The truckers and Peterson, along with other law enforcement at the accident, held traffic back as Stevenson and Dodges pulled through the accident scene and followed in behind the cradle-robbing truckers.

"She's throwing a fit, drivers. She's fish tailing that trailer. Crazy lady knows we got her pinned," Proud American informed the others.

Steel Jumper moved into the right lane just as he busted through the split. Betty followed him. Gambler and Lady Outlaw held back in the left lane, maintaining their speed with Steel Jumper.

"Get the hell out of my way, you stupid ass truckers." Betty laid on her horn.

"She's blowing her top. I guess she doesn't have a radio in that truck or I'm sure we'd be getting an ear full," Steel Jumper laughed.

"Yep, she's pissed," Lady Outlaw jeered. "Pull it back, Proud American. Gambler is going to roll this baby right beside her so I can get a hold of that handle. If looks could kill, I'd be dead. I think she's a little upset with us, Gambler." Lady Outlaw opened up her window on the passenger door.

"Once she pulls that bar, everyone needs to back off behind us. That trailer is going to go for a ride and it's hard to tell just where it will end up. We aren't rolling that fast, but it's going to be unpredictable," Gambler informed.

Gambler and Steel Jumper did their best to keep Betty pinned while Lady Outlaw stretched her body out her window. "Drop it back a bit, Gambler, and move over a little towards her rig."

Gambler complied.

"That's it, steady, steady, almost got it." Lady Outlaw screamed, "SHIT, the bitch sees me, she just moved her truck away from us. I got the hook, but I'm going to lose it if you don't help me."

Gambler punched the cruise button, put his legs on the bottom of the steering wheel to hold it steady and then pulled with both hands on his wife's hips. It was a crazy stunt, but it worked. Lady Outlaw fell back into the truck cab. "Move, baby, move. That trailer is loose and we need to get out of the way."

"What the hell is going on, Jack?" Shelby screamed as the front end of the trailer they had been sealed in for the last several hours hit the ground with a thud. Then Shelby and Jack could hear metal grinding on pavement as the trailer seemed to be sliding. Shelby and Jack grabbed for each other but were forced apart and thrown from what was once the floor of the trailer to the left. The trailer rolled once more, making the ceiling the floor before coming to a stop. Jack and Shelby had been thrown by the force of the roll to the front of the trailer that now rested with its front nose in the dirt. In a pile of two bodies mashed together, the couple did not move. The trailer lay still with only the plumes of dust swirling from beneath it and the free rotation of the four rear tandems that once carried the trailer upright down the highway behind the brown Pete.

Stevenson got on the radio. "The trailer is down. Dodges, back down and take care of those victims. I'm going to continue the pursuit with the truckers."

Proud American and Charmed One had already jacked down and pulled over near the trailer. Gambler and Steel Jumper were doing their best to hold Betty back now that she was bob-tailing it.

Betty screamed at the top of her lungs as she ran the front of her truck into the trailer belonging to Steel Jumper. "I'LL GET YOU, BARBIE. EVEN IF I HAVE TO COME BACK FROM THE GRAVE. I WILL GET YOU!"

Betty looked down at her air gauges and knew that she didn't have a lot of time. She pressed in hard again against Jumper's trailer.

"This stupid bitch is messing up the back door of my trailer."

Silverman objected, "You stop and let me out. I need to make sure those people are alright. If that crazy woman gets away, so be it. But I have to think about the lives that are at stake and what this is going to cost the agency."

Stevenson quickly pulled over and let Silverman out of the car. Before Silverman could barely close the door, Stevenson had the gas pedal clear to the floor board. Silverman yelled at Stevenson through the dust. "It's your badge if anyone but that psychotic witch dies!"

"This bitch is crazy, she's all over the road," Lady Outlaw explained.

Dodges keyed up his mic after receiving some information from the helicopter. "Stevenson, I got a couple drivers from that frack crew off the side of the road between Parachute and Rifle. I think you better listen to them."

"Okay, patch me through."

"This is Detective Stevenson. Who am I speaking with?"

A young male voice came over the radio. "Oh, this is Sexy White Boy and my friend Shorty. We run trucks for a frack crew out of Denver. But we've been listening to your transmissions over our radios and we think maybe we can help you out in stopping that lady driver. We have a chemical we use out here when we're fracking and it's called FR or Friction Reducer and it's real slimy. Anyways, we got some of that shit on our blender truck and Shorty and I were thinking we could put some of that across the road. I guarantee she won't be going anywhere but the ditch when she hits it."

Silverman thought for a few seconds and then keyed up his mic. "I like it, guys. Go ahead and put a bunch of that across the road. The rest of you that have been helping me, back your trucks down and let Betty go. I will get in front of you and put my lights back on. She will think that I'm the only cop pursuing her. She won't know what hit her when she hits the slime."

"Backing it down," Rubber Ducky complied.

"Me too," Lone Wolf reiterated.

Steel Jumper moved over and let Betty's bobtail pass. "There she goes, queen of the crazies."

Betty watched in her driver's side mirror as Detective Stevenson came around the other drivers. "So you think you can stop me with that little four wheeler do ya?" Betty pulled out the pistol she had taken off the cop she had killed. She placed it in between her legs. "You're going to get a bullet before you get me, cop."

Gambler and Lady Outlaw moved in behind Steel Jumper, letting Detective Stevenson follow behind Betty with his lights and sirens. "Thanks every one of you for helping me out here."

"No thanks needed, Officer. Just tell your buddies out there to let up on the regulations and tickets. We're just a bunch of ordinary people, doing an ordinary job, trying to take care of our families."

"I hear you, Gambler. I'll do my best to get the word out for you."

Shorty came over the radio. "Officer, sir, we done put that FR all over the road. I think I see her coming now."

"Yeah, I see you guys sitting up there. Make sure everyone is away from those trucks and away from where she's going to run through that stuff."

"Yes, sir, Officer, sir, we're moving everybody away right now. Oh, shit, gotta go, here she comes and she is coming fast."

Within seconds of hitting the wet spot on the road, Betty had no traction and the brown Pete spun in complete circles like a little toy top before hitting the dirt along the side of the median. The dirt stopped the spinning of the tractor, but gravity took over and sent the truck rolling end over end and side over side. The Pete came to a stop in a cloud of dust, weeds, glass, broken brown truck pieces, and bent metal parts. It lay on the driver's side.

Betty, still conscious but stunned at what had just occurred, moved to remove her seatbelt. She wiped a stream of blood that was slowly moving from the top of her head down her face. She scrambled to locate the weapon that she had placed between her legs. Between her now almost completely dislocated seat and shattered driver's window, lay the gun she needed. Suddenly, feeling the pangs of pain now shooting from what seemed every part of her body, Betty turned herself around and reached for the gun, from out of the dirt. She placed the gun in the back of her pants and stood up in the laid over truck. She put one of her feet in a steering wheel hole while pulling herself towards the now door-less passenger side of the truck. Betty struggled to free herself from the wreckage. "I'm not going back to prison. I won't give up until Shelby Mathews is dead and in the ground."

◊◊◊

"The truck is down in the median." Detective Stevenson let those listening to the CB radio know. "I don't see any movement, but the dust hasn't cleared yet. I'm going to go down near it and see if Betty is still alive." While Detective Stevenson waited for the cloud of dust to settle some, the truck drivers from the frack crew came back towards their equipment. Soon, all the drivers who had been involved in the pursuit of Betty lined the highway behind the detective's car. Several local police and sheriff units were arriving with EMS. Stevenson cautiously approached the now-destroyed Peterbilt.

Betty huddled behind the mangled steel of the truck waiting for who-ever would be brave enough to approach her. When she heard the rustle of brush near the hoodless engine, she stood up and pointed her gun in the direction of the noise. Detective Stevenson, took shelter behind the opposite side of the truck. He yelled towards Betty. "Don't make it any worse, Betty. Put the gun down and let me take you in. Things will go a lot better for you if you just give it up."

Betty fumed and let off another round from her gun in the same direction as before. "Never! I am never going back to prison!"

Stevenson knew that he was going to have to think of something to convince Betty to just give up. While he continued to talk to her, the CHP chopper flew down low near Betty's side of the wreckage. Betty pointed her gun at the chopper, but before she could get off the round lodged in the chamber, the CHP officer who was holding a twelve-gauge sniper rifle pulled his trigger. The bullet ripped through the middle of Betty's head, shattering the backside of her skull. The gun that Betty held in her hand slipped from her limp grip, and her body fell forward into the dust, matted-down weeds, and all the mangled pieces that remained scattered from the brown Pete.

Detective Stevenson moved from his covered position with the CHP cropper still hovering to cover him. He holstered his weapon and looked at Betty's body. With his hand he checked her neck for any sign of life. When he knew without a doubt that he would not find any, Stevenson waved off the chopper and motioned towards the highway for the EMS and local authorities to move in and take over the scene.

Stevenson walked somberly towards his vehicle. He hadn't slept in over two days but it was almost over. He spoke briefly with the truck drivers who had helped him capture Betty, thanking them again for all their help. He had hoped that things would have turned out differently as he drove back towards where the Mathewses were being extracted from their own mangled mess of metal.

He heard from Silverman that he and several of the truck drivers that had been first on the scene had cut through the wad of duct tape that Betty had placed over the chain and lock. Silverman detailed the entrance into the rolled trailer as daring and dangerous, and that they had successfully helped the EMS remove both Jack and Shelby Mathews from the wreckage with only minor injuries and one broken arm—Jack's right one.

As the ambulance left to take the couple to the hospital, Shelby reached out and took Jack's left hand. She sighed with relief, knowing she and Jack would live out their lives without the threat of one Betty Burton.

THE END

Read more from the Mother Trucker Book Series

Acknowledgments

I would like to thank Danielle H. Acee, Mindy Reed, Douglas Brown, and all those involved in editing and perfecting the text. Their guidance made the book release possible.

I also can't forget all of the individuals who supported me with their encouragement—my daughter-in-law, Cydney and my friends, Tina, Tamra, and Tammy. To so many others (truckers, friends, family members) who helped me in this endeavor, sometimes without even knowing it, thank you.

I will always remember all those who helped make this dream a reality.

With all my heart forever.
—Robyn Mitchell
robynmitchellauthor.com

ABOUT THE AUTHOR

Robyn Mitchell left the comforts of teaching in a classroom to explore the open road in an 18-wheel sandhauler. Her experiences and time on the road birthed Mother Trucker, a series of suspenseful thrillers based on the trouble and happiness Shelby Mathews—a well-educated, gorgeous blonde, wife, and mother of three grown men—finds while trucking.

Read More
Mother Trucker Book Series
Mother Trucker
Trucktress
Outlaws
Jumpers
Terror West